HALFHYDE AND THE ADMIRAL

BY THE SAME AUTHOR

Featuring Lieutenant St. Vincent Halfhyde, RN:
Beware, Beware the Bight of Benin
Halfhyde's Island
The Guns of Arrest
Halfhyde to the Narrows
Halfhyde for the Queen
Halfhyde Ordered South
Halfhyde and the Flag Captain
Halfhyde on Zanatu
Halfhyde Outward Bound
The Halfhyde Line
Halfhyde and the Chain Gangs
Halfhyde Goes to War
Halfhyde on the Amazon

Featuring Donald Cameron:
Cameron Comes Through
Lieutenant Cameron, RNVR
Cameron's Convoy
Cameron in the Gap
Orders for Cameron
Cameron in Command
Cameron and the Kaiserhof
Cameron's Raid
Cameron's Chase
Cameron's Troop Lift
Cameron's Commitment

Featuring Commodore John Mason Kemp RD, RNR:
The Convoy Commodore
Convoy North
Convoy South
Convoy East

HALFHYDE
AND THE ADMIRAL

Philip McCutchan

St. Martin's Press/New York

HALFHYDE AND THE ADMIRAL. Copyright © 1990 by Philip McCutchan.
All rights reserved. Printed in the United States of America. No part of
this book may be used or reproduced in any manner whatsoever without
written permission except in the case of brief quotations embodied in
critical articles or reviews. For information, address St. Martin's Press,
175 Fifth Avenue, New York, N.Y. 10010.

Library of Congress Cataloging-in-Publication Data

McCutchan, Philip
    Halfhyde and the admiral / Philip McCutchan.
        p.   cm.
    ISBN 0-312-04323-6
    1. Great Britain—History, Naval—Fiction.   I. Title.
PR6063.A167H26   1990
823'.914—dc20   89-78015
                                                                    CIP

First published in Great Britain by George Weidenfeld & Nicolson
Limited.

First U.S. Edition
10 9 8 7 6 5 4 3 2 1

ONE

Canon Rampling eased himself upright from his kneeling
position before the altar, assisted in this process by a small,
skinny man whose bow legs gave him the aspect of a groom,
which he was not. Churchwarden Tidy, as he had been until
Canon Rampling's recent retirement, was by trade a gardener,
a calling that he was about to give up to the canon's full-time
service.

'Thank you, Tidy.' For a moment Canon Rampling leant the
weight of his immense body on the faithful Tidy, for age was
catching up with him. In his cassock Canon Rampling looked
like a vast bat, the more so on the occasions when he lifted his
arms in supplication to the Almighty. 'A sad day, I fear.'

'Aye, Rector.'

'No, Tidy. You cannot call me that now.'

'Reverend, then. Reckon you'll always be that.'

'Yes.' Canon Rampling turned away from the altar and
moved down the body of the church, no longer his. The day was
bright, with high cloud scudding before a light wind blowing
fresh across the fells, and the dale was alive with daffodils.
Sheep grazed on the fellsides, a horse and cart moved lazily
along the dusty road running past the church and the rectory
close by. Canon Rampling, who had spent virtually his whole
ministry at St Botolph's except for a period when he had served
Her Majesty as a chaplain aboard her warships, being
accompanied by Churchwarden Tidy enlisted by special
dispensation of the Board of Admiralty as chaplain's yeoman,
would miss Yorkshire and the wide sweep of the dales. But he
had asked the Almighty for guidance and the answer had come

I

plain: he was to do his duty, and his duty was to a cousin living in distant Chile, an older cousin who had once, long ago, been his mentor and was now a widower in need of company.

With Tidy at his side Canon Rampling walked towards the rectory. 'You've seen to my packing, Tidy?'

'Aye, I have that, Reverend.'

'You've packed my galoshes?'

'Aye. Reckon you'll need more than galoshes, though. More like seaboots. You said the boat was small. Doan't see why we doan't go out in one o' them liners.'

'It is a question of husbanding our resources, Tidy. The Lord would not look kindly upon extravagance. Besides, we know the master of the *Taronga Park*, as I've said before. Aboard the *Meridian*, I formed the impression that Mr Halfhyde was a splendid seaman and a reliable gentleman of excellent character. Now that he has left Her Majesty's service, he will be no less so. And safety is of more importance than comfort. The sea holds dangers, as you know well, Tidy.'

'Aye.' Churchwarden Tidy, rector's warden for more years than he cared to admit to, trudged on beside the canon. Tidy had not enjoyed his naval service, which had been thankfully brief. Aboard the old battleship *Meridian*, bound as it had happened to Valparaiso for handing over to the Chilean Navy –Valparaiso which was once again to be Tidy's destination – his position had been somewhat nebulous. As chaplain's yeoman he had been regarded as having petty officer status; but the good petty officers of the battleship had been disinclined to accept him as such, and a compromise had been reached over his berthing arrangements insofar as he had been permitted to sling his hammock in the flat outside the petty officers' mess, thus being close to the door without being actually within, an example of class distinction that had not appealed to a good Yorkshireman.

And the day after tomorrow it would be back aboard ship again, though this time as a fare-paying passenger. That would of course be a different kettle of fish. There would be no nonsense from petty officers.

'Does it always rain in bloody England?' Victoria Penn asked disconsolately, staring from St Vincent Halfhyde's cabin port at a steady drizzle soaking into the dreariness of the London docks where the *Taronga Park* lay beneath the tall, blank-faced walls of the warehouses.

'Yes,' Halfhyde answered irritably, his mind on other matters.

'Take me back to bloody Sydney, then, mate.'

'You're free to go whenever you wish, Victoria.'

'Want me to, don't you?'

'I didn't say that.'

'Meant it, though. You don't bloody love me, never did. May as well admit it, eh?'

'I do love you,' Halfhyde snapped. Then he sighed and got to his feet; the girl had a dampish, about-to-cry look about her, the look that went as always to his heart. He strode across the cabin, bending his tall body to keep his scalp clear of the deckhead, and took her in his arms. She turned to him and held his face close to her own. He spoke somewhere down into her neck, feeling foolish. 'You must know me after all this time. I'm not demonstrative. And I've a lot to think about just now.'

She released him. 'Bloody cargo?'

'I've got my cargo arranged. It'll come aboard during the forenoon – a homogenous cargo of textiles. My concern is the passengers I've been landed with.'

'You're the master, why worry about bloody passengers?'

'It's because I'm the master and the ship's my own that I have to worry, Victoria.'

She gave him a shrewd look. 'This to do with you going up to the whatsit yesterday?'

'The Admiralty, yes.'

'Those buggers got their hooks into you again, have they?'

He said, 'I'm still a lieutenant of the reserve, Victoria. The Admiralty has a certain call upon me. Or if not precisely that, then their Lordships are in a position to make things awkward for me.'

'How?'

3

He shrugged. 'They can manipulate, Victoria. They can see to it, for instance, that I don't get cargoes – '

'If you don't obey their bloody orders?'

'Their requests.'

'Same bloody thing! Why not stand up for yourself, mate, tell them off a bit?'

'I have a living to make,' he said irritably. 'For you as well as for me. There are too many ships . . . and the *Taronga Park* is small, very small to face the competition.'

'There's something else, isn't there, eh?'

'What?'

She beat at him with small fists, her face angry. 'You bloody *like* being made use of! You bloody *like* taking orders from those bloody lordships! Like feeling you're half back in the bloody warships again. Eh?'

She had touched a raw spot and Halfhyde reacted angrily. He turned away and left the cabin, paced the master's deck outside. Victoria Penn . . . a mixed blessing, sometimes a virago like her namesake on the throne of England who through the medium of her Board of Admiralty was to interfere with his forthcoming passage across the seas to Valparaiso. Victoria Penn, rescued by his action from an unsalubrious life in Sydney some years before, had woven herself into his life until she had become a part of it that he could not reject. She attracted him greatly even while she infuriated him, and he knew her love for him was genuine and deeply felt. She had sailed the world with him, wife in all but name. Marriage was not possible; Halfhyde, separated from a haughty wife who had preferred horses to sex, knew there would never be a divorce. That wife's family would see to that: divorce was a social stigma. And he knew not whether he would have married Victoria had he been free to do so; she was too tempestuous, too forthright, too apt to put her foot in it with people who mattered to an owner-shipmaster with, as he had just said, a living to make in a very harsh world.

Halfhyde's thoughts went from Victoria to his visit to the Admiralty the day before. The visit that he had made as the result of a call upon him by a uniformed police constable bearing a sealed envelope with the Admiralty crest embossed upon it.

Halfhyde had gone by the Metropolitan District Railway from Shadwell to Trafalgar Square. Walking beneath the Admiralty Arch across the Mall, he had entered the building from Horse Guards Parade, giving his name to the uniformed custodian. The name had been checked against a list and Halfhyde had been escorted to the room of a rear-admiral, a portly man wearing a frock coat and gleaming linen. There were no other persons present. At Halfhyde's entry the rear-admiral turned from a tall window looking out over Horse Guards Parade and bade his visitor sit.

'Good of you to come, Halfhyde.'

'I think I had no option, sir.'

'Ah – perhaps not, perhaps not.' The rear-admiral, a fussy-looking man, took out a handkerchief and blew his nose with a sound like a trumpet. 'You'll want to know why you're here, what?'

Halfhyde said that indeed he would.

'Passengers,' the rear-admiral said, coming with naval directness to the point. 'I understand your ship takes passengers. How many have you booked?'

'Three, sir.'

'I see. And they are?'

'A Canon Rampling of the Church of England, once a naval chaplain, and his churchwarden. Also a lady, a widow as I understand – '

'Yes, I see. You have accommodation for two more, I trust?'

'At a squeeze, yes. And with the proviso that they're of the same sex. I have one spare cabin that can be made into a double berth.'

'Fortunate, that. Otherwise. . . .' The rear-admiral didn't go on with what he had been about to say; Halfhyde formed the impression that had there not been sufficient accommodation available he would have been told that Rampling and his churchwarden were to be struck out from the passenger list. The naval officer continued, 'Both are of the male sex, Halfhyde, so there is no problem. As it happens, you have met both these persons before. One is a Mr Mayhew of the Foreign

Office. The other is a detective inspector of the Metropolitan Police, by name – '

'Todhunter?' Halfhyde broke in. 'Why – '

'Todhunter, yes. They sailed with you recently to the Amazon, I understand. And it is precisely because of this that they and you have come together again. Or are about to.'

'I see. Am I under orders to take these persons, sir?'

The rear-admiral pursed his lips. 'I wouldn't go so far as to say that, Halfhyde. Not orders. A request, perhaps.'

'One that I would be unwise to refuse?'

The rear-admiral gave him a sharp look. 'You are now a merchant captain, Halfhyde. All should be grist to your mill. The passengers will be paid for, naturally.'

'And beggars can't be choosers.'

'It's very much to your advantage, surely? You have no objection to these persons?'

'None at all,' Halfhyde said, 'though both can become a little tedious. What concerns me is why this request is being made. If my ship is to be used in some way, as I suspect – going on past precedent – then I shall need to have an answer. The *Taronga Park* is a commercial venture, sir, and relies more upon her cargo, which does not need feeding and does not constantly complain, than upon passengers to maintain herself at sea. Any interruption – '

'Yes, yes, I understand, you may be sure. Should there be any such . . . er, *interruption*, then due recompense will be made by the Board of Admiralty, you have my word on that.'

'But not in writing, sir?'

The rear-admiral flushed. 'Not in writing. Am I not entitled to take it that you trust the word of an officer of flag rank in Her Majesty's Navy?'

'You are, sir, and I do. That was not the purport of my question. But the fact of nothing in writing suggests a degree of jiggery-pokery, and – '

'Jiggery-pokery indeed!' The rear-admiral, Halfhyde saw, was having difficulty with his temper. His face had gone a deep crimson colour suggestive of an apoplectic fit. 'I have studied your record of naval service, Halfhyde, and I have seen that you

6

were an officer much given to expressing himself in bald language to his superiors. To such an extent that you spent periods ashore on the half-pay list, an unemployed sea officer – '

'Which now I am not, sir. I must insist on knowing very precisely what is expected of me and my ship.' Halfhyde's voice was cold. 'I am well aware of the ways of the Admiralty and its propensity to dissociate itself from its minions when matters go adrift.'

'You – '

'I must have assurances, sir. I repeat, if I am to take these passengers who are clearly not ordinary travellers, I must be in possession of the facts.'

'There are other ships, Halfhyde – '

'Yes. But you have chosen mine. Why is that, sir? There are faster ships, more commodious ships. That you have chosen the *Taronga Park* does not suggest urgency. Yet I sense urgency in your very request. There is some dichotomy.'

The rear-admiral got to his feet and paced the room, his colour higher than ever. He made a hissing noise, like a fuse-line approaching a barrel of gunpowder. 'I dislike your tone and manner, Halfhyde. You are overbearing and arrogant.'

'I am sorry, sir. But – '

'Nevertheless I appreciate your position. I shall take you into my confidence – as I indeed I intended. Your ship has been chosen for the very reason that it is slow and, shall we say, unfashionable. It is no liner, such as attracts the attention of newspaper reporters among other persons. It is not the normal vehicle for gentlemen of the Foreign Office – for diplomats on sensitive missions. There is a degree of anonymity which aids secrecy. There is urgency of a sort, but the situation we are faced with is a developing one, so your slow speed is not of importance. For certain reasons, we do not wish Mr Mayhew and Todhunter to reach Valparaiso too soon.'

Halfhyde smiled. 'I am agog, sir.'

'What? Oh, yes. Well now. Again your past is catching up with you, Halfhyde, and this is another reason why you are being asked to assist.' The rear-admiral paused; Halfhyde sensed that weighty news was about to be given. 'You have served under Captain Watkiss, now Admiral Watkiss of the Chilean Navy – '

'The Brazilian Navy when last heard of, sir.'

'Yes, yes. Precisely. He has . . . er, transferred his flag. He now commands the Chilean Navy. I do not propose to go into the whys and wherefores of his change of allegiance. The facts are that he has made certain statements to the British Minister resident in Santiago, and certain despatches have reached this country as a result.' The rear-admiral lowered his tone as if instinctively guarding against spies with ears pressed to keyholes. 'Admiral Watkiss has come by intelligence that the Chileans are planning to exclude British shipping from their ports, preferring to trade with the German Empire. Undoubtedly this initiative has come from the Germans rather than from Chile. Do you understand?'

Halfhyde nodded. 'That explains Mr Mayhew, sir. What about Todhunter?'

The rear-admiral said, 'There is a suggestion, no more than that, that Admiral Watkiss may have upset his Chilean superiors. He may find himself in some difficulty – he may face arrest. It is thought that the presence of a member of the Metropolitan Police will be useful. The Chileans may be persuaded that any arrest would be more diplomatically carried out by a British subject and Admiral Watkiss transferred to Todhunter's custody for passage back to Britain.'

iv

Admiral Watkiss would not happily be transferred to anyone's custody, Halfhyde knew. Embarking again upon the underground railway, he found his mind filled with thoughts of Captain Watkiss as he had known him in his naval days. Short, fat, monocled, filled with a sense of his own importance, bombastic, given to strong language, calling all foreigners dagoes, yet often somewhat pathetic in his very bounciness and his utter certainty that he was always right. Admiral Watkiss as he had become when last they had met, glad enough to have a whole navy to command when the British Admiralty had had

8

no more use for him, yet angrily rejecting any suggestion that he was now a Brazilian subject. Out of the hearing of his political masters, he had fulminated about dagoes and how dirty were their habits. Why had he transferred from Brazil to Chile, and how had this remarkable transition been made? The answers to that would be intriguing. But there were worries attached: the *Taronga Park* could be steaming into much trouble, as could her master.

Halfhyde was thoughtful as he went back aboard his ship, and gave monosyllabic replies to Victoria's probing questions; and was still thoughtful that next morning when she accused him of a lack of love. There were matters more pressing than assurances of devotion; and one of them surfaced when St Vincent Halfhyde's passengers began to embark.

TWO

'Hey, mate!' Victoria turned from the port, full of news.

Halfhyde glanced up from his perusal of bills of lading and customs forms. 'What is it, Victoria?'

'You tell me! Look, there's a bloody parson come alongside!'

Halfhyde got up from his desk. 'That'll be Canon Rampling.'

'Canon?' Victoria giggled.

'Not a gun. A religious title, an important man. It would be as well if you became a little less Australian, Victoria.'

'But I am a bloody Aussie!'

'That's just what I mean. Bloody. We don't want to offend the canon by bad language.'

'Ha! You might not, mate, but I don't bloody care! I don't give a bloody fish's tit for no bloody canon. Bloody's a good word down under.'

'Yes, but you're up over now, and the cloth must be respected. So no bloodies in the canon's presence, Victoria, and that's an order.'

'Oh, yes? Where are you off to now?' she added as Halfhyde moved for the door.

'I'm going to welcome Canon Rampling aboard.'

As he went down the ladder from the master's deck to the after well-deck, Halfhyde heard words that sounded like 'bloody bullshit' following him down. Making his way aft for the gangway, he saw the large, beaming face of the clergyman, who was clad, though the day was warm and the drizzle had departed, in a voluminous ulster greatcoat of dark green tweed cloth. Currently Canon Rampling was paying off the cabby while Churchwarden Tidy clambered up the gangway carrying two hold-alls with leather straps. Two of Halfhyde's crew were lifting a vast round-topped trunk from the cab. The paying and unstrapping completed, Canon Rampling turned round and saw Halfhyde.

'Why, Mr Halfhyde, Captain Halfhyde I should now say, it is a long time since we met in South American waters, is it not?'

'It is, Canon – '

'And bound for South America again! Tell me, how do you expect the weather to be?'

'At this time of the year, fair until we're off the pitch of the Horn, where anything may happen.'

'Yes, yes.' Canon Rampling rubbed his hands together, jovially. 'But with your good seamanship, Captain Halfhyde, and of course God's good grace . . . ah, Tidy. You remember my good churchwarden, Captain?'

'Yes. Welcome aboard my ship, Mr Tidy. I trust you and the canon will have a comfortable voyage.'

'Well, I doan't know about that,' Tidy said grudgingly. 'Reckon I doan't relish being aboard ship, not all that much.' He looked around the decks, at the clutter of a ship ready to receive her cargo, at the swung-out derricks and the open hatches that yawned like great pits descending to the ship's bottom. Halfhyde was about to utter some sort of reassurance when there was a yell from outside his cabin.

'Hey, mate!'

Halfhyde looked up irritably. 'What is it, Victoria?'

'Tea's up. Want me to make some for the b – for the passengers, eh?'

Halfhyde raised an eyebrow at Rampling who said he would much appreciate a cup of tea and so would Tidy. Halfhyde said, 'Then come to my cabin, Canon. Once we're at sea, you'll find the saloon will provide for your needs.'

He turned and led the way up the ladders to his cabin, wondering how Canon Rampling would react to Victoria Penn, and vice versa; wondering also how he was to explain the girl's presence to the cloth. To his surprise, he found that Victoria was on her best behaviour, supervising Halfhyde's steward who was laying out the tea cups on a big kneehole desk.

Halfhyde made the introductions and as Canon Rampling shook her hand Victoria gave a kind of curtsey. The top of her dress appeared to be improperly laced; as she bobbed down, her neckline fell forward a little and some of her anatomy was revealed.

'Beg pardon,' she said and stuffed it back. 'Sort of thing that happens when it ought not, eh?'

'It's quite all right,' Rampling said, his face scarlet with embarrassment. 'Fr . . . hrrumph.'

'Eh?'

'I beg your pardon?'

'Said something, didn't you?'

Halfhyde came to the rescue. 'Canon Rampling was clearing his throat, Victoria.'

'Oh.'

The cups of tea were handed round by the steward who then departed. Victoria drank hers in a very ladylike fashion, little finger lifted delicately. Halfhyde and Rampling conversed on matters pertaining to the voyage that lay ahead; and about their last shared service under Captain Watkiss. Canon Rampling remarked that much water had passed since then; and that he was older now than when he and Halfhyde had last met, an obvious statement and a visible one. Rampling, though still large and in places indeed larger, had lost a good deal of his earlier bull-like appearance and, as he now said, some of his fire had gone out. '*Anno domini*,' he said with a sigh, and enquired if Halfhyde had kept in touch with Captain Watkiss. Halfhyde said that they had served together since, on quite a number of occasions, but maintained a discreet silence as to Watkiss' current whereabouts and employment. That was to be a matter strictly between himself and the Admiralty and, presumably, Mayhew and Todhunter when they embarked. While captain and canon conversed, Victoria maintained an unusual silence; Halfhyde, much relieved, fancied the girl was a little out of her depth; dignitaries of the church had not figured much in her life. Churchwarden Tidy was silent also, though he kept darting suspicious glances at Victoria. When offered a second cup of tea he refused.

'Not like Yorkshire tea, that isn't.'

'I'm sorry to hear that,' Halfhyde said coldly.

Canon Rampling blundered in. 'Really, Tidy. Tidy didn't mean to criticize, Captain – '

'Oh yes 'e did,' Tidy said at once. 'No offence, though. Just putting a point of view, like. I reckon I'm entitled. Folks down south likely doan't like Yorkshire tea. Fair's fair.'

There was an uncomfortable silence. Canon Rampling once again cleared his throat; and Victoria began to giggle. Halfhyde brought the social scene to a full stop, briskly. He had, he said, ship matters to attend to. He stood up. His guests also stood up. Canon Rampling uttered thanks and with Tidy he left the cabin. As clergyman and churchwarden went down the ladder, a clear voice floated down after them.

'Got a good look at me bloody tits, mate.'

Canon Rampling sucked in a horrified breath and avoided Mr Tidy's eye.

ii

The great doors of the warehouse were now slid open on their greased rails and the cargo for the *Taronga Park* was brought out and lifted aboard to be stowed under the watchful eye of Mr Hawkins, Halfhyde's chief officer. The scene was one of tremendous bustle and there was a good deal of noise and steam from the winches. Rampling and Tidy watched from the saloon ports, seeing a slice of life that neither had witnessed before – the loading of a merchant ship about to leave the London River for a destination many thousands of miles away. During loading operations, mischances were always liable to occur. They did this time. A sling from the dockside came adrift and a wooden crate dropped to the wharf and split open. In its fall it had struck a man, who now announced in loud tones that it had broken his fucking leg.

'What was that?' Rampling asked.

'Doan't know, Reverend.'

'I believe the man swore.'

'Aye, likely 'e did.'

'I think perhaps I should offer help, Tidy. He may be most seriously injured.'

'If I were you, I'd not.'

'Oh nonsense, Tidy, it's my duty. Come along.'

They left the saloon and descended to the dockside, their movement accompanied by yells of warning from both ship and shore. Halfhyde was already at the scene; the man, though not in fact badly injured, was making fresh reference to his fucking leg, but ceased when the cloth loomed and bent over him.

'It's me leg, sir.'

'Yes, I gathered that.' Rampling stood back; there was nothing he could do other than offer up a prayer for the injured man, which, with bowed head and clasped hands, he did.

'I'm not that bloody bad,' the man said. 'Am I?' He had suddenly gone quite pale, as though Canon Rampling were the Angel of Death in person. Rampling felt offended at the result of prayer. Clicking his tongue, he left the rest of it to Halfhyde. Shortly afterwards there was the urgent ringing of a bell and a horse-drawn ambulance dashed up, the animals in quite a lather, and the injured man was lifted and thrust into the innards of the vehicle, saying something about perishing parsons who put the fear of death into innocent men. But fortunately Canon Rampling, back in the saloon, failed to hear this. He was in fact discussing Victoria Penn.

'The woman with the tea cups, Tidy.'

'Aye. No better than she should be, I reckon.'

'Oh, I don't know about that, Tidy.'

'Doan't you? Then I reckon you ought, Reverend.' No specific mention was made of the escaping breast. 'She has the mark of sin.'

'Really. Well – perhaps. But we mustn't set ourselves up as judges, Tidy. The scriptures are quite specific on the point, as you know.'

'Aye. Casting of stones an' that.' Tidy's tone was full of meaning.

'Are you suggesting. . .?'

'Aye, I am,' Tidy said grimly. 'The woman taken in adultery, Reverend.'

'Well, really, such a thing to suggest, with absolutely no evidence at all! Captain Halfhyde's a man of honour, Tidy.'

Tidy gave a harsh laugh. 'Captain Halfhyde's a man, Reverend.'

'Well, so am I come to that, and you too, Tidy . . .' Rampling decided that enough was enough on that particular topic. He said stiffly, 'I was merely wondering what the lady's precise position in the ship's hierarchy might be, that's all. I think we should perhaps assume her to be Captain Halfhyde's house-keeper, come to sea with him in much the same kind of circumstances as you have accompanied me, Tidy.'

'Aye,' Tidy said sourly, 'perhaps that's reet. And perhaps it's not.'

iii

The loading went on throughout the day; after lunch in the saloon with Victoria, Canon Rampling and Tidy, Halfhyde went ashore to visit the customs authority and the local shipping office of the Board of Trade. Having much business to conduct, he was absent for some time. Shortly after the loading had been completed and while the hatches were being battened down and secured beneath their heavy canvas covers, a square-shaped lady disembarked from another cab and stood on the dockside surveying the ship with a critical look. Victoria was hanging over the rail of the master's deck, wearing a dressing-gown, having just completed an overall wash in the hand-basin in Halfhyde's cabin, a process known to Halfhyde as washing up as far as possible, and down as far as possible, but never washing possible.

The square-shaped lady was showing signs of restiveness. She called up to the deck, loudly. 'On deck there! You men. I have baggage to be brought aboard. Kindly come down at once and get it.'

Victoria watched with interest. Comment came from the hands working on the hatches, and guffaws. They were stopped by the ship's second officer, Mr Lewery. Two hands were detailed to bring the lady's gear aboard. A puff of wind, for a brief moment, blew Victoria's dressing-gown open and a whistle of longish duration came from below. This caused the square-shaped lady to glance up.

'You there. Are you the stewardess?'

Victoria glared. 'No, I'm not the bloody stewardess! This isn't no bloody liner, mate, we don't carry any bloody stewardesses. See, eh?'

The square-shaped woman bristled, her face reddening. 'Do you know who I am? I'm Mrs Weder-Ublick and I have a passage booked aboard the *Taronga Park*.' There was a short hesitation. 'I suppose this *is* the *Taronga Park*? I was told she was berthed here, but the common people have no intelligence, and – '

'It's the bloody *Taronga Park* all right, mate.'

A foot was stamped. By this time all the hands had stopped work and were listening with interest. 'Kindly stop addressing me as mate, I won't have it. And where's the Captain? I intend to report to him *every word* you've said!'

'You do that,' Victoria yelled. 'Just you do that, he'll bloody love you for it, mate.' She cupped her hands the better to ensure that her final broadside was heard beyond all doubt. 'Do that, and Captain Halfhyde, he'll have you off the bloody ship so fast we won't see your bloody arse for dust!'

There was a delighted roar from the deckhands. Victoria might not go down well with the passengers, but she was loved in humbler circles.

iv

'Are you trying to bankrupt me, Victoria?' Halfhyde was furiously angry, having been bearded by Mrs Weder-Ublick the moment he had returned aboard. 'Act like that again, and I'll be damned if I don't send you back to Sydney.'

'Sorry, mate.' Penitence didn't entirely suit Victoria; she giggled.

'And another thing: don't go out on deck in your dressing-gown again. This is a respectable ship, Victoria.'

'Maybe it is, but I'm bloody not. You bloody know I'm not! You've never moaned about it before.' She added, 'Who is this Mrs Weder-Whatsit anyway?'

'She's a passenger.'

'So she said, the fat bitch. I mean *who* is she? German, is she, with a bloody name like that?'

16

'She's not German, she's British – her late husband was German. That's all I know about her. That, and the fact she's going out to Chile to do some missionary work – '

'Missionary, eh?' Victoria gave a shrill laugh. 'God help the poor bloody natives! Any luck, they'll eat her up. Can't wait to see it.' Victoria, full of undampened spirits, wandered round the cabin, still in her dressing-gown. 'Cup of tea, mate, eh?'

'After Mrs Weder-Ublick,' Halfhyde said grimly, 'I need more than tea.' He went across to a cupboard secured to the bulkhead over his desk, unlocked it and brought out a decanter of whisky and a glass. He half filled the glass and, taking the whisky neat, threw it down his throat in a couple of gulps.

'Don't you go and get pissed, mate.'

'Hold your tongue, Victoria,' he said roughly. 'It's wagged more than enough for one day.'

She giggled. 'Think that canon bloke heard what I said about me – '

'I'd not be in the least surprised. You have a loud voice.'

'I know, it's me bloody cross. Why ever did you agree to take a bloody parson, mate, eh?'

'Because I need the fares.'

'Yes, but I thought seamen, they didn't go much on parsons. Bad luck, aren't they, aboard a ship? Make it sink, or something?'

'Don't exaggerate, Victoria. Anyway, superstition is the prerogative of the fo'c'sle crowd. I agree the hands may see Rampling as an omen, but there's no reason why we should.'

'Parsons,' she said musingly. 'Parsons, killing albatrosses, whistling at sea . . . you're all a rum bloody bunch. Reckon I've learned quite a bit about the sea and sailors since I joined up with you, mate. Now there's this old bitch. Bad luck for anyone, I reckon. Missionary! You know something?'

'What?'

'That makes two God botherers. I reckon you should be dead worried, mate.'

v

Mrs Weder-Ublick was settling in. She didn't like the cabin, it

17

was much too small but it would have to do. Mrs Weder-Ublick was a neat and methodical woman, always had been, and at the age of sixty was set in her ways and had made neatness a fetish. Out came her packing, to be set neatly in place. Silver backed hair-brushes and looking-glass, scent bottle – eau-de-cologne, not common scent – powder-bowl with puff, a pink puff given her by her late husband who hadn't quite brought himself to pay for the bowl itself. It wasn't that he hadn't got the money; he had been a wealthy man. It was his meanness. Mrs Weder-Ublick brought out her nightdress and laid it on the pillow of the bunk. Then the dressing-gown, which reminded her of the frightful woman who wasn't a stewardness (and what *was* she? Better, perhaps, not to know). Tooth glass – her own, for unknown glasses could carry disease – for receiving her false teeth at nightfall. Underclothing, yards and yards of it, into drawers that like the cabin were too small; outer garments into the wardrobe ditto. Everything in its place, that was the thing. After cleanliness, neatness.

With all in order Mrs Weder-Ublick knelt down by the bunk, knees creaking a little, put her face in her hands, and offered up a prayer of thanksgiving for a safe arrival through the dangers of London – footpads, dishonest cabbies, confidence tricksters who seized upon lonely widows in overnight hotels, chambermaids who stole, common prostitutes in every nook and cranny – and then another prayer for her continuing safety over the seas to distant Chile. Prayers over, she emerged into the short alleyway outside her cabin with the intention of exploring the vessel to find out precisely where everything was if they were overcome by disaster and had to abandon ship. That, after all, was a part of neatness, and of course it was one's duty to be prepared.

She all but bumped into a small, skinny man wearing a bowler hat with a length of black silk cord leading from its brim to an anchorage point on the lapel of his black coat. She said, 'Really!'

The bowler hat was lifted. 'Beg pardon, ma'am. Just come aboard.'

'I thought I heard a clumping noise on the deck.' She had

noted that the person, whose breath smelled, had very big feet. 'Who are you, may I ask? One of the crew?'

'No, ma'am, I assure you . . . Detective Inspector Todhunter of the Metropolitan Police Force. A passenger.' The man produced a pasteboard card that supported his contention as to who he was. 'I trust I've given no offence? I was merely passing by.'

'Quite.' Mrs Weder-Ublick thought him common. 'A policeman. Has there been a murder?' She smiled; this was supposed to be a joke.

'I trust not, ma'am, indeed I trust not. I should state that I am not expecting any such aboard the ship.'

'You're *just* a passenger?'

'That is so, ma'am, and not one who much looks forward to the prospect of rough seas, being inclined to seasickness. My old mother, my *late* mother I should explain – '

'Yes.' Mrs Weder-Ublick thought it in keeping with such a common little man that he should mention seasickness, an indelicate subject for discussion with a lady, but Mr Todhunter was not to be deflected, detectives of the Metropolitan Police Force never were, and he continued.

'On a sea trip aboard the paddle steamer from Clarence Pier in Southsea to Ryde pierhead in the Isle of Wight it was. Oh, she was dreadfully sick I do declare! But there was an angel of mercy, one of the stewards, who recommended Dr Datchet's Demulcent Drops, of which I have a supply.' Mr Todhunter delved into a pocket and brought out a small jar which he shook in Mrs Weder-Ublick's face. She stepped backwards involuntarily. 'They never fail, ma'am, never. If you should need – '

'Thank you. I shall *not* be in need. Please excuse me.' Mrs Weder-Ublick gathered up her skirts and more or less swept into Mr Todhunter, forcing a retreat. She proceeded along the alleyway and emerged into the dockland daylight somewhere amidships, though this she didn't know, where there was a strange grumbling noise coming from beneath her feet, from beneath a sort of skylight from which came a hot smell, oily and disagreeable. She peered down, being of an inquisitive nature, and saw a kind of platform with a rail running round it, no doubt for safety, and a man on it, blackened and very nearly naked. Looking up at that moment he caught her eye and gave her a wink. This she met with a stony glare and turned away. She began to regret her resolve to travel to Chile, to regret even more that she had not booked aboard a liner of the Pacific Steam Navigation Company, which would have transported her in comfort and dignity to begin her mission to the unfortunate natives, the ignorant peasantry of South America. But immediately these thoughts came to her she rejected them, steeling herself to her duty, reminding herself that her late husband's money was not to be spent upon frivolities such as comfortable passages and the fawning attentions of stewards and stewardesses who in the ships of the PSNC would scarcely be comparable with the abandoned woman in the dressing-gown. There must be suffering and she must not weaken.

Turning, she once again encountered Mr Todhunter. He seemed to have followed her, which she didn't like. Helpfully, he pointed down the hatch. 'The engine-room, ma'am.'

'I see.'

'The fount of movement, in the absence of sails.'

'Naturally. I – '

'Dependable, ma'am. Wind or no wind, they drive us on. You need have no fear about safety, ma'am – '

'I never – '

'And Captain St Vincent Halfhyde, ma'am, is a fine and experienced seaman, both in the Royal Navy and now in command of his own ship – '

'Do I take it you have sailed with Captain Halfhyde before?'

'I have indeed, ma'am,' Todhunter said, placing something on the deck as though for a long conversation. For the first time Mrs Weder-Ublick noticed the detective's Gladstone bag. 'Twice before now.'

'Then perhaps you can throw some light on the woman, Mr Todhunter?'

'The woman? Oh, yes. Miss Penn, Miss Victoria Penn – '

'Not his wife, then. I confess I thought not. What is she?'

'Ah,' Mr Todhunter said, clearing his throat in some embarrassment. That was sufficient for Mrs Weder-Ublick; she snorted. Her view had been tacitly confirmed.

Early, very early next morning, shortly before the *Taronga Park* was due to sail, the last of the passengers arrived aboard: Mr Mayhew of the Foreign Office, coming alongside with a degree of pomp and fussiness as befitted the arrival of an important personage, a senior clerk in Her Majesty's employ, an official who, though his style had the unfortunate sound of one labouring in lesser spheres such as a bank, an insurance office or a firm of wholesale corn merchants, was in sober fact the next most senior person after the Permanent Assistant Under-Secretary of State himself. And Mr Mayhew was second-in-command of the South American desk. So he disembarked not from a common hackney carriage but from a brougham furnished by the Foreign Office, and he wore a tall hat and a frock coat. He also had a large amount of luggage – thirty-nine pieces in all, which followed behind the brougham in the body of a station waggon.

Halfhyde looked down impatiently from the bridge.

'Mr Mayhew!'

Mayhew looked up two ways at once; he was slightly cross-eyed. 'Ah, Captain Halfhyde, we meet again. Good morning to you.'

'Good morning.' Halfhyde indicated the station waggon. 'What's all that? Am I embarking a half battalion of troops?'

Mayhew, a sallow man with a bad-tempered expression and a black moustache which he had a habit of tweaking in order to emphasize points, replied that the waggon contained his luggage.

'God help us all!' Halfhyde murmured. Then he called down, 'Get it aboard double quick, Mr Mayhew – I'll send some hands. The tugs are due shortly, and I have to catch the tide. Had you been ten minutes later I would have already sailed without you.'

'And thereby incurred the displeasure of –' Mr Mayhew broke off, recalling that his mission was at this stage supposed to be cloaked in a degree of secrecy and that it would be unwise to invoke in person Her Majesty's Secretary of State for Foreign Affairs. He amended what he had been going to say. 'Of certain persons of whom you know.'

'To hell with certain persons, Mr Mayhew – '

'There's no need to be peremptory, Captain Halfhyde,' Mayhew stated in an admonitory yell. Halfhyde eschewed further argument, passing an order down to the bosun for all hands that could be spared to empty the station waggon at speed. The gear was roughly handled; already the tugs with the mud pilot aboard one of them were approaching the lock gate, where the caissons were standing open in readiness. Mr Mayhew hovered in some distress, urging the men to have a care as his boxes were dumped unceremoniously on the deck, fuming at Halfhyde's tone, at his gibe about half battalions, really! Persons highly-placed in the Foreign Office could not possibly travel like other people; they had appearances to keep up, after all. Her Majesty would wish her representative to be properly dressed at all times – even at sea aboard such a trumpery vessel as the *Taronga Park*. And while the sea voyage could be cold and wet, Chile was at times a hot land; thus the thirty-nine pieces of Mr Mayhew's luggage contained items to deal with a variety of needs: many thick vests and the new-fangled flannel combinations that protected an important person's lower parts, an assortment of shirts with starched cuffs and collars for both day and evening wear, nightshirts of varying thicknesses to be worn as the climate dictated, and a large assortment of white jackets and trousers for informal wear in Chile where the sweat penetrated and showed yellow patches thus enforcing frequent changes. All this in addition to the formal dress that might be required during his mission: dinner jackets both white and black, tails, frock coats, and levee dress of dark blue embellished with gold-laced frogging for use if he should be bidden to a party given by the British Minister or by the President of Chile, when Mr Mayhew would also be expected to wear, or anyway carry, a cocked hat like an admiral. All this, common seamen could not perhaps be expected to understand; though Mr Mayhew believed that in fact the wretched Halfhyde understood it only too well. Mr Mayhew remembered from his voyage to the Amazon with Halfhyde that the latter had a sharpish view of persons whose careers were largely spent behind desks.

'Well, goodbye bloody England,' Victoria said as the *Taronga Park* emerged into an early-morning mist over the Thames, known to seafarers as the London River. 'You know something, do you?'

'No.'

'Right, I'll bloody tell you, then! That Mrs Weder-Whatsit she's a bloody snob. Bloody missionaries, they've no right to be snobs, eh?'

'In what way is she a snob?' Halfhyde's attention was on the tugs, which were about to be cast off.

'Thinks I'm common. Wouldn't bloody talk at dinner. And when I went along to ask her if there was anything she wanted, women's things, she sort of fluffed her bloody skirt at me as though I was some sort of disease carrier.' Suddenly Victoria giggled. 'Know what? Her cabin stank of bloody moth balls. There's a photo of her husband there, or I reckon it's him. Right old geezer with side-whiskers and a boozer's nose. Rat trap mouth, like hers. Dog collar beneath all the bloody fluff. Did you know?'

'That he was of the cloth? No, I didn't. It's scarcely remarkable, though.'

'I reckon a German reverend is. *Do* the Germans have reverends?'

'I see no reason why not. Lutherans or some such. I – '

'Could explain the missionary lark, I reckon. Bloody old cow. Anyway, she ought to be a good mate for that canon bloke.' She paused. 'Where was he at dinner last night, eh?'

'He said he was going ashore.'

'Say why?'

'I didn't ask, Victoria.'

She gave one of her giggles. 'Dockland Daisies, could be. Reckon I may have set the old goat off by letting me tits show.'

THREE

In April, Chile was moderately hot; in the port of Iquique, on the northern seaboard fronting the Atacama Desert, it was very hot. Admiral Watkiss, Commander-in-Chief of the Chilean Navy, was very hot indeed after an exhausting forenoon spent in inspecting his one and only battleship, lying off the port in brilliant sunshine and a stifling lack of breeze. The ship, like the old battleship *Meridian* that he had years before brought out for transfer to Chile as a sale offer from Her Majesty Queen Victoria, had once been British, sailing the seas under the White Ensign and manned by smart British bluejackets, orders being given largely by bugle blown by a bugler of the Royal Marine Light Infantry, everything done with precision when, for instance, coming to anchor; anchor let go in the same split-second that the lower boom and quarter-boom were swung out and the accommodation-ladder lowered and the Union Flag broken out at the jackstaff, that sort of thing.

It was different now. HMS *King William IV* was now the *Almirante Smith*, renamed on transfer in honour of one Admiral Smith, another Englishman who had commanded the Chilean Navy some sixty years before Admiral Watkiss – it was good to know, of course, that the damn dagoes preferred Englishmen to command their fleet, but still. It was all so different from Her Majesty's ships; and Iquique, a smelly place, was very different from the Royal dockyards of Portsmouth, Chatham and Devonport. Ashore, persons defecated in the street, no better than the dogs that did the same. Harlots abounded, but that of course was *not* so very different from the British seaports where sailors would be men and why not for heaven's sake – it was *dago* harlots that irritated Admiral Watkiss. And upon occasions, he had to confess, tempted him which was perhaps why they irritated . . .

The *Almirante Smith*, supposed to have been prepared for the Commander-in-Chief's inspection, had been filthy. Absolutely filthy and very unseamanlike. Captain Salvador del Campo was no Lord Nelson, his executive officer Commander Manuel Latrinez was no Earl of Clanwilliam, that stalwart disciplinarian who had been rumoured to have once eaten a midshipman for breakfast and who had commanded the Flying Squadron under sail when Admiral Watkiss had been a younger officer.

The ship's company's washing had trailed on lines running from the signal bridge to the jackstaff in the bows where the slips and cables showed rust. Among the washing were strange garments – strange, that was, to find aboard a warship.

Admiral Watkiss had poked at one of these garments with his telescope and screwed his monocle more firmly into his eye. 'What's this, Captain?'

'Knickers, *Almirante.*'

'Oh, damn it, I'm aware of that, I didn't come down with the last shower! I meant *why* knickers?'

Captain del Campo's English was not good; and Admiral Watkiss refused to learn any dago language, whatever it was the Chileans spoke which he believed to be Spanish. Captain del Campo shrugged and said, 'For modesty, *Almirante.*'

The telescope was waved dangerously close to Captain del Campo and Admiral Watkiss bounced on the balls of his feet. 'Oh, God give me strength, I'm aware of that too! Why are the blasted things hanging on your damn washing line, that's what I want to know – and why's the damn washing there at all? We don't carry on like that in the British Navy, you know.'

Captain del Campo answered the first question first. 'The ladies' knickers – '

'Whores, harlots.'

'You say?'

'I said whores and harlots. Not ladies. Go on.'

'Yes, *Almirante.* The – female persons, they are permitted

25

aboard when it is not convenient for the men to be given shore
leave, such as now when they have been busily cleaning ship for
your – '

'Cleaning! Damn ship's a blasted disgrace, and that's fact, I
said it. I've never heard of such a thing in all my life, whores
allowed aboard! It's to stop instantly, d'you hear me, Captain
del Campo? *Instantly!* And no more blasted hanging out of
washing – of any sort. Not in port. Doesn't matter so much at
sea.'

'But *Almirante,* we do not go much to sea – '

'I'm aware of that.' There was a coldness in Admiral
Watkiss' voice. He disliked the reminder that his command was
mostly a landbound one. 'You must make other arrangements.
And get those women off.'

Captain del Campo sighed and muttered something at his
executive officer, who yelled in an unseemly fashion at a person
Watkiss took to be a petty officer, though the man was not
wearing any identifiable uniform. Watkiss proceeded on his
inspection, finding fault frequently. There was a mess on the
deck, large and splodgy, and again the telescope was brought
into play.

'Good God, look at that!'

'Excellent guano, *Almirante* – '

'Oh. I call it birdshit.'

One thing led to another. Admiral Watkiss went below to
tour the messdecks and flats. He enquired about the heads.
This British naval term was misunderstood, and Watkiss
explained irritably. 'Latrines, Captain.'

Commander Latrinez came forward. 'Yes, *Almirante?*'

'Not *you!*'

Shortly before Admiral Watkiss left the ship, refusing the
offer of a glass of sherry in the wardroom, which he had already
noted was a filthy place with slack stewards loafing about and
even sitting in the officers' chairs, a strange procession formed
up for embarkation in the *Almirante Smith*'s cutters, brought
from the lower boom to the accommodation-ladder. The
whores and harlots, summarily ejected and all yelling at once,
probably about the loss of earnings, Watkiss supposed. They

were of all shapes and ages – fat, thin, young girls, old women with sagging breasts and stomachs, all scantily clad to the point of indecency.

Watkiss said, 'Well, you've obeyed my order promptly enough I must say, Captain. I'm obliged.'

'*Gracias, Almirante.*' Captain del Campo seemed ill-at-ease despite the praise. 'There is a difficulty, I am so sorry. Your galley . . . it has had a hole made by bumping against a ringbolt in the side of the ship. *Almirante*, I am desolated . . . but of course you may use the ship's boats . . .'

Admiral Watkiss went willy-nilly back to the shore in company with the whores and harlots. When he had gone del Campo and Latrinez took a strong drink together, sitting outside the Captain's quarters on the sternwalk and watching the cutters go inshore with the harlot-swamped Commander-in-Chief. They talked in their own language about Admiral Watkiss. The man was an imbecile, an imbecile who didn't even know his own naval history. Why, the great Vice-Admiral Nelson of the Nile, Duke of Bronte, victor of so many glorious sea battles, had permitted women aboard his line-of-battle ships. It was well known that the British naval expression 'son of a gun' came directly from intercourse beneath the muzzles of the cannons, and that sons so born were honoured in the British Fleet and many had become great heroes like Lord Nelson himself. The British Admiral, now a Chilean, was a stupid fiend and very rude. But perhaps, said Captain del Campo, his reign as Commander-in-Chief might not last for much longer.

'So?' asked Commander Latrinez with eagerness.

Captain del Campo laid a finger alongside a rather sharp nose. 'I hear stirrings in Santiago. There are enemies, men close to the President. *Almirante* Watkiss has been a little indiscreet over certain matters. I say no more, and this is strictly between you and me.'

ii

It was a long and uncomfortable journey by coach to Valparaiso, where Admiral Watkiss was due to inspect the port installations. He decided to spend the night, as he had spent the

27

previous night, at the local lodging house of the Salvation Army, British and well run. The Salvation Army respected persons of his position and in any case always welcomed seamen. And the bed that Admiral Watkiss had slept in the previous night had been reasonably comfortable and very clean – naturally, being British. Admiral Watkiss trudged from the somewhat derelict jetty where the *Almirante Smith*'s boat had dumped him, and dumped was the word since the sternsheets-man hadn't been up to his job and Admiral Watkiss had nearly been projected into the water on disembarkation with the harlots. He trudged through the terrible heat and dust and the attentions of roaming dogs filled with mange, past tired-looking natives slumped on the ground beneath big straw hats, wearing his full-dress uniform as Commander-in-Chief, a curious mixture, largely of his own invention, of British and Chilean formal wear. Overlong white shorts flapped about his knees, emphasising the skinniness of his legs beneath the portly stomach covered by the white tunic – once starched, now limp – that was itself adorned with various medals and orders bestowed upon him by the President of Chile. A number of gold tassels swung as Admiral Watkiss trudged, and sweat poured down his face from beneath the cocked hat from the top of which sprung the feathers of an ostrich. His full-dress sword, British naval pattern, dangled from a patent-leather sword-belt concealed beneath the white jacket. This was troublesome to walk with for long, and Admiral Watkiss seized it in his left hand and held it clear of the dust and other things that lay along the way.

As he began to approach the citadel of the Salvation Army, he saw Major Barnsley, the citadel's commanding officer, emerging and coming to greet him. Barnsley, who had told Admiral Watkiss that his last citadel command had been in Valparaiso where he had met many men of the British Navy, was a good fellow: respectful and humble.

'You look hot, Admiral. May I suggest the cup that cheers? Mrs Barnsley has the kettle on.'

'Thank you, Barnsley. Not as strong as this morning. I don't like it. Kindly tell her.'

'I will, sir, I will. Though I must say the sailors seem to like it – '

'Oh, common seamen would.'

Major Barnsley fell into step beside Watkiss. 'Mrs Barnsley's tea was a landmark of life in Valparaiso, known to, and much appreciated by, most of the seamen passing through the port. It may be because it was, and still is, issued free of charge,' he added humbly.

Admiral Watkiss grunted and lashed out at an attack from flies. As he and the major entered the citadel, Watkiss removed his cocked hat and handed it to Major Barnsley to be put in a place of safety. He was then ushered into the Barnsleys' private sitting-room, a small slice of England acting as an oasis in the doubtful surroundings of Iquique. There were antimacassars on the chair-backs, a sick-looking aspidistra gloomed in a pot in the window, china dogs smiled from the mantelpiece, the paintwork was dark brown, and a huge paper fan reposed in the otherwise empty fireplace. There was a horsehair settee upon which Watkiss sat, rising perfunctorily to his feet when Mrs Barnsley entered with the tea tray. The tea was accompanied by rock buns, and half a seed cake.

'The cup that cheers, sir.' Mrs Barnsley was an echo of her husband and had a similar physical aspect, both of them being stout, round and merry. 'Just fresh mashed, like.'

'Oh. Er – thank you, Mrs Barnsley.'

'It's no trouble, sir. It's an honour to have such an important gentleman visit us.' Mrs Barnsley sat down to pour and having poured remained where she was. Admiral Watkiss shifted fretfully; it seemed he was to have the woman for company while he drank his tea. The major, too; for Admiral Watkiss had scarcely lifted his cup before the salvationist came in, rubbing his hands and looking cheerful.

'I 'ope you had a successful day, Admiral,' he said.

'Ship was filthy,' Watkiss snapped.

'Oh dear, dear. I call that a shame when you – '

'I call it more than a shame. Damned disgraceful. I shall have my work cut out, I can tell you, to bring the fleet up to a reasonable standard, a fleet in which one can take pride.'

Admiral Watkiss dislodged a beetle that had crept onto his white tunic. 'But I need hardly say I shall achieve results, and that's fact, I said it. By the time of my next inspection the flagship will be a different story or I shall know the reason why.'

'Yes, indeed, sir.' Major Barnsley, somewhat out of his depth in present company, hummed a hymn tune, wondering what to say next. He chose the wrong tack. He said, 'I'm sure you'll work wonders, sir, with the Lord's help. I've no doubt you think of yourself as a Chilean now, sir – '

Watkiss reddened. 'No, I damn well don't! Kindly refrain from impertinence, Major Barnsley.'

'Oh, dear, I never meant – '

'I can't damn well *stand* foreigners,' said the Commander-in-Chief of the Chilean Navy. 'They're not damn well *British*!'

iii

In a huff, Admiral Watkiss retired to his bedroom, furnished from England like the sitting-room. There was a large double bed with brass knobs on the bedposts, decent linen sheets covered by a white counterpane embroidered with a view of Scarborough; there were two hard upright chairs, a washstand, a small desk like something from a schoolroom, a flimsy wardrobe and a cupboard for the bedroom utensil. There were also mosquitoes, and the brass bedstead had been provided with a mosquito-net. The room was the Barnsleys' private spare room and Admiral Watkiss had been grudgingly grateful; but it was all a far cry from the splendid accommodation provided for flag officers of the British Navy on their tours of inspection. Fine mahogany wardrobes, bedroom, study and drawing-room provided, excellent dinners with whisky, sherry, port, brandy, liqueurs, cigars . . . no Yorkshire-mashed tea. And plenty of well-disciplined stewards.

Nevertheless, Admiral Watkiss was not without a servant, and that servant should be here now, attending upon his master. After a short interval, Watkiss left his room and bellowed down the stairs for Major Barnsley.

'Where's that man of mine?'

'Coming, sir,' a voice answered, and a moment later Petty

30

Officer Steward Washbrook appeared with a basket of fruit. 'Bin shopping, sir.'

'Oh.' Admiral Watkiss went back into his room. He didn't much like Washbrook, but at least the fellow was British – Watkiss, on transfer from Brazil to Chile, had insisted on a British personal steward and representations had been made to the British Admiralty that a steward of Petty Officer rank might be sought and offered the billet as Commander-in-Chief's servant. The Admiralty, where Watkiss still had a few enemies posing as friends, had done better than that. Files were examined and a name was chosen and signals were made that landed in the cubby-hole of the Drafting Master-at-Arms in the barrack hulks in Portsmouth Dockyard. Petty Officer Steward Washbrook was awaiting Court Martial for sundry offences that included embezzlement of mess funds from the wardroom of HMS *Lord Rodney*, his last ship; selling stores from ditto for his personal profit; and being drunk and incapable when supervising the wardroom stewards on the occasion of a visit from Her Majesty Queen Victoria to her fleet when he had uttered insulting remarks to Her Majesty in person, accusing her, for reasons of his own concerned with the earlier loss of a good-conduct badge and with the subsequent drop in pay, of being as tight as a gnat's arse. His later insistence that what he had really said was 'light of a nation's hearts' was not accepted; but in view of the personal nature of this insult, and the pain that would be caused to Her Majesty by any publicity attending upon the Court Martial, it was not considered wholly desirable that a trial should be proceeded with; and Admiral Watkiss' request had come at a very opportune moment. Petty Officer Steward Washbrook was offered transfer to the Chilean Navy and attendance upon its Commander-in-Chief. There was glee at the Admiralty; the two would be a penance to each other, each in fact deserved the other, and two birds were killed with the one stone. Admiral Watkiss, naturally, was not told of Washbrook's service record.

'What have you got?' Watkiss demanded, peering into the basket.

'Luscious fruit, sir, very luscious. Cost a fair lot it did.'

Washbrook multiplied the actual sum by three. There were melons, oranges, apples and other things, local produce strange to Admiral Watkiss. Washbrook said some of the fruit was imported, hence the price. He had in fact made an advantageous arrangement with the bosun of a recently arrived steamship carrying fruit, the bosun being also on the nick, but he felt no need to report this.

Admiral Watkiss ate some of the fruit: it kept the scurvy at bay and was excellent for the bowels and the apples were reminders of England. Eating them, he was overcome by a wave of nostalgia. He would give much to see Portsmouth again, the town filled in the evenings by roaring crowds of libertymen, seamen in bell-bottomed trousers with smart blue jumpers and collars, the names of their ships laced in gold thread on their cap-ribbons, lusty men seeking drink and women . . . the Naval Town Patrol in their gaiters and with side-arms marching the streets and arresting the more exuberant spirits before murder was committed . . . the stirrings of the bushes in Victoria Park or on Southsea Common where seamen, long deprived of women whilst at sea, cavorted with the town whores.

'Damn this blasted place, Washbrook.'

'Aye, sir.'

'Rat-infested hole.'

'Aye, sir, it be that, sir.' Washbrook had a crafty face, not unlike a rat himself. 'Better off, sir, in Valparaiso or Santiago, sir.'

'Yes. Much better. I rather wish I'd gone by the coach this evening.'

'Bumpy roads, sir, very bumpy.'

'They'll have to be faced tomorrow, Washbrook.'

'They will that, sir.'

'The train,' Admiral Watkiss said with a far-away look in his eye. 'The train from Waterloo to Portsmouth. The comfort!'

'Aye, sir, very comfortable it be, sir.'

'England in April.' Admiral Watkiss got to his feet, a sudden resolution made. 'You'll join me in a drink, Washbrook. Naturally, I have never made a habit of drinking with the lower deck. But we're two British exiles in a damn dago country and I intend to stretch the regulations for once. We shall drink to Her Majesty.'

'Thankee, sir, thankee very much, sir.' The Petty Officer Steward looked on in some alarm as Admiral Watkiss approached the cupboard containing the bedroom utensil. In the cupboard was a bottle of whisky and in the Commander-in-Chief's absence aboard the *Almirante Smith* Washbrook had helped himself and then topped the bottle up with water. But all was well; Admiral Watkiss didn't appear to have noticed when, after pouring, he drank; his mind was far away in England's green and pleasant land. Almost with tears in his eyes, he proposed the toast to Her Majesty.

Between them admiral and steward finished the bottle; when it was empty Admiral Watkiss brought out another from a locked portmanteau. They grew maudlin; Petty Officer Steward Washbrook embarked on a rambling reminiscence of his early days as gunroom steward, when what he spoke of as 'them young whipper-snapper gennelmen, sir, them midshipmen', had made life hell for those attendant upon them, and then boozily apologized because Admiral Watkiss had himself once been a midshipman. They began to sing loudly, nostalgic songs of glory about Hearts of Oak, and Soldiers of the Queen, and Goodbye Dolly Gray, and Rule, Britannia. The noise caused consternation below in the citadel, but Major Barnsley didn't like to remonstrate with an admiral so it was allowed to pass.

Petty Officer Steward Washbrook at length fell from his chair and in so doing crashed against the flimsy wardrobe, which also fell, and in turn dislodged another portmanteau placed upon its top. The portmanteau came open and discharged its contents. The two began attempts to clear up the mess, and Major Barnsley at last looked in. Shocked, he nevertheless offered his assistance.

'Go away, blast you.'

'But – '

'Oh, bugger off!'

'Oh, dear me. Oh, dear, dear.' His homely face crumpled in

dismay, Major Barnsley went away and left them to it. Admiral Watkiss would be contrite in the morning without a doubt, and sick too. A prayer went up from the staircase as Major Barnsley entreated the good Lord to look with compassion upon those who erred and strayed from their ways, though in all conscience neither Admiral Watkiss nor his man looked much like lost sheep. In the bedroom Watkiss flailed about among his possessions and a worn leather case came open and a number of photographs were lavishly scattered. Washbrook assisted as best he could with recovery and sat for a while staring at what appeared to be a family group. The young Watkiss in a sailor suit, two middle-aged parents, the father in the uniform of a captain RN. A little apart from the group stood a young woman, square shaped and with a grim expression, in a pinafore that was too small for her, and hair not yet put up.

Petty Officer Steward Washbrook gave a series of hiccups, then asked, 'Your young lady, sir? Your lady wife, sir, maybe?'

'Fiddlesticks, man! Young lady be buggered . . . it's a f-f-family group and that's my blasted sister . . .'

'A handsome young lady, sir.'

'Oh, balls and bang me arse, quite the reverse. Back of an omnibus. Character to suit . . . can't stand the woman, never could. Got worse . . . married some sort of blasted foreigner, damn Hun . . . can't stand blasted Huns, worse than most dagoes. Never corresponded with her since. Only kept the damn photograph because my father and mother . . . pity about my blasted sister ruining it. I think we should h – have another drink, Washbrook . . .'

'Begging your pardon, sir, there ain't any left.'

'Oh. In that case you may dismiss. And pull yourself together. I'm going to turn in.'

In the morning, Petty Officer Steward Washbrook, who had been berthed in the common seamen's dormitory where many of the occupants had been in a condition similar to his own, came to Admiral Watkiss.

'What you said about Huns, sir. Germans, sir.'

'Yes, yes.' Admiral Watkiss' head spun in circles; the pain was excruciating. 'What did I say, Washbrook?'

34

'Ar, sir.' Washbrook had, as a result of long experience, already assessed the situation: Admiral Watkiss was unable to recall much of what he had said. 'Said a lot, you did, sir. About Huns, sir.'

'*What* did I say?'

'Said they were dishonest buggers, sir. Not to be trusted, sir. Said they was scum, sir, not fit to lick a British officer's boots, sir. A lot like that, sir.' Washbrook pursed his lips. 'They do say sir, in Santiago, sir, that them Germans is taking a hinterest in Chile, sir. That emperor, sir. 'Er Majesty's grandson, sir.'

'Leave the Queen out of this, Washbrook.'

'Yessir.'

'Nobody heard me.'

'Begging your pardon, sir, I did. And Major Barnsley, sir.'

Watkiss blew out his cheeks. 'He couldn't possibly!'

'You was declaiming loud, sir. About your sister, sir, what 'ad married one o' them buggers, sir. Major Barnsley, sir, 'e 'ad 'is ear glued to the key'ole like a leech, sir.'

Admiral Watkiss mopped sweat from his face with a corner of the sheet. 'What are you suggesting, Washbrook?'

'Me, sir?' Washbrook was all innocence. 'Why, sir, nothing, sir. Not up to me, sir. But if I was you, sir, I'd watch it. I'd use care in what I said, sir, if I may say so without offence. An' if what you did say already ever came out, sir, then the Chileans might not like it, sir. That's all, sir. I reckon you get my meaning, sir.'

Watkiss did. He was now in the hands of his own steward and a major of the Salvation Army. The implications were unpleasant. There had, he was aware, been mutterings against him in high circles in Santiago: his position as Commander-in-Chief was not all that secure and although Chile was a frightful place for a Briton he was at least an admiral in it . . .

Petty Officer Steward Washbrook gave a discreet cough into his hand. 'I bin thinking, sir. My duties as your steward, sir, they be fairly honerous. Long hours an' that, sir. Not that I mind, sir, o' course,' he said unctuously. 'But in the British Navy, sir, as you know, officers what get extra care from their stewards, they reward them, sir. Extra pay, sir. Out o' their own pockets, sir, they do.'

Slowly, Admiral Watkiss reached for his purse on top of the utensil cupboard. He brought out a gold *peso* coin and flung it ill-temperedly at Washbrook.

'Thankee, sir. Thankee very much, sir. That's what I call generous, sir.'

Admiral Watkiss hissed through clenched teeth. This, he knew, was only the start. He blamed it all on his sister. If that photograph hadn't emerged he would never have mentioned Huns.

FOUR

When Canon Rampling had gone ashore, still clad in his heavy tweed ulster greatcoat, for it might rain, nothing had been further from his mind, naturally, than the Dockland Daisies hypothesized by Miss Penn. He was simply fulfilling a promise made to the clergyman who had succeeded him in his Yorkshire parish that he would pay a call on the vicar of St Luke's in London's dockland, the two men being brothers, and convey messages of goodwill. Churchwarden Tidy had been left aboard the *Taronga Park*, complaining of tiredness after the long train journey from York; and as Canon Rampling emerged from the dock gate, he wished fervently that he had Tidy with him, for there was no mistaking the character and calling of the young woman who approached him.

'Evening, mister.'

'Good evening, madam.' Canon Rampling, drawing in a shocked breath, tried to push past but the young woman, hussy would be a better word, stood in his way.

'Off a boat, mister?'

'Yes, I – '

'Give you a good time I could. What's your fancy, eh?'

'Fancy?' Canon Rampling looked round wildly for a policeman, without success.

'Well, you know.' She indicated her tariff, verbally. 'Just a florin for basic like. Extra for the rest. Coming with me, are you?'

Canon Rampling drew himself up. 'Really! I most certainly am not! I have never heard of anything so disgraceful, never.'

She glared at him. 'Mean old sod.'

'I am not mean. That is scarcely the point, I fear. Can you not see the evil of what I take you to be suggesting, my poor girl?'

'No,' she said blatantly, looking him full in the face. 'I give a service, don't I? Seamen what have been a long while heaving about on the bloomin' sea – '

'I am not a seaman. I am of the cloth.' Canon Rampling opened his greatcoat in a wide gesture, revealing the clerical collar. 'There! What have you to say to that, may I ask?'

The fallen girl stared, then gave a hoot of laughter and – Canon Rampling devoutly thanked his Maker – turned away. That was when both she and Rampling saw the policeman advancing from a side street. There was a warren of side streets and into one of them the girl vanished. Letting her go, the policeman advanced on Canon Rampling, who had buttoned his coat right up again.

'Well now. Off a boat.' The constable rocked back and forth on his heels, hands clasped behind his back, a large battery lamp fastened to his leather belt. 'Flashing, was you?'

'*Flashing?* My good fellow, it is not I who has the lamp.'

'I'm not speaking of me lamp, sir.' The constable had recognized the voice of a gentleman. 'I see you open your coat up, sir, to the young woman. A shocking act, sir.'

'Well, really! How can that possibly be shocking? I was merely doing what I could to repel the advances of that deplorable young woman.'

'May I enquire as to how, sir?'

'By revealing that I am in holy orders.' Canon Rampling once again opened his greatcoat. 'There. My collar.' He added on a jocular note, 'It appeared to be successful. Like the devil confronted by the Cross.'

'Yessir.' The constable touched his helmet. 'Beg your pardon, sir, I'm sure. Case of a mistake. You're not used to this part of London, I take it, sir?'

'No – '

'Evil lurks, sir, and that young woman was one of thousands. May I ask where you're going, sir?'

Canon Rampling told him; the constable was helpful,

offering to accompany him to St Luke's vicarage. They set off together; the day was darkening fast by now, and shadows flitted before the approach of the law, diving into more side streets. There was certainly plenty of evil around. When they parted the constable said the reverend had best ask his host to send a man to the police station, not far away, and an escort would be provided back to the dock gate. Thanking the constable, Canon Rampling was still unsure as to why the man should have imagined him to be flashing a lamp, and even if he had been, surely it was no crime? He mentioned it to the vicar of St Luke's, who was as baffled as himself, and was much concerned to learn about the way the canon had been approached by sin.

ii

In the morning, at a dreadfully early breakfast after the ship had moved out into the river, there were the attentions of Miss Penn to contend with.

'G'morning, Reverend. Have a good time ashore, did you?'

'Yes, thank you.'

Victoria giggled. 'Good on yer, mate! Really enjoyed it, eh?'

'Oh, very much indeed.'

'Missed supper, you did.'

'I was provided with a most excellent dinner.'

'You don't say! My God, you wouldn't have been, not in bloody Sydney! All for free?'

Canon Rampling was beginning to feel uncomfortable, knowing that for some reason the wretched girl was laughing up her sleeve at him. With dignity he said, 'Of course. I would hardly be expected to pay, would I?'

'Dunno, mate. You live and learn, eh? I'm glad you enjoyed it. But remember what it says in the Bible – you pay later. That right?'

He was amazed that she had ever heard of the Bible. He quoted her the relevant chapter and verse but she seemed to lose interest and left the saloon. After her departure, Mrs Weder-Ublick came in for her breakfast, served by the steward. She and Rampling exchanged good mornings and she sat down briskly, pulling her chair forward beneath her with almost a male movement, not waiting for Rampling to rise to his feet – which he did a trifle late – and thrust it under her.

'Please don't get up, Canon. No ceremony for me.'

'Ah – no. Yes.' Rampling sat again. Bacon and eggs, fried, were brought for Mrs Weder-Ublick. Rampling attempted some conversation. 'I dare say we'll not be as comfortable as this once the ship is out upon the sea.'

'Possibly not.'

'I heard one of the seamen saying – '

'No doubt. I don't talk at breakfast, never did.' Mrs Weder-Ublick brought out a book from somewhere inside her skirts and opened it, propping it against a jar of marmalade. The book, Rampling saw, was a treatise on South American Indians. The meal finished in a silence broken only by a loud champing sound from Mrs Weder-Ublick's false teeth as she chewed toast.

iii

By 10 a.m. the *Taronga Park* had cleared the London River and was making around the North Foreland for the Downs. Halfhyde paced the bridge with the channel pilot, who would be dropped once the ship was off Dungeness, clear of the shifting sands of the Goodwins, when course would be set for the Bishop Rock in the Scillies whence he would, in the nautical parlance, take his departure for Funchal in Madeira where bunkers would be taken to carry the ship on for South America.

Halfhyde, glad to be at sea again, free of the port's constrictions and the endless filling of forms for this, that and the other, to say nothing of the expense of harbour dues, of tugs and pilots, sniffed the air gratefully. There was a light south-westerly breeze and already the *Taronga Park* was lifting and falling a little to the movement of the water. He wondered about his passengers' sea-legs, and their stomachs. No doubt there would be a thin muster for dinner that evening; the pilot had spoken of more wind off Land's End and the Bishop, and the *Taronga Park* was small, liable to be severely thrown about in anything of a real sea . . .

Off Dungeness the pilot boat was seen coming off from the shore. The pilot made ready to disembark, wishing Halfhyde a successful voyage. The pilot dropped, the ship was on her own. Halfhyde spoke to the second officer, who had the bridge watch.

'I'll remain, Mr Lewery. You may go below.'

'Aye, aye, sir. Thank you, sir.'

Halfhyde nodded. It was his custom always to remain on the bridge when his ship was in coastal waters; there was always a lot of shipping in the Channel, vessels to be stood clear of, deep-water ships, paddle-steamers coming out from the piers at Hastings, Brighton and Worthing that might come suddenly across his bows from starboard so that he would need to alter course to cross their wakes. Lewery was capable enough, but the final responsibility was Halfhyde's as Master and he felt his responsibilities keenly, thus he would remain on the bridge for most of the thirty-hour passage to the Bishop.

Shortly after the pilot had left, Mr Mayhew of the Foreign Office clambered up the ladder to the bridge. Halfhyde saw that the diplomat was wearing black patent-leather shoes and grey spats beneath black trousers and frock coat, an unsuitable rig, in Halfhyde's view, for seagoing.

'Good morning, Captain. I – '

'Passengers are not usually permitted on the bridge, Mr Mayhew, other than by invitation.'

'Ah. Then may I, perhaps, assume the invitation?' Mayhew coughed. 'There are matters that should be discussed, and – '

'Later, much later, if you please, Mr Mayhew. I must remain on the bridge for some while yet. I take it you'll wish any discussion to be privately conducted?'

'Ah yes, most certainly, most certainly.' Mayhew took in the helmsman and the bridge lookout with his two-way glance. 'Later, then. Perhaps you'll let me know?'

Halfhyde said curtly, 'I shall send for you when I'm ready, Mr Mayhew.' The Foreign Office man flushed a little before he turned away; he hadn't liked the idea of being sent for. The lack of deference was unfitting to his Foreign Office background. Halfhyde, keeping a watch all round and now and again using his telescope to view the shore and anything that might emerge, found his thoughts veering towards Admiral Watkiss who was, it seemed, the reason behind Mayhew's presence aboard. When last Halfhyde and Watkiss had served the Queen together in South American waters there had been another gentleman embarked from the Foreign Office. . . . Mr Petrie-Smith, for reasons of secrecy travelling under the name of Luckings and attached to the battleship ostensibly in the capacity of an assistant paymaster. Halfhyde grinned to himself as he recalled the then Captain Watkiss' reaction to men from the Foreign Office. A load of pimply clerks, he had called them, and much else. He had informed Mr Petrie-Smith on one occasion that the whole blasted lot of Foreign Office clerks would benefit from a two-year commission on the lower deck of a man-o'-war; and had sent him back from his cabin to the ship's office with a threat that if he should fail to mind his Ps and Qs he would demand his reasons in writing and his balls for breakfast. It had been a case of no love lost. Halfhyde wondered what Captain Watkiss would have made of Mayhew's spats.

iv

As a simple precaution, Mr Todhunter had taken two of Dr Datchet's Demulcent Drops just after breakfast and felt a great deal safer, giving thanks to his old mother now in God's hands for having introduced him to the excellent panacea. During the morning he walked the deck, lurching a little from side to side in a sort of crablike movement as the ship rolled. Walking, he was hailed by Mrs Weder-Ublick.

'Mr Todhunter!'

'At your service, ma'am.' Mrs Weder-Ublick's tone had been peremptory but Mr Todhunter was always polite. His chief super at the Yard always made a great point of the need to be polite to the public even whilst arresting them – unless, of course, they were criminals of the commoner sort, thieves, footpads, prostitutes and so on. Politeness didn't matter with them; they wouldn't understand it anyway. Gentlemen were different, even murdering or swindling gentlemen. And Mrs Weder-Ublick was undoubtedly a gentleman – lady, Mr

Todhunter corrected himself; it was easy to make the mental error.

He went across, skirting the after hatch to the port side of the well-deck.

'There seems to be no deck steward,' Mrs Weder-Ublick said. 'Not like the PSNC I'm *quite* sure.'

'I agree, ma'am.'

'Then you'll do. I'd like a deck chair. Put it where there's no *smell*.'

'That'll be on the windward side,' Mr Todhunter said, displaying his nautical knowledge. 'The smell is from the engine-room, and the funnel.'

'I know that, thank you. Will you please *hurry up*? I don't like the motion.'

'I did offer you my cure for – ' Todhunter began mildly.

'Don't mention that word. Just go and do what you're told.'

Mr Todhunter lurched away on a hunt for a deck chair. Very likely the *Taronga Park* was not equipped with such luxuries. He was feeling somewhat ill-used. Detective inspectors of the Metropolitan Police were not stewards, not dogsbodies to be sent hither and thence, and he wondered where his chief super would draw the line. He found, as it turned out, no deck chairs. But when he went back dismally to confess failure, he found that Mrs Weder-Ublick had already been provided with one. With two, in fact. In the other sat Mr Mayhew of the Foreign Office. Mr Todhunter went below to obey a call of nature, leaving them alone.

The deck chairs, not large ones, not large enough to contain Mrs Weder-Ublick's form with ease, had come out of one of the thirty-nine items of luggage that now lay cluttering up the tween-decks. Mr Mayhew, seated comfortably himself, without revealing his mission for the Secretary of State, began chatting casually of Germany.

FIVE

'Dresden, such a charming place.'

Mrs Weder-Ublick looked sideways. 'You think so, Mr Mayhew?'

'Yes indeed. I went there some years ago, on a cycling tour.'

'A *cycling* tour? One of those dreadful people in knicker-bockers?'

'Knickerbockers, yes. Comfortable – on a bicycle. But Dresden . . . Herder called it the German Florence, you know.'

'No, I didn't know. Who is Herder?'

'A German writer, dear lady. Johann Gottfried von Herder.'

'A *von*, an aristocrat? I should know him. Perhaps I do after all.'

Mayhew coughed. 'He lived from 1744 to 1803, as I expect you'll recall – '

'Ah yes, I do, now I come to think of it.'

'He was once chief pastor at Buckeburg, and after that Weimar.'

'Ah yes. I've heard my husband speak of him.'

'An erudite man.' There was no point in speaking further of Herder; Mrs Weder-Ublick clearly had not the faintest idea of what he was talking about and had simply reacted to the *von*. But Mr Mayhew continued talking of Dresden; it was a good lead towards cultivating the woman, who as an obvious snob would perhaps warm to an educated man and release the sort of information that he wanted. He had been disturbed to find someone with a German name aboard the *Taronga Park* and considered the Admiralty to have been lax – either them or Halfhyde. He proceeded, as Mrs Weder-Ublick watched the rise and fall of the distant coastline to starboard and then, because of the effect of this upon her stomach, closed her eyes.

'The banks of the Elbe, such a splendid setting. The Erzebirge, you know. And the south bank in particular, the *handsomest* part of the city, would you not agree, Mrs Weder-Ublick?'

'Yes, yes – '

'The Brühl Terrace, quite magnificent, and the square at its eastern end – '

'Western.'

'Ah yes, I'm so sorry, western,' said Mr Mayhew who had made a deliberate error. 'The Albertinum and its wonders of archaeology . . . the statues of Semper, and Ludwig Richter, and the Elector Maurice of Saxony. The Art Academy, the royal palace. And the Zwinger!'

'Yes.'

'All those old masters.'

'Yes.' Mrs Weder-Ublick was giving the appearance of one asleep. She showed no apparent interest in art, old masters, the law courts, the synagogue, the Johanneum Museum, Schilling or Kircheisen, the Japanese Palace or the Körner Museum, all of which Mr Mayhew tried. She was a Philistine; Mr Mayhew essayed the Lutheran church and achieved some success. Mrs Weder-Ublick, whose husband had been one of the Old Lutherans and probably, Mayhew thought, a bigot, spoke at length and rather venomously about the Reformed Church – Swiss, Scottish Presbyterian, Anglican and so on, and went on and on about the doctrine of justification by grace through faith, managing to lose Mr Mayhew intellectually. It took the Foreign Office man some while to extricate himself from theological discussion as such and to get the lady onto mission work. She was going, she said, to do good. Her late husband had always wanted his money after death to be spent on doing good, and he had a fetish, if that was the word, about the unfortunate Indian races of South America who lived in a constant state of being ground down by the wealthy *hacienda* owners and such. Animals and crops, Mrs Weder-Ublick said, were of more account in South America than human beings,

45

who dwelt in squalor, victims of every disease known to man, their babies dying or being devoured by alligators and crocodiles, poisoned by noxious snakes or ripped to pieces by *piranha* in the muddy waters of the rivers. Through God, through the power of love, she would change all that. Mr Mayhew, though he found little love about Mrs Weder-Ublick, took the point concerning God. If God could be brought to the people of South America, Mrs Weder-Ublick said, if they could only be persuaded of the eternal truths, then they would rise up and make their presence felt.

'Scatter their enemies, Mrs Weder-Ublick?'

'Precisely that, Mr Mayhew.'

'H'mmmmm.'

She opened her eyes. 'What exactly do you mean by that noise, Mr Mayhew?'

He reassured her. 'Oh, nothing, nothing. Just that – '

'You don't believe it will work. I assure you it will. I shall see to that and that's a promise.'

'I wish you every success, Mrs Weder-Ublick.' He paused. 'As an Englishwoman living in Germany . . . I am making the assumption you are of British birth, Mrs Weder-Ublick?'

'Of course I am! I wouldn't be anything else. You are about to ask how I took to living in Germany, I think?'

'Yes.'

'I didn't. It was an awful country, quite, quite appalling. All those square heads and moustaches, don't you know. Every-thing run on military lines. Of course, they're very clean, not like London for instance, and orderly, which I must say I *did* like. But they're hard, very unyielding . . . of course I made the best of it for my husband's sake. It was his country and his calling – the church, you know – and it was up to me to put my best foot forward, and so of course I did.'

'But you're glad to have left for England?'

'For *South America*,' she corrected him. 'I dislike England as well. Only one good thing about it and that is Her Majesty the Queen, a most saintly woman, *most saintly*, and clean. So tragic, the loss of dear Prince Albert.'

'A long while ago now – '

46

'That is what is so splendid about her. She has *never* forgotten and reveres his memory daily.'

Mr Mayhew thought fleetingly of the awfulness of the Albert Memorial in Hyde Park, so vulgar. Having at last got Mrs Weder-Ublick started, he prodded further; but for now the source had dried up. Mrs Weder-Ublick said suddenly that she felt unwell and would Mr Mayhew please leave. He made solicitous offers of help but was rebuffed. As he moved away he was aware of Mrs Weder-Ublick moving for the ship's rail. Mrs Weder-Ublick was thinking that the man Todhunter was a fool: the *Taronga Park* was heading slap into the wind, so there was no windward side, no leeward. When her stomach refused to be contained any longer, the results were spectacular.

ii

Late next day, with the Bishop Rock now behind his ship, Halfhyde left the bridge finally in the care of his chief officer, Mr Hawkins. It was now dark; a meal had already been brought to Halfhyde on the bridge. In his cabin, tea awaited him, hot and strong; also Victoria Penn.

'Wotcher, mate. Tired, eh?'

'Yes.'

'Not too tired?'

'For what?'

'You know bloody what.'

'Later, Victoria.' He drank the tea. 'There's work to be done. Mr Mayhew . . . he wanted to speak to me.'

'Oh, let him bloody wait, why not?'

'Can't. Duty calls. I must see him alone, Victoria.'

She glared. 'Mean you want me to piss off, eh?'

'It's a way of putting it.'

'Well, I'm bloody not! This time of night – where am I to go, eh?'

'The saloon –'

'With that lot of dead-beats, mate? Bloody likely! A reverend, a missionary and that dick, Todhunter! You've got a hope!'

He said firmly, 'It's an order, Victoria.'

47

'Order me arse.'

'And one you'll obey. As master of this ship – '

'Master!' she said with a shrill laugh, putting her hands on her hips. 'You're not master of anything, mate, you're the Admiralty's bloody bum boy, jumping to do what you're bloody told – '

'That's enough, Victoria. Kindly stop talking and acting like a fishwife.'

She came at him, face red and angry, small fists flailing. He laughed and stepped aside, got a firm grip on her body, swivelled her and sat down on a hard chair with her across his knees. Pulling up her dress, he gave her six hefty smacks while her legs wriggled helplessly. She roared out, 'Leave me bloody bum alone, will you?'

'So long as you're going to be good.'

'All bloody right!'

He released her. She stood panting, a small animal at bay. She was irresistible. He took her in his arms, held her close and kissed her. 'Now get below,' he said. 'I'll not be long.'

Halfhyde sent his steward down to tell the Foreign Office man he would see him now. Within five minutes Mayhew was in his cabin, complaining about the long delay.

'I've waited all day, Captain Halfhyde. All day.'

'I'm sorry. The ship comes first – the ship and the safety of all aboard. What is it you wished to talk to me about, Mr Mayhew?' He added, 'Would you care for a drink?'

'A brandy, perhaps. Yes, a brandy.'

Halfhyde's steward brought brandy, with whisky for Halfhyde. When the man had gone, Mayhew said, 'It's about Mrs Weder-Ublick. Frankly, I'm amazed.'

Halfhyde lifted an eyebrow. 'About what?'

'The fact she was married to a German. I consider there has been laxity at the Admiralty, but then of course they're not the Foreign Office. Simple seamen basically, playing at diplomacy. Enquiries should have been made into Mrs Weder-Ublick's background before she was permitted to board, or a ship other than yours chosen for – what we have to do in Chile.' Mayhew paused, shooting an interrogatory look at

48

Halfhyde. 'Did you, or did you not, inform the Board of Admiralty of her presence?'

'I did not. That is, not by name.'

'Why not?'

Halfhyde compressed his lips. 'Kindly do not catechize me aboard my own ship, Mr Mayhew. The reason I did not tell them was that I was not asked. And it didn't appear to be particularly important.'

'Not even in view of the German connection, the trade business in Chile?'

Halfhyde waved a hand, dismissively. 'My dear fellow, Mrs Weder-Ublick is a churchman's widow, not a spy, or a merchant dealing with shipments to and from Chilean ports! I suggest you keep a sense of proportion.'

'And I suggest that you on your part have a sharper eye for possible trouble, Captain Halfhyde. I say again, there has been laxity – and I admit I consider the blame to be chiefly the Admiralty's.'

'Thank you,' Halfhyde said. 'I hold no particular brief for the Board of Admiralty, with whom I had disagreements many years ago and ultimately terminated my service in the Queen's ships accordingly. So let us start on an even footing, Mr Mayhew. What do you propose I should now do about Mrs Weder-Ublick?'

Mayhew frowned and seemed ill-at-ease. 'As it so happens, I think we should not be hasty.'

'I am in agreement. But why the *volte face*?'

'It's not exactly a *volte face*, Captain. The fact is that the delay in my being allowed to speak to you enabled me to have discreet words with Mrs Weder-Ublick.'

'I see. Well?'

Mayhew pursed his lips. 'A curious character, one with scant interest in culture, unexpected in a churchman's wife or widow – '

'I don't see why.'

Mayhew shrugged, as if to say that seamen would not understand culture in any case. He said off-handedly, 'Well, that was my impression, Captain. Also she is a snob, one who would be a social climber in England if she had the chance. She pretends to acquaintanceship with people with whom she has never had any sort of contact.' Mayhew didn't go into details about Mrs Weder-Ublick's tentative claim to have known dead von Herder. He went on, 'Further and more importantly, she claims a dislike of both Germany and England, obviously very deeply felt. And there is her mission to South America . . . this has an unfortunate ring about it. A mission to disaffect, through God, the South American Indians from their white masters. There was much talk of their poverty, and their death rate from disease and malnutrition. There was a ring of – of – '

'Of what, Mr Mayhew?'

Mayhew answered indirectly. 'I was about to ask her if she read the works of Karl Marx, who after all was a German, but she became seasick.'

Halfhyde kept a straight face. 'Yes, I see. So you suspect a political involvement, is that it?'

Mayhew said, 'Politics are already involved, Captain, insofar as there are the trading interests being manipulated against Great Britain. But now – yes, there may be more than that. I dislike even mentioning the word . . . but there could be a communist taint about Mrs Weder-Ublick. I fear that very much indeed.' He frowned again, with a baffled look on his face. 'Yet there is a strange dichotomy – if she has communist views, that is.'

'Yes?'

'She reveres Her Majesty.'

'More than the German Empress?'

'She didn't mention the Empress, only the Queen. Natural, she being of British birth. But Her Majesty . . . Mrs Weder-Ublick considers her most splendid, particularly as to her continuing devotion to the memory of Prince Albert.'

'A German,' Halfhyde said tongue-in-cheek. 'Another cause for suspicion.'

Mayhew gave a vigorous nod. 'Yes, indeed, you're quite right. But, you see, reverence for the Queen scarcely ties up with this new scourge of communism, don't you agree?'

'Oh yes, I do, certainly.'

'So I am in a quandary. There are two ways of taking Mrs Weder-Ublick. One, she is a convinced communist who may have links with disaffected persons in Germany – '

'Or in England, or South America?'

'Yes, there too. Oh, it's a great worry and of course I'm acting in the room of the Secretary of State, himself, so the worry is the greater. But there is the other possible aspect – that Mrs Weder-Ublick is a somewhat stupid woman of little intellect but a liking for the aristocracy of which she is not a part, and one who sees nothing beyond her desire to spend her late husband's money on good works without considering the social consequences of upsetting the natives. You follow?'

'Yes, indeed. And I see nothing wrong in an attempt to improve the lives and conditions of the South American Indians.'

'No, no. I didn't mean to suggest . . . though in my view charity begins at home and the Amerinds and *mestizos* are a shiftless lot. But various balances can be so easily upset by persons poking about into other persons' business and missionaries are noted for being a confounded nuisance at the best of times. We do not wish British nationals, or those born British to – to stir up trouble. Admiral Watkiss, it would seem, does quite enough of that.' Mayhew sat forward in his chair. 'Captain Halfhyde, I would be glad of your opinion. Which aspect of Mrs Weder-Ublick would you consider the one to settle for?'

Halfhyde had mentally settled for the silly woman aspect but wasn't going to say so. 'That's your province, Mr Mayhew. It's not up to me to make any attempt to state an opinion or sway the Foreign Office as so ably represented by yourself – '

'Thank you, Captain, thank you. I do my best. But I am still in a quandary.'

'Then I suggest you keep a close eye on Mrs Weder-Ublick for the rest of the voyage.'

'Oh, I shall, you may be sure! I would ask you to do the same, and the detective, Todhunter as well – I shall speak to him. A little sleuthing, if I may put it that way?' Mayhew laughed at what was meant to be his joke. 'If you have any suggestions, Captain, I would be most grateful.'

'Funchal,' Halfhyde said.

'Funchal?'

'We take bunkers and fresh water there, entailing an all-day stay in the anchorage.'

'Yes?'

'Make use of your Foreign Office acumen, Mr Mayhew. Watch for messages being passed by boat between ship and shore. And *vice versa*.' Halfhyde's tongue was still in firmly in his cheek.

iii

Victoria, eschewing the doubtful company in the saloon, had sat on the after hatch, gloomily, her knees clasped in her hands, facing for'ard so that she could see when Mr Mayhew left Halfhyde's cabin. Light was coming down from the officers' cabin ports. Chief Officer Hawkins, a married man missing his wife as he ploughed on towards Funchal, found his concentration on his watch diminishing as the light fell on the white gleam of knickers. He found it necessary to send many looks aft, as if seeking out vessels that might be approaching from astern. After some while Victoria began to count his sternwise looks and when she reached forty-three she called up to the bridge.

'Hey, mate!'

'Yes, Miss Penn?'

'Keep your bloody peepers off me privates.'

Mr Hawkins started as though hit by a bullet. 'Oh, I'm sure I didn't intend anything of the sort, Miss Penn!'

'Bloody likely,' she said with a snort, and then saw that Mr Mayhew had set foot on the ladder leading down from the Captain's deck. Obviously, he had overheard; he could scarcely have done otherwise. He scurried past with averted eyes once he reached the deck. Victoria said cheerily, 'I didn't mean you, Mr Mayhew,' but he made no response beyond a shocked sucking in of his breath.

With a giggle, Victoria climbed to Halfhyde's cabin. 'Took your time,' she said. 'What did he go on about, eh?'

'Mrs Weder-Ublick.'

'Wouldn't anyone, that old bag. She's succumbed again, by the way – puked her guts up, didn't have any dinner.' Victoria made no enquiry as to what aspect of Mrs Weder-Ublick had been under discussion. After long acquaintance with Halfhyde, she knew when to ask leading questions and when not. If he wanted to take her into his confidence, he would do so in his own time. In any case she had other matters on her mind and when Halfhyde said he proposed having a second glass of whisky she tapped the clock secured to the cabin bulkhead and said, 'It's getting latish, mate.'

'Nonsense, Victoria – '

' 'Tisn't nonsense and anyway you know what whisky does.'

Halfhyde laughed. 'It increases the desire, Victoria.'

'And mucks up the performance.'

'Not unless taken to excess.'

'Don't be excessive, then, mate. You know something? I'm the only woman aboard this bloody ship.'

'There's Mrs Weder-Ublick.'

'Don't be daft.'

'What are you suggesting now?'

She said, 'Oh, never mind.' She pirouetted round the cabin for a few moments, humming a tune. 'What I mean is, there's plenty of other men.'

'Yes, indeed. Canon Rampling, Tidy, Todhunter. Mayhew.'

'I said *men*. Your bloody crew, mate! Some of them have bedroom eyes. You want to watch it.'

Halfhyde laughed again, got to his feet and took her in his arms. Ostentatiously he opened the wash-basin cabinet and poured the contents of his glass into the basin. 'I take the hint,' he said. He knew he had no need to worry; Victoria's past was behind her now and she would stick to him like a loving leech just as she had done during all the voyages they had made together over the past years.

iv

The weather predicted by the pilot off the Downs had failed to materialize at the time Halfhyde had left the bridge, but he had noted a fall in the barometer reading and a coldness in the atmosphere that meant rain to come, and with it wind. He had left orders that he was to be called immediately if the wind reached Force Five on the Beaufort Scale; and the call came at six bells in the middle watch, the graveyard watch as it was known to seamen, the lonely watch that lasted from midnight to 4 a.m. The voicepipe from the bridge whined in his ear and he woke at once and answered, and without delay pulled on jacket and trousers, thrust his bare feet into his seaboots, and took up his oilskin and sou'wester. Victoria rolled over and murmured in her sleep but didn't wake. Halfhyde climbed to the bridge where Second Officer Lewery had the watch. The ship was already labouring and there was a continuous creak of woodwork.

'Wind's in the sou'west, Mr Lewery.'

'Aye, sir, slap on the starboard bow.'

A good deal of water was coming over on to the fo'c'sle. Halfhyde said, 'Send down to the bosun, Mr Lewery. He's to check the hatch covers.'

'Aye, aye, sir.' Lewery called to the bridge lookout, sending him below to rouse out Bosun Haggerty. Halfhyde stood against the canvas dodger at the fore part of the bridge, feeling the wind strong against his face. It was increasing; he judged it to be already at Force Seven, a moderate gale, and the glass was falling further. Soon there was a whip of rain, a mere scatter at first, and then it came down strongly, drenching Halfhyde through his oilskin. Within a couple of minutes he saw the light of a lantern: Haggerty, at the fore hatch carrying out his inspection.

Halfhyde cupped his hands. 'All right, Bosun?'

'All secure, sir. I'll go aft now, sir.'

The gale buffeted the ship. There was an eerie howl in the wind, like a banshee in the bogs of Ireland. As a heavier gust came Halfhyde passed a warning to the engine-room and then gave Lewery a small alteration of course to bring the ship's head directly into the wind and sea. The alteration made, the *Taronga Park* rode more easily. Bosun Haggerty came up to the bridge to report the hatch cover secure aft.

'I'll stand by a while, sir.'

'No need, Haggerty. Turn in – I'll send down if you're needed again, but I doubt you will be. She's taking it well enough.'

Haggerty went below. Halfhyde remained on the bridge with Lewery; and was there still when Mr Hawkins came up a little before 4 a.m. to take over the watch. The wind had strengthened further and was tending to back. As the force of it came onto the port bow Halfhyde ordered another alteration of the course and just as he did so a big wave took the ship and lifted her, slewing her head to starboard sharply, giving her a nasty lurch as the sea passed beneath her plates and lifted the stern in passing, a sick-making corkscrew motion. Three minutes later the saloon steward came to the bridge to report an accident: Mrs Weder-Ublick had fallen from her bunk.

Halfhyde said, 'Inform Miss Penn, and ask her to act as nurse.'

SIX

'On me bloody own? Who's going to lift her back, eh?'

The steward said, 'I'll give a hand, miss. And the reverend gentleman's there already, seeing to the lady.'

'She in her nightdress?'

'Yes, miss – '

'The reverend'll enjoy that.'

'He's wrapped 'er in a blanket,' the steward said, sounding shocked.

Victoria pulled on her dressing-gown and went below, lashed by wind and rain as she went fast down the ladder, in the open until she reached the door into the passengers' accommodation. Her hair was all rats' tails as she went along the narrow alleyway to Mrs Weder-Ublick's cabin, where the missionary lay on the deck, whale-like and angry. She had, she said, hurt her back and her cries had attracted the attention of Canon Rampling, who had hastened to her aid. Her heavy face peered from the blanket, like a cow in labour, Victoria thought. Canon Rampling was looking panic-stricken, having no idea how to cope.

'Get her back in the bunk,' Victoria said.

'Oh, I think that would be unwise – her back, you see. We might do damage. She needs a doctor.'

Victoria stared. 'Where do we get a bloody doctor, eh?'

Mrs Weder-Ublick groaned. Canon Rampling said, 'Well, I really don't know. I suppose the Captain could return to a port somewhere.'

'Take time, that would. She going to lie on her back till we get somewhere?'

'Certainly not!' Mrs Weder-Ublick said. Her position was undignified as well as uncomfortable, and her nightdress was rucked up. She had been mortified thinking about what Canon Rampling had already seen, though as a gentleman he had averted his eyes at once and had passed the blanket down behind his turned back. 'I believe I am merely bruised – there is nothing broken, and I do *not* wish a doctor. Will somebody please lift me back to my bunk?'

With a helpless glance at Victoria, Canon Rampling volunteered for the lift. The steward came to his assistance. With Rampling at her head and the steward at her feet, Mrs Weder-Ublick was with some difficulty hoisted, like a cargo sling, to the level of the bunk. It was quite a reach to get her heavy body over the bunk itself and Canon Rampling's end was already sagging.

The steward suggested swinging her.

'First to port, sir, then to starboard. Get her moving, sir, and let go when she's in position, if you get my meaning. Kind of like a church bell, sir.'

'Well, not exactly.'

'Lead line, then, sir, when taking soundings.'

Mrs Weder-Ublick suggested they got on with it. They did so, the steward giving the time. '*Hup*, swing port . . . *hup*, swing starboard. Oh my Gawd, sir, not that way!' Canon Rampling did not know port from starboard and Mrs Weder-Ublick took a twist, giving a high scream.

'Oh dear, it's all right, dear lady, we shall try again.'

They did. '*Hup*, swing left, *hup*, swing right . . . and again, sir. Right, sir, that's it – let go!'

Mrs Weder-Ublick dropped with a thump, luckily dead centre. She panted and groaned again, closing her eyes. Canon Rampling enquired, 'Are you all right, dear lady?'

'Yes, I think I am. Thank you for your help. Now please go away. The stewardess will stay.'

'I am not the bloody stewardess,' Victoria said, 'for the second time of telling.'

Mrs Weder-Ublick opened her eyes. 'Oh. You're *that* woman. The Captain's – er.'

'Right. I'm the Captain's er. Don't worry, I'll stay, reckon I'm used to insults by now. Where does it hurt, eh?'

'Not with men present.'

Canon Rampling and the steward took the hint. They departed. Mrs Weder-Ublick said, 'There.'

ii

' "There" was right above her arse,' Victoria reported to Halfhyde during the forenoon when the weather had moderated. 'I had to turn her over.'

'Bad?'

'Bloody great bruise, that's all. Found some liniment in the medical bag and rubbed her with it. She'll be all right, no worry.' There was a gleam in Victoria's eye. 'Your turn next, mate. She wants to see you, pronto. In her cabin. I said you'd be along. Do right, did I?'

'No,' Halfhyde said. 'But I suppose I'll have to do as she asks – she's a fare-paying passenger after all. Is it proper?' he added with a grin. 'A woman in bed – '

'She's covered up like a dead nun in a shroud, mate. Best go and get it over with, eh?'

He did. He went below. A knock at the cabin door produced a peremptory voice. 'Who is it, pray?'

'Captain – '

'Come in, come in. Leave the door open.'

Halfhyde entered. There was a smell of the liniment applied by Victoria, who seemed to have overdone it. Halfhyde was about to offer condolences but was not given the chance. Mrs Weder-Ublick was very angry.

'*This ship!* This would never have happened aboard a PSNC ship, Captain Halfhyde. I call it *disgraceful* that one should be – be *cast* from one's bunk in the middle of the night to end up upon the deck! The bunk board was unsuited to its task, as you can see.' Halfhyde did; the bunk board lay in splinters of wood-work. It had been subjected to an unfair weight. Mrs Weder-Ublick went on. 'I think your seamanship leaves much to be desired, Captain Halfhyde. Surely you could have handled your ship better than to bring about such a terrible motion?'

58

'The sea is mostly unpredictable, Mrs Weder-Ublick. I assure you, a vessel of the PSNC – '

'Nonsense, rubbish, fiddlesticks! In the liners *no-one* is cast about in such a fashion – and that's fact, I said it.' She went on and on; Halfhyde was scarcely listening. The phrase she had used had hit him like a blow on the head from a blunt instrument. *'That's fact, I said it.'* He saw, all of a sudden, certain mannerisms, certain turns of other phrases, certain physical resemblances. The face that reddened quickly with anger, something about the capacity of the eyes to glare, the square shape of the body. Give her a monocle and a telescope, put a naval cap upon her head . . .

He interrupted the flow of complaints, unceremoniously. 'Your pardon, Mrs Weder-Ublick. Do you happen to have a relative who has served in Her Majesty's ships, by any chance?'

She stared at him. 'Yes, as a matter of fact . . . yes, I have. Why do you ask?'

'Is his name, perhaps, Watkiss? Captain Watkiss at the time – '

'Yes, it is.' Mrs Weder-Ublick was clearly astonished. 'Do you know him, Captain Halfhyde?'

'Very well indeed. I have served under him, when I, too, was in Her Majesty's service.'

'And why do you connect me with him, may I ask?'

Halfhyde smiled. 'A certain phrase. *That's fact, I said it.* Captain Watkiss – '

'Yes. Captain Watkiss is my brother. Was, perhaps – I've not heard anything of him for very many years. He may be dead. The phrase was our father's, made frequent use of when we were children. Our father was often a tiresome man. Like my brother. When did you last serve with my brother, Captain Halfhyde?'

'Some years ago,' Halfhyde answered cautiously. There were current complications in regard to Captain, now Admiral, Watkiss. It was not up to him to reveal any information, at least not until he had spoken to Mayhew. But his reticence, if indeed it had been noticed, appeared not to matter. Mrs Weder-Ublick went on to say, with venom, that she had always detested her brother, who was pompous and conceited and over-bearing, even when playing the games of childhood. He had cheated in order to win, she said, and had when challenged blandly denied the accusations. He was, she said, always right in his own opinion.

'That phrase,' she said. 'Am I to understand my brother still made use of it after all these years?'

'It was virtually his trade mark,' Halfhyde answered solemnly.

Mrs Weder-Ublick's response was brisk; she appeared to have forgotten about her back, for she gave a violent movement in her bunk. 'In that case, I shall *never* employ it again myself,' she said venomously, 'and that's fact, I said it.'

iii

'Goodness gracious me!' Detective Inspector Todhunter said in amazement. He had been brought into the discussion, along with Mr Mayhew, he being concerned with the eventual extraction, if matters went so far, of Admiral Watkiss from Chile. 'Admiral Watkiss' sister! What an extraordinary coincidence, Captain Halfhyde, sir!'

Mayhew indicated that it might well be no coincidence at all. 'Some dastardly design,' he said, remembering Mrs Weder-Ublick's possible communism and the fact of her German marriage.

'In what way?' Halfhyde asked.

'I can't say as yet. Matters must be allowed to develop. It's fortunate in one sense, unfortunate in another, that you brought the relationship to light, Captain Halfhyde. One thing is certain: Admiral Watkiss must not be discussed further between you and Mrs Weder-Ublick. I leave myself the freedom to bring out further details myself if I see fit. I may be able to discover something, who knows?'

'Who indeed? But myself, I see no guile in Mrs Weder-Ublick. She came out with it quite openly when I asked. There was no attempt to hide anything whatsoever.'

Mayhew nodded. 'Yes, that's a point, certainly. Well – we shall see. I find it most curious that the sister should be bound for Chile at a time when the brother is in – shall we say difficulties with his employers, the government of Chile.'

'Possible difficulties,' Halfhyde corrected. 'I think that at this stage it's only surmise that the Chileans may turn against Admiral Watkiss – '

'Yes, yes – '

'And past experience has taught me never to under-rate the capacity of Admiral Watkiss to crawl out from under any onslaught, to turn matters to his own advantage.'

'Really. I see. Well, we must hope nothing unfortunate takes place.' Mayhew pondered, frowning. 'When do we reach Funchal, Captain?'

Halfhyde said, 'In approximately eight days from now. Why do you ask, Mr Mayhew?'

Mayhew shrugged. 'As you yourself suggested not long ago, that is when we must watch carefully. Do you propose allowing the passengers ashore, Captain?'

'Perhaps, perhaps not. It must depend how long we're held there. Sometimes it's necessary to wait for bunkers – they move but slowly in Madeira, and often there is no availability of coal. If we're in port for long, I'll have to let the passengers, and crew as well, stretch their legs ashore.'

'Yes, very reasonable.' Mayhew squinted across the cabin at Todhunter. 'We must make arrangements, you and I, Todhunter.'

'Arrangements, sir?'

'With regard to a watch. If Mrs Weder-Ublick goes ashore, it would be prudent, in the circumstances that have now arisen, to – er, to see that she . . . er – '

'Comes to no harm like?'

Mayhew nodded. 'A way of putting it, Todhunter, yes.'

The conference ended; Mr Todhunter proceeded towards his shared cabin, still employing his crab-like motion, for the night's gale, though it had subsided as quickly as it had arisen, had left disturbance behind it and the *Taronga Park* moved uneasily, with a rather nasty roll. Wakened by the gale sounds during the night while Mr Mayhew had slept on in the bottom bunk, Mr Todhunter had found it necessary to re-stow much of his luggage, for things had come adrift and some drawers had come open and had spilled their contents on the deck, or floor as

Mr Todhunter thought of it. The silver-framed photograph of his late mother stared up from the deck or floor much as she had stared in life, with love for her only son. Todhunter had picked up the photograph and thrust it down between himself and the bulkhead against which his bunk was fixed. Now, with the ship's motion easier and never mind the roll, he replaced the photograph on the chest-of-drawers and thought about his mother.

She had been filled with pride when he had been accepted into the Metropolitan Police Force, with more pride when he had transferred to the plain-clothes branch and had been made a sergeant. When he had become a detective inspector she insisted upon his bringing his chief superintendent to tea. Mr Todhunter had been bashful about putting the request to his chief super but he could refuse his mother nothing and as it happened the great man had been pleased to accept.

Mr Todhunter smiled now with inward loving memory of the tea-party. Oh, there had been a tremendous fuss! A nice fuss, of course; his old mother had been much honoured. There was China tea as well as Ceylon, there was cream, and loaf sugar, there was a splendidly iced cake, another of fruit and cherries, another of seed; there were rock buns, macaroons . . . preceded of course by scones and the thinnest possible slices of bread-and-butter. In addition, for this was high tea, there was ham, cold roast beef, cold Bath chap, salad and pickled onions. Mr Todhunter's old mother had presided with love and pride and had greatly embarrassed Mr Todhunter by relating tales of his childhood, of his little escapades such as tying a string across the street from old Mrs Shuttleworth's door-knocker to that of crotchety old Mr Higgins opposite, and then banging upon one of the doors before running away. He had been, said his old mother, a naughty little boy as little boys are, but of course there had never been any guile about him and he had always owned up. There had been, however, something in his chief super's eye when the door-knocker-tying episode had been raked up that said that in his opinion it was a doubtful background for a detective inspector . . . but nothing had ever been said and the chief super had left the house with a glazed look and a full stomach. There had, nevertheless, been an

62

unfortunate ending: fish-paste sandwiches had been on the menu but off their best, and that night neither Mr Todhunter nor his old mother had had much sleep. And the chief super hadn't appeared in his office the next day.

Mr Todhunter had remonstrated with his old mother and she had burst into tears. This he now recalled with regret and sorrow. She had done her best, after all, and with the very best intentions. And she had been so proud of him and his achievements. It wasn't every old mother in Skellhorn Street, E. that had a son who was a detective inspector of the Metropolitan Police Force. Mr Todhunter knew he had to live up to a vision; his old mother would still be looking at him, down from heaven, noting what he did, noting his further achievements. At Funchal, if Mrs Weder-Ublick should give cause for concern, he would put his best foot foremost. Funchal might well be his great moment, the moment when perhaps, after it was over, he might be able to write a report to his chief super of the unmasking of a diabolical spy ring centred upon Berlin and dealt its death-blow, by his agency, in far Madeira; but somehow he didn't really believe he would.

iv

Canon Rampling called along the alleyway outside his cabin. 'Mr Tidy, where are you?'

There was no answer; and the churchwarden was not in his cabin; Canon Rampling had already checked that. But after the second call there was a sound from the end of the alleyway, the flushing of the lavatory. Canon Rampling, embarrassed, went back into his own cabin and a minute later Mr Tidy appeared.

'Here I am, Reverend.'

'Ah, Tidy.' Canon Rampling tried to look as though he had not heard the flushing of the lavatory. 'It's my communion set. I can't find it anywhere.'

'It's not in here, Reverend.'

'Oh, dear. I do hope you brought it, Tidy.'

'Aye. I brought it along all reet, no fear.' Mr Tidy, caught somewhat on the hop, was adjusting his braces. 'Got it in my cabin, for safety like.'

'Oh good, what a relief.' Canon Rampling paused. 'Mrs Weder-Ublick wishes to take communion, Tidy.'

'When?'

'This very morning. Quite soon. She will call out when she is ready.'

'I'll just polish oop chalice,' Mr Tidy said.

'Oh, it's quite all right, I'm sure – '

'Matter o' pride,' Tidy said obstinately. 'It's t'sea air, like. Won't be a tick.' He went off on his bandy legs and Canon Rampling, sighing a little at his churchwarden's stickiness on detail, for the polishing of the chalice wasn't going to make the slightest difference to the holy significance of the occasion, proceeded to the tween-deck to root out his cassock and surplice from the round-topped trunk, not fully unpacked on account of the lack of stowage space in his cabin. He went thoughtfully; at first he had been a shade doubtful about administering Holy Communion to a member of the Lutheran church; he was unsure of his ground on that one. Of course, they were all Protestants together, no taint at all of Rome or anything like that, but still. It *was* a different church and Canon Rampling was not well up on Lutheran practice or ritual – not *ritual* exactly, that was Roman, and he cast the word from his mind immediately. However, all had been well: Mrs Weder-Ublick had remained Church of England. 'I wasn't going to change to anything *foreign*,' she had said upon his making representations of his doubts. 'My husband didn't like it, but I was quite determined on the point.'

So that was all right.

The chalice came back polished; and, cassocked and surpliced, Canon Rampling awaited the call, sitting on his bunk because it was more comfortable, and more ample too, than the chair. The call came and Rampling obeyed. Mrs Weder-Ublick was still in her bunk, the blanket drawn tight to her chin, concealing every part of her body including her arms, which were pinioned like a trussed duck. She must know she would need to reveal those arms in order to clasp the chalice when the time came, and to receive the wafer, but there was no need to mention indelicacies just yet.

64

Canon Rampling knelt by the bunk, resting his elbows on the mattress just clear of Mrs Weder-Ublick's rump, the bruised section. She gave a little scream.

'Not there! Move farther down. By my feet.'

'Certainly, dear lady.' Canon Rampling shifted awkwardly and then began his abbreviated form of service. He offered up thanks to the Almighty for having calmed the raging of the waters and for having brought all the souls aboard the *Taronga Park* safely through the darkness of the night with its attendant dangers; he offered thanks for the saving of Mrs Weder-Ublick from worse injury, and besought the Almighty to look upon her with love and pity and to ease her suffering.

'It's not as bad as that,' Mrs Weder-Ublick said briefly and rather crossly. 'I'm certain God recognizes exaggeration.'

'I'm sorry, dear lady – '

'The whole point is, I wish to bare my breast. In regard to my brother, who is or was a sailor.'

Canon Rampling, who had started as if struck by lightning, misinterpreting the use of the word breast, resumed his equilibrium. 'Your brother?' he enquired.

'Yes. I've recently been reminded of him, very recently. It's brought back thoughts. Those thoughts are not kindly, and of course they should be. Am I not right, Canon?'

Rampling nodded. 'Oh, most certainly, yes.'

'There you are, then! I detest my brother and I shouldn't. My thoughts worry me. I am not by nature a vindictive woman.' Canon Rampling remained silent and Mrs Weder-Ublick said irritably, 'Well? Do you understand my need or don't you?'

'Oh yes, I do indeed. You wish to make your peace with your brother through the Almighty. I – '

'No, I don't wish that at all. I wish to make my peace with *God*, because of my *thoughts* about my brother. That's different, don't you see?'

'I – I suppose I do, dear lady.'

'Good. Now I have just one question, and it's this: if my thoughts were to continue, would God's forgiveness continue?'

'I would rather doubt that, I'm afraid.'

Mrs Weder-Ublick clicked her tongue in annoyance. 'But His forgiveness will extend up to my present thoughts?'

'Oh yes, certainly, provided you are contrite, that is.'

Mrs Weder-Ublick's response to this was unclear; it was little more than a sound in her throat. Canon Rampling, a man of conscience, pressed. 'Do you believe your thoughts will henceforward take a – a more kindly turn?'

'No.'

'You will continue to . . . denigrate your brother in your mind? That is what you mean, dear lady?'

'Yes.'

'But really, to ask – '

'I'm sure you can find a formula to cover it, Canon. My husband always did in similar situations. Will you please get on with it?'

Canon Rampling gave a deep sigh, considering Mrs Weder-Ublick to be a disgrace to the Church of England and wishing she had become a Lutheran. But he got on with it since she had asked and was in pain and, after all, she had basically the right idea; she was confessing her sin through himself to the Almighty and that was to the good and perhaps the future could be left in God's hands. Canon Rampling in his silent prayers prayed for her somewhat dubious soul and besought God to clear her mind and in due course Mrs Weder-Ublick's arms emerged fatly from the blanket to receive chalice and wafer. Canon Rampling took himself off with his communion set for Tidy to clean, feeling most dissatisfied. Later, he would himself try to talk to her, acting for God in the matter of mind clearing. As for himself, he felt in urgent need of a confessor, or at any rate someone to talk to about what he now saw as his weakness in administering communion to a person who was not spiritually ready for it. Tidy wouldn't do; Tidy was a Yorkshireman, with all a Yorkshireman's obduracy and forthrightness and sturdy opinions. Tidy would be scandalized and would say so in no uncertain terms. Who else was there to whom he could turn? No-one. Yet there was Captain Halfhyde, a sound and sane man, worldly yet with stout principles of his own – in most things; there was, of course, Miss Penn, but that was simply part of a very human frailty.

Captain Halfhyde . . . Canon Rampling knew from his service as a naval chaplain that the captains of Her Majesty's ships of war often considered themselves to be God Himself, their reasoning being that aboard their ships on foreign service they represented Her Majesty the Queen, who as head of the Church of England represented God . . . the naval mind was a fairly wondrous thing. And Captain Halfhyde, though now of the Merchant Service, was, in the official words inscribed in the ship's articles of agreement, the crew's Bible, Master under God.

Yes, he would do.

Canon Rampling waited for a suitable moment. This came later in the day when the shades of evening lengthened over a now calm sea and the splendid colours of God's sunset overlaid the *Taronga Park* and, most suitable of all, Miss Penn had been seen talking to Mr Mayhew, a long conversation in the fore well-deck, so that she would be absent from Captain Halfhyde's cabin.

Canon Rampling climbed the ladder, and knocked at the cabin door. Captain Halfhyde made him welcome; and listened to what he had to say. And it was while he was expounding on Mrs Weder-Ublick and her undying hatred for a long lost brother that something swam strongly into the canon's mind, some echo from the past, an echo that quite quickly became a blinding shout, for of course he, like Captain Halfhyde, had sailed in the old battleship *Meridian* to Chilean waters, and the *Meridian* had been commanded by the eccentric and terrible Captain Watkiss of the Royal Navy. That brother, who had been or still was a sailor . . . Canon Rampling could now see the extraordinary family likeness, the manner, the peremptoriness, the curious ability to turn any situation to his or her own benefit and to force people into wrong positions. And so on. There had been so much to Captain Watkiss.

Canon Rampling voiced his thoughts. 'It's incredible, but I believe it to be the fact, Captain Halfhyde.'

Halfhyde was circumspect. 'An interesting theory, Canon. I agree the similarities without a doubt. But I must ask you not to speak of this to anyone else aboard my ship. There are good reasons for this, but I'm not at liberty to say what they are. Have I your assurance, Canon?'

'Yes, indeed. I shall not utter.' Canon Rampling paused. 'Do you think I did wrong to administer Holy Communion in the circumstances, Captain?'

'By no means. She sought comfort for her state of mind, and it's an important part of your duty to give that. The friction will be solely between God and Mrs Weder-Ublick. I advise you not to worry.'

v

Victoria had listened from beneath an open port, crouched down in a corner, an angle of the deck. She had not been noticed by Canon Rampling on his exit. She went into the cabin giggling. 'Missed your vocation, mate. Should have been a Holy Joe yourself, I reckon. Almost, what, shrove him, eh, silly old geezer. And what's all this about that other old geezer, eh?'

'What old geezer?'

She jeered. 'Come off it! You know who I'm talking about. The old bloke on the Amazon who held his bloody nose at me, time you sent me ashore to waft my charms at him so he wouldn't see what you was up to when – '

'Victoria – '

'That Watkiss bloke. All right, mate.' She grinned, urchin-like, lovable. 'I reckon I got cloth ears, eh? Just for once, anything for peace and bloody quiet.'

68

SEVEN

The *Taronga Park* dropped down south, down on Madeira and the port of Funchal lying beneath the six-thousand-foot eminence of Pico Ruivo. The days were idyllic now, the gales of the early stages of the voyage well in the past. Mr Todhunter disported himself on deck, walking daily round and round the ship wearing his bowler hat with its retaining toggle until he had by his estimate (derived from counting his footsteps) completed a full mile, thus keeping his bowels in good order as always insisted upon by his old mother and also, as it happened, by his chief super whose dictum it was that a constipated detective was a slow-moving, slow-thinking detective who would never be a credit to the Force. Mrs Weder-Ublick came from her bunk, her bruise now gone. She could be seen often in conversation with either Mr Mayhew or Canon Rampling and sometimes both; although Mr Mayhew having brought only the two deck chairs in his thirty-nine articles of luggage, Canon Rampling had to squat on the deck at Mrs Weder-Ublick's feet amid a clutter of deck gear. Mr Tidy spent many hours reading a book of sermons preached by an Archbishop of York long departed and in thinking about the glorious sweep of the Yorkshire Dales, and the sheep, and the waterfalls, and the church he had lately left, and wondering if he was going to settle easily to Chile, which he hadn't much liked when he'd been there with the reverend on his naval service. He recalled sundry undesirable persons who would never have gone down in the North Riding; he recalled things that had gone on in the streets, if you could describe them thus, that would have shaken Wensleydale to its core. They were a different lot, the Chileans, with a different outlook and different morals if they had any at all. Mr Tidy believed, had believed all along, that the reverend was making a mistake in going out to Chile but he did of course recognize that he had a duty to his cousin. Families naturally came first. Mr Tidy had none of his own, or he would have stuck by them rather than accompany the reverend across the world to heathen parts. Mr Tidy had never married; he believed his bandy legs to have been an impediment. A young woman who had subsequently married a farmer in Swaledale had once remarked, scornfully, that they could be useful to a child as a hoop. Mr Tidy had never forgotten that remark. He recognized that it had coloured his approach to life, or anyway to young women. Thoughts now of young women arose when, on deck, the shadow of Miss Penn was thrown by the sun across the book of sermons.

'Wotcher, mate. Lovely day, eh?'

'Morning,' Mr Tidy said ungraciously, not looking up.

'Get out of bed the wrong side, did you, eh?'

Mr Tidy grunted something.

'Oh, well. Takes all sorts, I reckon. Me, I like to be friendly.' She glanced at his book. 'What's that you're reading, mate?'

'Book of sermons. Do you good to read 'em an' all.'

'I don't bloody think so, thank you very much. Tell you something. Do you more good to get up off yer bum and walk like that peeler.'

She went away, giggling. Mr Tidy was flabbergasted at the way she had spoken, using the word bum. She was an abandoned woman, of course, and he should, but didn't, feel charitable towards such unfortunates. The Scriptures . . . God moved in a mysterious way and no mistake; Miss Penn moved in a different way, leggy, provocative. She certainly hadn't got bandy legs. Despite himself something stirred deep in Mr Tidy. Bum, indeed! Ashamed of his thoughts, Mr Tidy returned to the sayings of the Archbishop of York.

ii

Funchal, and a day of stifling heat and blinding sun. During the approach to the port Bosun Haggerty and his deck gang had

rigged canvas awnings over the bridge and the well-decks fore
and aft, thus providing some welcome relief to the bridge
watchkeepers and the passengers. After ringing off his engines,
Halfhyde awaited the arrival of the port authorities, who came
out, a motley bunch of persons in dirty white suits and panama
hats, after more than an hour's delay. After a session of signing
documents pertaining to his stores, cargo and crew and
passenger lists, Halfhyde established that his ship would not
take her bunkers until the following day. There was a shortage
of labour, due to some dispute about wages and the unpleasantness of working in clouds of coal-dust. When the port officials
had gone back inshore from the anchorage, Halfhyde sent
down for Mr Mayhew.

He came quickly to the point. 'We were speaking about shore
leave, Mr Mayhew. I'm told we'll be here for some forty-eight
hours.'

'At anchor, Captain Halfhyde?'

Halfhyde nodded. 'We coal from lighters. They'll not take us
alongside. So there's the question of getting everyone ashore –
my crew will take shore leave in watches, of course, the
passengers being free to do as they wish subject to the
availability of my seaboat.'

'You have Mrs Weder-Ublick in mind, Captain.'

'Not in my mind, Mr Mayhew. In yours.'

'I have my duty to do, you realize. I am responsible to – '

'Yes, very well. I am merely informing you that your spy is
likely to go ashore, that's all. I am giving you due warning for
your vigil. The rest of it is up to you.'

'And Todhunter, who understands my point of view better
than you do, I fear.'

Halfhyde waved a hand, dismissingly. 'As I have just said,
it's up to you. You're perfectly free to waste your time.'

Mayhew went off angrily, clad now in a suit of white sharkskin, well starched and ironed back in London, and with a
topee on his head against the sun. He was already sweating
profusely and dark patches had appeared beneath his arm-pits.
The sun was really quite ferocious, unusually so, he believed,
for Funchal where normally the climate was moderate. On

deck he encountered Detective Inspector Todhunter, still with his bowler hat and wearing his blue serge.

Todhunter asked, 'Have you had words with Captain Halfhyde, sir, as to – '

'Yes.' Mr Mayhew reported his interview. 'You and I shall go ashore in the boat together, if Mrs Weder-Ublick herself does likewise, that is. It will appear perfectly natural up to that point, though it would be better if we sat at opposite ends of the boat and parted when reaching the shore.'

'Of course, sir.' Mr Todhunter was well aware of class distinctions: gentlemen of the Foreign Office did not hobnob socially – going ashore was social, sharing a cabin was *force majeure* – with policemen. That was proper. Todhunter went on, 'Do I take it, sir, that we shall each watch the lady but from different positions?'

'Yes. That way we shall make doubly sure.'

'Yes, indeed, sir.' Mr Todhunter's chief super had ground it into his inferiors that everything should if possible be double-checked and that the evidence of a witness should be corroborated by that of another witness, nothing ever being left to chance. He gave a cough. 'Beg pardon, sir. What is it you expect the lady to do, sir, precisely?'

'I've no idea, really. We just watch, Todhunter, in case she does . . . well, something. I'm sure you understand.'

'Oh, yes, sir, of course,' said Mr Todhunter, who didn't. Frankly, he was flummoxed. Mrs Weder-Ublick in his eyes was no more than the usual tiresome middle-aged, middle-class woman who considered herself – and rightly, of course – to be set irrevocably above those who had to work for their living. Autocratic, demanding – Mr Todhunter remembered his scurry round for a deck chair at her orders – but a criminal lady, never. However, Mr Mayhew of the very superior Foreign Office, now in a sense acting as his chief super, had spoken so that was that. He would watch devotedly, largely in the self-interest of his own promotion on return to the Yard.

iii

Ahead in Chile, May was hanging onto the tails of April and the weather had grown hotter and more sultry in Santiago, which Admiral Watkiss had now reached via Valparaiso and a further inspection, this time of a seedy cruiser that had lately been refitted but was nevertheless as filthy as the *Almirante Smith* had been. The seabirds had been busy and no-one had bothered to clear away their deposits. When Admiral Watkiss had ordered the immediate turning-on of the wash-deck hoses they had failed to operate satisfactorily, producing only a thin stream of water that had itself appeared a dirty brown. Admiral Watkiss had danced about the deck with rage, scarlet in the face, and when representations had been made to the engineer officer in his dark and smelly hole below decks, there had been a sudden emanation of white-hot steam from some unauthorized aperture in the funnel that had only just escaped boiling Admiral Watkiss.

'Stupid buggers!' Watkiss had roared out, and had at once realized that bugger was a fairly universal word, easily enough comprehended even by the Chileans, and he had smirked unctuously and turned his expletive on its head. 'Pellucid udders.'

There was puzzlement. '*Si, Almirante?*'

'An engine-room term used by the British Navy.' He'd known they wouldn't understand *that* one. He had gone ashore in a vile temper to embark aboard the railway train for Santiago, a very hot journey of Chilean standards of discomfort that made his temper worse. Reaching at last his official residence he found he had a visitor, a senior member of the staff of the British Minister.

'Oh, thank God, a white man. You'll have a drink? I'm going to.'

'Perhaps a glass of sherry, Admiral.' The emissary was thin and pale, with spots, a typical sherry drinker. Watkiss himself, attended by Petty Officer Steward Washbrook, took whisky.

'To Her Majesty the Queen,' he said.

'And to His Excellency the President of Chile.'

'Oh, yes, all right.' They drank, standing; then sat down. Letting his monocle drop from his eye Watkiss said, 'Blasted dagoes.'

'I beg your pardon, Admiral?'

'You heard what I said. Filthy ships, no damn discipline, I'd flog the lot, let them kiss the gunner's daughter as we used to say in a proper navy. There was a damn midshipman aboard that wretched cruiser, with his nose running down to his damn mouth and no handkerchief, but no-one took any blasted notice. If it had been a British ship, by God! The little bugger'd have been sent aloft to sit on the foretopmast cross-trees for a fortnight!'

'Yes, I see – '

'I don't suppose for a moment you do,' Admiral Watkiss said energetically, waving his telescope. 'Soft life in British embassies and whatnot, never got your blasted hands dirty, never kept a watch in a gale of wind, never – '

The pale man got a word in. 'Admiral, really, I – '

'Never faced up to hardship, any more than those dago buggers, and that's fact, I said it. Well? What have you come for, may I ask?'

'I was attempting to tell you, Admiral. I am instructed by my Minister – '

'*He*'s not up to much. Minister my backside! He hasn't stood up for me as I would expect, letting those buggers ride roughshod over him, and him Her Majesty's – '

'Yes, Admiral. I mean no. He's working behind the scenes, as – '

'So far behind as to be damn well invisible. But go on, do.'

'I come with a warning. I – '

'Warning?'

'Yes, Admiral. I'm sorry, but it's my duty to warn you that the President is in . . . shall we say, an unconciliatory mood. His Excellency – '

'Excellency my bottom. Nothing excellent about the bugger, he's a dago maniac, and that's fact – '

'Admiral, please.' The pale man sat forward earnestly, determined to utter untrammelled. He was tougher than he looked; and his urgent manner penetrated. 'For your own safety, you must listen.'

'*Safety?* Dammit, I'm the Commander-in-Chief of the Navy!'

'Yes. But your . . . your rigorous nature, your dedication shall we say to maintaining standards – '

'Hah! Raising standards, you mean!'

'Yes, perhaps I do, Admiral. But you have aroused strong emotions. You should remember walls have ears. You have made reference to dagoes and so on, words unpleasant to Chilean ears as I am sure you would agree – '

'Of course I do. They were meant to be, you fool.'

'But unwise. Very, very unwise. Also there is the other matter.'

'The blasted trade business, and the Huns?'

'Yes. Germans, as my Minister prefers them referred to. The President believes you to have exceeded your brief as naval Commander-in-Chief – '

'I merely did my duty as I saw it. My duty to report jiggery-pokery.'

The pale man was patient. 'It is appreciated, of course, Admiral. But I have to ask, your duty to whom?'

'To Her Majesty, of course. To Great Britain. What a ridiculous question.'

'But that's it precisely, Admiral! You have no duty to Her Majesty now. Your duty is to His Excellency – '

'Don't keep on calling the bugger that!'

'But – '

'I am *not* a blasted Chilean! Come to that, Admiral out here I may be, but I'm still a captain on the Retired List of the Royal Navy. You may put that in your damn pipe and smoke it!'

The pale man nodded. 'It's a very valid and important point and it has by no means been forgotten you may be sure. That is partly why I am here, Admiral. Certain efforts are being made on your behalf, since it would be very unfortunate, and diplomatically most undesirable, for a retired British captain to be arrested in Chile – '

'*Arrested? Me?* Fiddlesticks, sir! I have never heard such blasted rubbish in my life!'

'It is not rubbish, Admiral. It is a very real possibility I fear. The Chileans – '

'Arrested, simply because I have been outspoken in my comments? Balls and bang me arse, man, that's ridiculous!'

'Your *manner* would not be the charge, Admiral, nor would it be the official reason. This would be that you have passed information about the German trade intentions to us, to my Minister.'

'That was intended as a helpful act to Her Majesty!'

'Yes, we all realize that. Unfortunately the President does not, or so we are led to understand by certain persons friendly towards Britain. I have to repeat, Admiral, that your allegiances have perforce changed now.'

'Perforce or per anything else, my dear fellow, they have *not* changed and they never damn well will. I refuse to be hounded by a bunch of blasted foreigners!' Admiral Watkiss had got to his feet by now and with his monocle screwed back in his eye was storming up and down the ornate drawing-room of his head-quarters, past portraits of former presidents of Chile, portraits of commanders-in-chief long gone, many of them British like himself, and other portraits, of women with seductive looks who for all Watkiss knew could have been to his predecessors what Emma Lady Hamilton had been to Lord Nelson, for the Chilean air corrupted the morals. Noises of anger came from Admiral Watkiss while the pale man finished his hitherto neglected sherry and waited for the storm to pass, which it did. Admiral Watkiss had recognized that this time bluster was not enough: the threat was to be regarded as real and potent.

He simmered down. 'When is this abominable arrest to take place?'

'We don't know. But we believe it to be imminent.'

'At any moment?'

'Yes, I'm afraid so.'

'Then,' Admiral Watkiss said firmly, 'in that case I demand – ask – the sanctuary of the British Minister. I shall be safe there, unless he's more pusillanimous than I suspected – '

'I'm sorry, Admiral, but that cannot be.'

'But dammit, I'm a British – '

'I'm afraid the Chilean aspect takes precedence now.'

'Oh, what balls!' Admiral Watkiss brandished his telescope, getting it tangled in the black cord of the monocle. 'Damn.' He extricated it and replaced the glass. 'It's already been agreed

76

that I'm a post captain of the British Navy on the Retired List. I have never been struck from that. I now quote my rank and nationality and demand sanctuary from these blasted ruffians.'

The pale man shook his head. 'It simply can't be done. We have instructions from London that we are on no account to upset the Chilean government. But you are not being left without help, Admiral, be sure of that. A mission cloaked in secrecy is on its way aboard ship, steaming to your assistance under a sea-captain well known to you.'

'Who?'

'His name is Halfhyde, Admiral. Together with Foreign Office representation, and a man from the Metropolitan Police Force. If you will listen carefully, I shall explain fully.'

iv

The explanation had acted as a goad. Todhunter, Watkiss remembered well; also Mayhew, the clerk as Watkiss thought of him, a man who sat upon a high stool at a ledger. It seemed that it was hoped he could be taken into protective custody by Todhunter acting under the authority of the Foreign Office before the Chileans had got their hands on him. Then, according to the pale man, it would be too late for the Chileans to react. If they did react, then it would become necessary for Admiral Watkiss to be smuggled out of the country, probably aboard the *Taronga Park*. Watkiss enquired as to the difference between such smuggling and the provision of sanctuary on British soil as represented by the residence of the British Minister. The pale man's answer was unsatisfactory and Admiral Watkiss came to the conclusion that the British Minister simply didn't wish to become personally involved. Clandestine operations were safer; and afterwards any blame could be attached elsewhere, which in Watkiss' view was typical of the Foreign Office and of the Admiralty as well.

That, however, was for the future. Currently there was the question, the pale man said, of what to do with him. The advice, never of course to be quoted, was that he should vanish, and remain vanished until the arrival in Valparaiso of the *Taronga Park*.

EIGHT

'Canon Rampling!'

Rampling turned from the guardrail and his distant inspection of Funchal from the anchorage. 'Yes, dear lady?'

'I should like to go on shore. The ship is constricting. Besides, I would like to look at the natives.'

'Yes, an interesting study I'm sure.'

Mrs Weder-Ublick gave a heave of her ample serge skirt. Canon Rampling was not quick in the uptake. 'I shall of course need an escort.'

'Ah.'

'If you would be so kind.'

'Oh . . . yes, indeed. Of course, dear lady.' Rampling's tone was glum. He was not feeling very well; he didn't know what it was but his insides were uneasy. The food, no doubt, or the water brought out in the tanks from England and by now not fresh. And the heat was almost intolerable. But he felt it to be his duty; as a fellow churchman, up to a point, of her late husband . . . the clergy, he felt, should stick together. Also, he was the only suitable escort apart from Mayhew, who had made himself scarce since the ship's arrival in Funchal. Tidy would hardly do, nor would the policeman. 'When do you wish to start?'

'When the boat's ready, of course. Perhaps you would make enquiries.'

ii

The *Taronga Park*'s seaboat left the ship's accommodation ladder at four bells in the forenoon watch, Mrs Weder-Ublick seated in the sternsheets with Canon Rampling, clutching at his panama hat, beside her. Just before the boat was cast off, Mr Mayhew arrived at the ladder and, embarking, sat to starboard just for'ard of Mrs Weder-Ublick. After a short pause, Detective Inspector Todhunter also embarked, taking his place to port next to Canon Rampling with not a single exchange of glances with the gentleman from the Foreign Office. The orders were given and the boat was pulled away. Canon Rampling gazed ahead at the encroaching land, which appeared to be immensely rocky, though there was cultivation on the terraced mountains. It was, he thought, a pleasant enough place, so far anyway, though of course it could hold dangers such as were to be expected in any foreign land. He spoke cordially to the detective inspector. 'Very refreshing, Todhunter.'

'Sir?'

'To see strange places I mean. So good for the mind, don't you know.'

'Ah yes, sir, yes indeed. As a child, sir, I used to be taken by my old mother to Southend-on-Sea. Very different from London that was . . . all that ocean, and far across it the continent as I used to be told.'

'Yes, quite. The mind roves, does it not, with imagination.'

'Indeed it does, sir, yes.' After this exchange, a mere matter of politeness on Canon Rampling's part, as Todhunter seemed to understand, the conversation lapsed and Mr Todhunter's mind went backwards to the days at Southend-on-Sea with his then not-so-old mother. They used to make sand-castles with a spade and a little tin bucket his mother bought from a vending stall behind the beach, and on the completed castle the small Todhunter used to plant a flag, the Union Jack. Of course the sea always came in eventually and washed it away, and Todhunter recalled how he had cried the first time that happened though later he became accustomed to the destruction of their shared handiwork. He also recalled how one day a man had got into conversation with his mother, a perfectly respectable excuse ready to hand in that the man had trodden with large feet, policeman's feet, on the sand-castle. He had raised his hat and apologized profusely, addressing little

Todhunter as 'my little man,' and had then sat down saying that at his age – he was about sixty, Todhunter thought – he felt the heat of the day badly and would she mind? She didn't mind. He had seemed very respectable, like a retired bank manager. He was certainly no policeman. He had kept shooting glances at his 'little man', and had assisted him with the re-building of the castle, getting somewhat close up to him as he did so. After a while he had asked if the 'little man' would like to walk along the sea-shore with him and perhaps seek a lollipop from a vendor. That was when his mother had suddenly changed and in a sharp voice had asked the man to go away before she called a policeman, and he had gone away very fast indeed.

The young Todhunter had had no idea of the whys and wherefores of it all. Not until many years later, when his duties as a policeman brought him into contact with strange men, and then it had come to him, and he had blushed in shame and horror and had been devoutly thankful that his mother had ticked over in time.

He looked sideways at Canon Rampling, as if fearful that somehow his thoughts could have been transmitted across the bench. What the reverend gentleman would think!

His mind shifted tack.

This expedition on Mr Mayhew's orders. Glorious thoughts of spy-catching had receded. It was a fool's errand. What could Mrs Weder-Ublick do in Madeira? But Mr Mayhew must know his onions, presumably. Todhunter concentrated, thinking hard. Of course, Madeira was, he understood, Spanish. Or was it Portuguese? Like Malta, say, was British. Both Spain and Portugal were funny countries and doubtful ones. They could have links with Germany, and Germany was behind the doings of Admiral Watkiss in Chile. Perhaps Mr Mayhew had all that in mind, though he had never precisely said so.

Time would tell. Or anyway, it might. You never knew, as his chief super always said. You had to be ready for the totally unexpected, on your toes to nip in quick. His chief super was a wonderful man; he had sent a splendid bunch of flowers to his old mother's funeral, out of the station funds, and afterwards had spoken warmly of the tea-party.

There were carriages waiting at the small jetty to which the boat went. Madeirans called out to the disembarking passengers, offering their services for a tour of the island.

'How very nice,' Mrs Weder-Ublick said.

'Yes, dear lady.' Canon Rampling had noted that, not far behind the jetty, there was an hotel with a wide verandah upon which were chairs and tables and people some of whom looked British sitting at them. 'May I suggest a cup of coffee?'

'Thank you, but no. Make arrangements with those natives, the carriage drivers. Remember to bargain, Canon, and choose the cheapest. One should never overpay natives, it goes to their heads.'

'I would really rather – '

Mrs Weder-Ublick set her jaw. 'We've had coffee for our breakfast, Canon. I do wish to look round the island.'

Canon Rampling removed his panama hat and mopped at his forehead and his streaming cheeks with a handkerchief – silk, part of his leaving present from the parishioners of his late living. He understood: too much coffee taken into the body led to problems later and the tour might be a long one. But for his own urgent reasons he stuck grimly to his guns.

'A short rest, dear lady. On the verandah, which is shady.'

He set off, rather fast, and Mrs Weder-Ublick had no option but to follow, which she did crossly. Behind them Mr Mayhew and Todhunter had moved apart, one to the right, the other to the left. As the other two moved, so they also moved, but with circumspection. They observed their targets, sitting a minute or two later at one of the tables. Some altercation seemed to be in progress. (There was, of a sort. Mrs Weder-Ublick was saying she wanted no coffee and Canon Rampling was agreeing but saying she would perhaps excuse him for a while. He would be back as soon as possible.) Mrs Weder-Ublick, disliking being left on her own in a foreign public place, was looking upset. Canon Rampling disappeared inside the hotel, where after a search he found a man who directed him to the gentlemen's lavatory.

With the dusty street between them, Mayhew and

Todhunter exchanged glances. Was it, perhaps, the canon they should be watching?

Canon Rampling reappeared but didn't sit down; he and Mrs Weder-Ublick walked back again, down to the carriages that had had no custom. Mr Mayhew and Todhunter walked the other way, with backward glances. Canon and widow went aboard a carriage and Mayhew and Todhunter strolled back again, meeting briefly as if by purest chance for a short discussion. Todhunter was to follow in another carriage, at a discreet distance. Mayhew would remain in the port, watching any developments there. Todhunter hired his carriage and set off, feeling back in his proper place and function. In the Metropolitan Police Force he had followed behind many a hansom cab and the results had often been interesting and fruitful, but he didn't believe they would be this time. However, it was a nice day, and he would be sitting at his ease with much to tell his chief super when he got back at last to the Yard, all about native customs and the splendours of a foreign land.

Things could be worse.

Mr Mayhew walked around, observing, getting to know his local geography in case of some sudden dramatic happening. In basis he was looking out for Germans, upon whom he might be able to eavesdrop; his German was good, so was his Spanish and Portuguese. After an interval he went to the hotel, which seemed to be the only one in the port. There were two men, thick and square like Mrs Weder-Ublick, seated at a table drinking. Mr Mayhew sat close by and listened, but they turned out to be speaking, he thought, Dutch. He had no Dutch.

iv

'The man Todhunter is behind us, Canon.'

Rampling turned and looked to the rear. 'Oh yes, so he is.'

'One wonders why.'

'Oh, it's of no consequence.'

'He's a detective and that makes me uneasy.'

'I think there's no cause for unease, dear lady.' Rampling wondered what was in her mind; she was a widow, he was unmarried. They could scarcely be the object of any snooper trying to involve them in one of these modern divorce beastlinesses. He reassured her. 'All the tours doubtless follow the same route. If you remember, we were offered no alternatives.' Then he recalled Captain Halfhyde's adjuration that for some reason undisclosed he was to refrain from mentioning to anyone that Mrs Weder-Ublick was the sister of Admiral Watkiss. Was there some connection, something underhand that Todhunter was watching out for? No, there couldn't be. Mrs Weder-Ublick was certainly not underhand. She was too direct; that was her principal fault. But she persisted.

'I do *not* like the feeling of being followed, Canon Rampling. Stop the carriage. Call out to the driver. We shall let the man Todhunter pass by.'

Rampling obeyed, and the carriage stopped. The driver jabbered at them but they took no notice. Behind, Mr Todhunter was in a quandary, but only for a short time. Clearly, he had to go past but he could look out astern and watch just as well, and if the carriage didn't get under way again, well, he could always stop his own carriage and make his way back with discretion. As it happened, they were at the point where the dusty track ran between irrigated groves thick with fruit trees.

Canon Rampling waved as Todhunter went past. Todhunter lifted his bowler hat. Mrs Weder-Ublick sat with her hands folded in her lap and her gaze fixed ahead. Mr Todhunter rattled away. Just here the road was dead straight and after a while he looked back.

The other carriage stood empty.

Mr Todhunter ordered a stop. He scratched his head. What was he to do now? Well, of course, reconnoitre backwards as he had told himself just a few minutes ago. He spoke to the driver, hoping his English would be understood, saying the man was to wait and he would be back shortly. He then entered the groves and made his way back in good cover towards the vicinity of the stationary vehicle. It was quite a long way, but Mr Todhunter made haste, realizing that he could have chosen the wrong side of the road if there was any clandestine meeting taking place, but that could not be helped. Even his chief super made mistakes at times and would understand.

He heard a sound, and stopped dead. Crackling of undergrowth and something else unidentifiable. He moved very cautiously forward and thrust his head through a gap in the foliage. Mrs Weder-Ublick turned her head and saw Mr Todhunter's face, framed in green.

She screamed. 'You *disgusting* man!' she said. 'How dare you!' Later, Mr Todhunter saw Canon Rampling emerging from the trees on the other side of the road. Oh, dear! He should have guessed.

v

It was late in the day when a footsore Mr Todhunter arrived back at the jetty: his driver, paid in advance, had mistaken his words and had gone. So, from the jetty, had Canon Rampling and Mrs Weder-Ublick. Mr Mayhew was there and in a foul temper.

'Where have you been, Todhunter?'

Mr Todhunter explained. He was shame-faced about what he had inadvertently seen. 'Not my fault, Mr Mayhew. I'm not that sort, never was. I felt I was doing my simple duty, and now she or the canon will be making a report to Captain Halfhyde, and the good Lord knows what'll transpire if my chief super gets to hear – '

'Never fear, I shall explain to Captain Halfhyde, Todhunter. But it seems we've drawn a blank.'

'You also, sir?'

Mayhew nodded. 'I fear so,' he said glumly. 'And now we must await Captain Halfhyde's pleasure.'

'You refer to his sending the boat back for us, sir?'

'Yes. We can only hope it occurs to him.'

'Oh, I'm sure it will, sir.'

It did, two hours later. By this time the evening air had become chilly and Mr Todhunter shivered, not having brought his thick vest. He could only hope he wouldn't take cold. It was a cold trip back to the ship, too, and the rowers slopped a certain amount of water aboard the boat from their oars, which was unpleasant.

When they reached the *Taronga Park* and clambered up the accommodation ladder they were met by Victoria Penn. She said, 'Get a good view, did you, mate? Sooner you than me, that's for sure.'

NINE

'You're a blasted scoundrel,' Admiral Watkiss said furiously 'and if I had you back in England, by God, I'd have you keel-hauled and – and damn well *flogged*!'

'Begging your pardon, sir – '

'Oh, hold your tongue, Washbrook, I refuse to listen to you.' Admiral Watkiss bounced up and down his drawing-room from which the Minister's emissary had departed some while ago. Watkiss had sent immediately for his steward, whom he suspected of having reported some of his recent conversations to the Chilean authorities. Stewards always eavesdropped, that was sheer routine, they were scum. Of course, the blackmailer Washbrook had denied the charge as vigorously as he had been permitted – that also was routine. He had virtually cringed, however, overdoing it. He had wished to accompany Admiral Watkiss in his disappearance from official life; and Watkiss knew very well why. The man would have further opportunity for spying on him and reporting. But Washbrook had advanced another reason: without Admiral Watkiss he would himself be redundant, and as such he would be recalled to England by the Admiralty who had permitted his Chilean employment in the first place, for he was still on the active list of the Royal Navy, being merely on secondment to Admiral Watkiss' personal service. And upon his return to British naval service he would face those disciplinary proceedings followed by imprisonment for theft and other matters that, only a few months ago, he had escaped by the skin of his teeth.

Watkiss was in a cleft stick: he wished nothing better than to leave Washbrook to his just deserts but knew he would be quite

86

unable to face his banishment without a servant to attend upon him. He moved up and down, red in the face, his monocle banging about on his stomach at the end of its toggle, his telescope clasped like a club ready to strike his steward down.

He stopped, chest heaving, and faced the man. He flourished the telescope and stamped his foot. 'You're a blasted disgrace to your uniform, Washbrook!' Then he remembered that the man was wearing the uniform of the Chilean Navy so it didn't really matter. 'Your *British* uniform, which I thank God you haven't on your back at this moment.'

'Beg permission to speak, sir – '

'No! And don't damn well speak to your superiors without permission. Don't even *ask* without permission, do you understand me?'

'Yes, sir – '

'Hold your tongue!'

Washbrook was in a familiar quandary. To speak was to disobey orders, yet dumb insolence was still a charge in the British Navy and Admiral Watkiss had made it so in the Chilean Navy as well. And just to remain silent could in some circumstances be construed as insolence. But Washbrook was not too worried; in the end Admiral Watkiss could always be relied upon to do the talking and to arrive at a conclusion satisfactory to himself; and this time was no exception.

'I have considered the matter,' Admiral Watkiss said loftily a few moments later. 'Your request. You shall accompany me.'

'Thankee, sir.' Petty Officer Steward Washbrook gave a discreet cough. 'Beg pardon, sir. But have you anywhere in mind to go, sir?'

'Go?' Watkiss seemed distrait.

'Hide like, sir.'

'No.'

'Then, sir, with respect, I have.'

'Have what, Washbrook?'

'In mind, sir. Where to go, sir. To hide, sir.' Another cough. 'Course, there'll be palms to be greased like, sir.'

'Whose?'

'Friends o' mine, sir.'

'British?'

'Oh, no, sir. Chileans, sir.'

'Well, I suppose it can't be helped in the circumstances, Washbrook. I'm obliged to you. How much?'

A sum was named. With an angry grunt Admiral Watkiss foraged in his purse and brought out a number of gold *peso* coins.

ii

It had been Canon Rampling who had prior to the detective inspector's return aboard reported Todhunter's apparent Peeping Tom activities to Halfhyde. Mrs Weder-Ublick, he said, had been much distressed. She had not told him in so many words what had happened, but it was plain enough what had; nor had she wanted the incident made the subject of a report. But Canon Rampling had felt it to be his duty, since Todhunter was to accompany them all for a very long way yet, and in the close confines of a ship at that.

'A storm in a tea-cup,' Halfhyde said.

'I disagree, Captain.' Rampling's tone was stiff. 'The act can be repeated, can it not?'

Halfhyde shrugged. 'It *can*, I suppose, but it's highly unlikely I would have thought – '

'But really, with such a man, and a policeman – '

'I'd have thought the one look was ample.'

Rampling reddened. 'You are being flippant, Captain Halfhyde. It is a serious matter.'

Halfhyde sighed. 'Oh, very well, I'll have a word with Todhunter.'

'Without letting Mrs Weder-Ublick know you know? I have your word on that?'

'Yes, yes.'

Canon Rampling departed. Victoria came into the cabin from the steward's pantry where she had been helping to prepare an evening meal, which Halfhyde intended taking in the privacy of his own cabin. She said, 'Poor old Todhunter, eh.'

'You heard?'

'Course I bloody heard, mate. Know something, do you?'

'What?'

'That Medusa. Serpents for hair. Bloody great claws and big teeth, turned people to stone, didn't she?'

'What's all that got to do with – '

'What Todhunter saw? Well, I reckon the sight must have been a bloody shock, that's all. So I say poor old Todhunter.'

'Do you indeed. Anyway, you're not to talk about it, Victoria. Not a word – all right?'

She grinned cheerfully. 'Won't be able to help meself, you know me, mate.'

He aimed a cuff at her and she dodged, laughing. In due course, the boat came off shore for the second time, bringing the latecomers. Halfhyde's next visitor, before he had summoned Todhunter to his cabin, was Mr Mayhew, come to fulfil his promise to the detective inspector. Todhunter had been doing his duty, no more and no less, and the encounter had been not of his making and was most unfortunate. Todhunter was very embarrassed. Halfhyde was glad enough to let the matter drop, never to be mentioned again. There was, however, a corollary: the *Taronga Park* would take further bunkers en route for Valparaiso – at St Helena, the Falkland Islands, and Puerto Montt; also fresh water and stores. There would be further opportunities for Mrs Weder-Ublick to go ashore; if and when she did, it would be necessary to watch her just as here at Funchal. But she had already made it quite plain, Mr Mayhew said, that if the man Todhunter went ashore then she would not. If Todhunter remained aboard, the watch would be very difficult, for Mr Mayhew could not be everywhere at once and was less experienced at sleuthing than was the detective inspector.

Halfhyde said, 'We'll cross that bridge when we come to it, Mr Mayhew.'

iii

No Chileans came that day to Admiral Watkiss' residence; there was no arrest, and the dilatoriness, as Watkiss saw it, of the dagoes allowed leeway. Petty Officer Steward Washbrook went off with his gold *pesos* and a promise of more to come, and Watkiss roved his residence restlessly, shooing the Chilean peasantry who supplemented Washbrook out of his way. The whole thing was too bad, was blatantly unfair upon a man who had done his best for such a filthy lot, such a useless country. There was no gratitude anywhere; the British Admiralty had served him no better in the past, come to that, but at least they were British and that made all the difference. They were gentlemen, with a gentleman's instinct for dismissing officers politely in a civilized manner.

It was near dark when Petty Officer Steward Washbrook returned to the residence. He had, he said, made satisfactory plans. There was a young lady, a friend he had made in Santiago, he said, who lived on her own on the city's outer fringe, and was poor. For *pesos* she would help. She would give Admiral Watkiss and Washbrook sanctuary for a while. Not long, for that might be dangerous once the hunt was up, Wahbrook said.

'I'm not a blasted fox, Washbrook.'

'No, sir, begging your pardon, sir, you're not, of course. Just a manner o' speaking, sir.'

'Find a more suitable manner. Go on.'

'Yes, sir.' Washbrook drew a hand across his nose. 'I reckon, sir, we'd best head for Valparaiso after a while. That's where you said the ship would be coming, sir – '

'Yes, yes, yes. When?'

'Well, sir, soon as it's possible like. I'd say we have to take it day by day.'

'Yes, I suppose so. This young woman is reliable?'

'Oh, yes, sir, very reliable, sir.'

Admiral Watkiss sniffed, making the guess that the young woman was a prostitute. But in his present position he was forced to take what was on offer. He said, 'Well, it seems satisfactory, I suppose, as a temporary measure. Of course, we shall not go in uniform, Washbrook.'

'No, sir, oh no.'

'Lay out one of my white' plain clothes suits. And pack properly. I don't propose to pig it.'

'Well, sir.' Washbrook rubbed at the side of his nose. 'The young lady's house, sir, hut I should say, it isn't like this.' He waved a hand around the opulence soon to come to an end. 'Not posh, sir. Onc o' your suits, sir, they'd – '

'Yes, yes, yes, all right, I take your point. Certainly I've no wish to stand out like a bishop entering a brothel.'

'Oh, 'tisn't a brothel, sir, not – '

'I didn't mean that, you fool.'

After dark, Admiral Watkiss was ready. He was clad in an affair made of sacking, worn over dirty white canvas trousers that Washbrook had brought in a wicker basket. On his head was a sombrero and he carried the basket in his hand like a peasant selling eggs or whatever. There was no telescope, no monocle visible, no gold braid or feathered cocked hat. Petty Officer Steward Washbrook was somewhat similarly clad though not quite so extreme. Watkiss fancied he was wearing his normal shore-going, out-of-uniform rig, very scruffy and nondescript. As the moon began rising over Santiago, the Commander-in-Chief of the Chilean Navy, not in fact yet displaced as such, left the residence in company with his steward, sliding anonymously into the darkness.

iv

A curious *rapport* had begun to develop between Mrs Weder-Ublick and Canon Rampling as the *Taronga Park* dropped south from Funchal towards the tropics and the Doldrums. Canon Rampling observed that it had really started after the episode in the orchard; what Todhunter had seen had in some way drawn them together, and the ever-present detective inspector seemed by that very presence to draw them even closer, for they shared a dreadful secret – or it would have been secret had it not been for the deplorable Miss Penn. Now, it seemed, everyone aboard the ship knew about it; and the drawing close continued even more because of it. Canon Rampling, for one thing, believed himself to be in some degree to blame. He had been Mrs Weder-Ublick's escort and he had failed her. Of course, it was a delicate matter but perhaps he should have stood guard since there could have been, but weren't, Madeirans in the

91

vicinity. Canon Rampling remembered an episode in the North Riding of Yorkshire, some years ago just after he had completed his naval chaplaincy and had recently been appointed to his parish. One day he had driven the daughter of a local landowning family to a tea-party in a neighbouring parish – neighbouring as the North Riding went, a matter of some ten miles over the fells. He had driven her back afterwards; it was winter and it was dark, though there was no snow fortunately. When still some five miles from her home, the young woman had asked him to stop, which he did, pulling up the pony and trap by the side of a worked-out mine – lead it was – in Swaledale.

The young woman had got down and vanished into the darkness. For a while there had been silence and then had come the furious barking of a dog, the scream of the young woman, and the flashing of a battery torch. The young woman had been pin-pointed very cruelly indeed and then Rampling had seen her running towards him holding up what had looked like a whole draper's-shopful of intimate clothing. He had at once turned the other way, thanking God that the dog, still barking, was on a leash, and the young woman had bundled in beside him, coming in through the door in the back like a bundle of washing, he remembered. She had upbraided him; a gentleman, she said, would have stood guard, even reconnoitred ahead. At the time he had been most terribly embarrassed and had thought the young woman much too forward and indelicate, but in retrospect he had seen her point. It all came back to him now. Yes, he had let Mrs Weder-Ublick down very badly indeed, but it was much too late to apologize or anything like that.

They sat on deck, beneath the awnings that were still spread. They talked of this and that; of the terrible heat, of the sea's current deep blue calmness, of Germany and the Lutheran religion. Canon Rampling politely extolled the virtues of the Church of England. They didn't speak of Mr Todhunter, who on occasions passed by raising his bowler hat but looking the other way. They spoke a good deal about missionary work and the great need to improve the lot of the natives everywhere. It turned out that Mrs Weder-Ublick had done some earlier missionary work in Africa.

'Ah, darkest Africa,' Canon Rampling intoned. 'Most interesting I'm sure.'

'Dirty, though. Dirty habits, the natives. They seldom wash, and the smell is appalling. I disliked that.'

'Oh, naturally, dear lady, naturally.'

'Yet there is a charm about the people. So child-like, so primitive. So stupid too, I regret to say. Christmas in the bush I found amusing, however. The idea of God, the whole concept of the virgin birth, you know, of an Almighty Being who didn't live on a totem pole. I found the witch doctors trying I confess. All that painting of faces, and bones through their noses, and the gibbering, and the dances which were really quite threatening at times. I was chased by them once, right out of the village. I was really terrified, but I dare say they meant it kindly enough – it was just their way. Such simple people.'

Canon Rampling drew in his cheeks in horror. 'They failed to catch you, I take it?'

'Yes.' Mrs Weder-Ublick had some knitting with her, and she knitted a little before going on. 'A district officer I think he was, turned up in the very nick of time, with a revolver. That settled them! I didn't go back to that village again.'

'I should think not indeed! What a dreadful experience, dear lady.'

'I took it in my stride, don't you know. We British . . .' Mrs Weder-Ublick, with a click of her false teeth, bit through a strand of wool. 'We have to show what we're made of, we're not like foreigners. I always think it's *most* unfortunate for people who aren't born British, don't you, Canon?'

'Yes, certainly,' he said, recalling that he had once heard her brother Captain Watkiss say almost the very same thing. Mrs Weder-Ublick had gone on to remark that a missionary's life was a very lonely one and she would, once started on her work in Chile, miss her late husband more than ever.

'Such a dear man, so supportive,' she said, casting his meanness from her mind. 'I think one needs that.'

'Yes, indeed.'

'A companion . . . especially, of course, someone sympathetic, with a background of the church.'

'Of course. Er . . . the Lutheran church?'

'Well . . .'

There was a moment of panic that a suggestion had been made, however discreetly. Canon Rampling shied away from anything like that; he might be considered very highly suitable as a companion but he was not the marrying sort, and what would Tidy think? He was saved further comment by the arrival of Mr Mayhew, who loomed over them looking both ways at once and spoke sharply.

'Ah, Canon. I see you have my deck chair.'

'I was merely speaking to Mrs – '

'*My* chair. I brought them aboard. Please don't move, Mrs Weder-Ublick.'

Taking the broad hint, just short of a command, Canon Rampling got up and moved away, quite thankfully really. On the other hand . . . there was always another hand. His elderly cousin in Chile might prove to be a burden, and the sharing of burdens with a wife could be a blessing, but of course that would be sure to conflict with Mrs Weder-Ublick's missionary work and she would not be slow to say so. So no, most positively no.

Mr Tidy thought the same, more or less. He had been watching the reverend with Mrs Weder-Ublick. Soppy, he thought it was, the way the reverend pandered to her. He thought Mrs Weder-Ublick was like a Wensleydale heifer, one without charm, and lumpy. Mr Tidy believed she had an eye on the reverend; being already used to clergymen, she might very well see him as a sort of life-line to cling to the nearer the *Taronga Park* got to Chile and all those heathens, and if the reverend was daft enough, then what would become of himself? He might become redundant, and that would never do. But Mr Tidy cheered himself up; Mrs Weder-Ublick knitted. Sooner or later the reverend would find himself shushed when he was talking: sooner or later Mrs Weder-Ublick would count stitches. Mr Tidy reflected on an aunt who had knitted. She had seemed to him as a nipper always to be knitting and his

94

uncle by marriage had seldom been listened to, seldom allowed to speak at all in fact. Auntie had counted on, through everything he had ever said. One day Mr Tidy's uncle by marriage, goaded beyond endurance, had said he was going out into the farmyard to shoot his bloody self, and his aunt hadn't taken a blind bit of notice until she heard the shot and by then it had been too late.

v

'Balls and bang me arse, Washbrook, you don't surely expect me to live in *that*?' Admiral Watkiss pointed.

'I did say, sir, it was a hut like. And the young woman, sir, she's partial to British seamen. Not like some, sir.'

'Oh, very well,' Admiral Watkiss said bad-temperedly and moved on through the night towards the simple dwelling at the end of a line of similar huts, making his way past an open drain that stank to high heaven. Mangy dogs roamed, with bared teeth, and Admiral Watkiss lifted his sacking clear of the teeth.

'Shoo them away, Washbrook, don't just stand there.'

'Begging your pardon, sir, them Chileans might get upset, sir.'

'Oh, what balls, you fool, no foreigner has any feeling for animals, they wouldn't be in the least upset. Kick that brute at once.'

'Aye, aye, sir.' Washbrook raised a foot; the dog seized his boot in his teeth, growling. In the moon's light the eyes appeared red flecked. But all was well. A voice screamed from a hovel doorway and the dog let go of the steward's foot and slunk away, its tail between its legs.

'I told you so, Washbrook.'

'Beg pardon, sir.'

They reached the hut recommended by Washbrook. A terrible stench came from it but grew a little less when a pig emerged, rushing into the night past Petty Officer Steward Washbrook, egged on by a goad and a stream of Spanish invective. Admiral Watkiss felt his heart sink lower. Having no option really, he entered the dwelling. It appeared to consist of a single room with doors at front and back. It was lit by an oil lamp that smoked horribly to the ceiling. In this light Watkiss saw what he took to be the young woman who was partial to British seamen and he had something of a shock: she was indeed young – when British seamen felt the urgings of nature in foreign parts they were often inclined to view as young those who were not – and good-looking in a Spanish way. Dark hair, dark eyes, tall and slim.

Washbrook made the introductions. 'Señorita Maria, sir.' To the girl he said, 'Friend o' mine.' Turning again to Admiral Watkiss he said, 'I 'ope you'll excuse the liberty, sir.'

'All right, all right.' Watkiss spoke to the girl, very slowly as was customary when speaking to natives. 'I am obliged to you, young woman – '

'It is all right, señor. I am pleased to meet you.'

'Good heavens! You speak English?'

'Yes, señor.'

'I'm most surprised I must say.' Admiral Watkiss sounded a little offended; natives had no right to speak English so well, it was scarcely proper in a hovel like this. 'May I ask where I am to sleep?'

The girl reached out a hand and drew him towards a corner of the room. She indicated a pile of straw. Watkiss was horrified. 'That's a blasted pig's damn bed!' he said.

'No, no, the pig he was not my pig. A neighbour's pig. I do not permit pigs to sleep in my home, señor.'

'I'm glad to hear that,' Admiral Watkiss said. 'Where does Washbrook sleep?'

Once again the pile of straw was indicated, the same pile. Watkiss drew in his breath: he was to sleep with his steward, was he? The young woman seemed to understand his reluctance and made haste to reassure him. 'For start of sleeping only, señor. Later the other señor moves.'

'Oh. Where to?'

She pointed again. There was another pile of straw in the opposite corner. 'There, señor.'

'*Your* pile?'

'Yes, señor.'

'Washbrook!'

'Yes, sir?'

'You needn't bother with the proprieties.'

'Beg pardon, sir?'

Watkiss snapped, 'Oh, for heaven's sake, man . . . don't you come anywhere near my damn bedding!'

TEN

The young woman prepared a meal of black bread and some rather nasty beans with a little tough meat. Admiral Watkiss was unable to face it, and pushed the earthenware dish away.

'You do not like it?' Maria sounded sad and apologetic.

'It's not that I don't like it.' Admiral Watkiss was always well disposed towards respectful and good-looking young women, a different side of his nature showing through. 'I'm not very hungry. That's all.'

'There is fruit, señor.'

'Yes, all right. What fruit, may I ask?'

'Apples, oranges, apocarpous fruits – '

'An apple.' Apples could be washed, and God alone knew what apocarpous fruits were, something heathen no doubt. The apples were produced, Watkiss enquired as to whether they had been washed, and upon being told they had been, crunched. The apple was quite good and he was becoming used to the smell left behind by the departed pig. In fact, the wretched hovel was quite clean. Washbrook hadn't done so badly, all things being considered – *all* things. It was far from what any admiral was accustomed to, but admirals were also unaccustomed to having to hide. The great Lord Nelson had never hidden himself: he was ever to be seen, at the enemy's throat. The sense of unfairness descended again and Admiral Watkiss grew morose. The young woman tried to draw him out and he discovered that she was quite intelligent. Watkiss believed she was no common prostitute such as were to be found in the world's seaports, which of course Santiago was not. Possibly there was a superior variety in Santiago. Maria spoke of art – she was, she said, or she wished to be, an artist. Perhaps one day she would be. In the meantime she made pottery, in a shed attached to the rear of the house or room in which they now sat. She also liked music, flamenco in particular but also the works of the great composers.

'You like music, señor?'

'Some music.' Admiral Watkiss thought of 'Hearts of Oak' and 'Rule, Britannia' and other stirring British patriotic tunes. The girl seemed glad they had struck, as it were, a mutual chord; she went out of the door at the back and returned with a machine that Watkiss recognized as an Edison phonograph, such that registered vertically the sound vibrations on tinfoil. Maria cranked up this machine, in which a cylinder had already been inserted. Sound filled the hovel, sound that went unrecognized by Admiral Watkiss. The young woman was plainly enthralled, and so was Washbrook unless, as Watkiss suspected, he was merely being sycophantic against the favours of the night to come. Watkiss asked him what the machine was playing.

'I understand, sir, it was writ by a gennelman called Bee summat, sir.'

'Oh. Beethoven I suppose, and bugger Beethoven!' Admiral Watkiss was immensely disappointed. Patriotic music would have been heartening, and the blasted Beethoven was, or had been, a Hun, Watkiss believed. But he had to make the best of it and wait for the cylinder to finish rolling. It took some time, during which the young woman seemed ecstatic, swaying her slim body to the most unlikely dirge that came from the horn of the machine. But at last it ground to a halt. When asked, Watkiss said he didn't want any more.

'You not like?'

'Not much, no.'

She shrugged. 'You are a seaman, señor,' she said in acceptance of philistinism.

After a pause Admiral Watkiss said ungraciously that he was indeed a seaman. The young woman commented that the other señor, also a seaman, had told her that he was forced to attend upon a most terrible admiral, a man of no feeling but much bad temper. Admiral Watkiss glared at Petty Officer Steward Washbrook, who looked abashed. 'Is this true, Washbrook?'

'In a manner o' speaking, sir.'

Before Watkiss could utter, the young woman spoke again, squatting now beside her pile of straw, hands clasped around her knees. 'Perhaps you have suffered under cruel officers,' she said.

'Certainly not!' Then Watkiss remembered his shabby treatment at the hands of the British Admiralty; but that was not to be spoken of to the native peasantry – he was a loyal officer, a most loyal subject of the crown and never mind the fools at the Admiralty. Instead he spoke of the glories of the British Navy, of great fleets at sea around the world, showing the flag to awe-filled natives, driving boldly into mountainous seas while the seamen ran aloft with carefree abandon, at any rate in the days of sail, to obey the smallest whim of the Captain. He spoke of the great victories of Trafalgar, and the Nile, and Copenhagen. He spoke of the Glorious First of June when Admiral Lord Howe had scattered the many enemies of His Majesty King George III – a Hun, but no matter really, he had been made British or anyway English, by that time. Admiral Watkiss, when wound up, was a rival for Edison's phonograph; going backwards in time, he pulled himself up with a round turn when he was about to mention the singeing of the King of Spain's beard and the Armada. It would not be tactful, and he was currently dependent upon the young woman, though he had to admit that she hadn't seemed to be paying much attention and might possibly have failed to catch the Armada.

All she said when he had finished, gazing at him with her big dark eyes, was, 'You are a seaman but you have no tattoos.'

'Oh yes I have.' Watkiss pulled back his sacking garment to show the head of a colourful snake that wound round his forearm. 'There!'

She seemed disappointed. 'That is all?'

'On the other arm as well.'

'The other señor has on his – '

'Yes, yes, but we'll not go into that.' Admiral Watkiss, who had once seen Petty Officer Steward Washbrook sluicing

100

himself down when the normal facilities of a Chilean warship had failed them and the deck hoses had had to be used, knew perfectly well what was tattooed on his body and where. Shortly after this the three of them went to bed, or anyway to straw. Sleep did not come quickly, and Admiral Watkiss found his mind filled with alarm at the course the future might take. Never had he sunk so low as to be forced to find shelter in a virtual pigsty. Washbrook, on the other hand, seemed content enough. Admiral Watkiss wondered what on earth the young woman could see in him, apart from the tattoo.

ii

By now the *Taronga Park* had entered the Doldrums, that part of the South Atlantic Ocean that lay between the north-east and south-east trade winds, an area of almost total calm where the ships under sail had been frequently without wind for weeks at a time beneath a cloudless and torrid sky, the oppressive calm being broken occasionally by violent squalls, torrential rain and severe thunderstorms.

This, Canon Rampling, on deck again with Mrs Weder-Ublick, explained. She said the atmosphere was like that of a steam bath, unpleasant to be in for so long a time.

'Yes, indeed, you have it precisely,' Rampling said, his big face beaming. Rampling was unable to avoid giving a beaming appearance even when he didn't mean to; his face was built thus. 'A steamy haze upon the waters, dear lady. But of course we depend upon steam,' he added humorously, 'for our motion, and really that is fortunate. We shall not be so very long in the Doldrums.'

'You spoke of possible bad weather.'

'It can come very suddenly,' Rampling said, 'and very violently. But you must not worry if it does. The ship is sound and Captain Halfhyde is very experienced and reliable.'

Mrs Weder-Ublick gave a snort. 'Is he, Canon?'

'Indeed, yes – '

'I do not see,' Mrs Weder-Ublick stated, keeping her voice low, 'how a man can be *reliable* when he consorts openly with that dreadful young woman.'

'Ah.'

She looked sideways at him. 'What do you mean by that, pray?'

Rampling dithered. 'Very reprehensible, of course. As one who wears the cloth, I am bound to disapprove, naturally. Yet there is good in the young woman – '

'I have failed to see it, Canon.' Mrs Weder-Ublick knitted, but not very briskly. The heat was so enervating, and perspiration dampened the wool and made it sticky so that it didn't travel well around the needles. Mrs Weder-Ublick cast it aside; the natives of Chile would have to wait for their comforts. She resumed the discussion of Miss Penn. 'A very common young woman.'

'Australian . . .'

'Yes, that's what I meant. I don't believe Australians are very well-bred. And such an awful accent, is it not? Worse than cockney. And the constant use of that particular dreadful word. Is the word endemic to Australians, Canon?'

'I understand it is, dear lady.'

'Very unfortunate. And Captain Halfhyde appears to be a gentleman.'

'Yes, indeed he is. A long naval history.'

'Really?' Mrs Weder-Ublick inclined an interested head.

'An ancestor at Trafalgar, serving under Lord Nelson himself, not in the *Victory* but aboard the *Temeraire*.'

'As captain?'

'Not as captain, no, dear lady. As a gunner's mate.'

'Gunner's *mate*? Oh. Not an officer?'

'No.'

'Then Captain Halfhyde can scarcely be considered a gentleman, Canon.'

'It was a long time ago,' Rampling said.

'Perhaps, but never mind that. Lineage counts. What you have told me explains the woman.'

iii

The woman was on the bridge with Halfhyde, who was taking his noon sight of the sun to fix the ship's position on the chart.

From long experience Victoria knew that if she spoke to Halfhyde while he was manipulating his sextant, and then working out the complications of logarithms that followed, the wrath of God would fall upon her. So she remained leaning over the rail and looking out across the fore well-deck and the fo'c'sle. In the well-deck was Mr Todhunter, who had largely kept himself apart from the other passengers since the unfortunate affair at Funchal, and was currently sitting on the fore hatch reading a volume of police procedure. Over his head a long rope was heavy with washing, drying out in the heat of the sun. The saloon steward, who attended also on the passenger accommodation, was responsible for the washing of the ladies' and gentlemen's laundry, a task in which Miss Penn had volunteered to help him. The results of their labours were a sight from which Mrs Weder-Ublick had earlier turned her eyes and had gone aft: it was all too obvious that the vast bloomers with elastic where they met the knee were hers and not Miss Penn's. They hung now like sails drying out after a gale, along with a number of petticoats and vests and thick stockings and so on, all mixed up with articles of male underwear, a juxtaposition that Mrs Weder-Ublick thought indelicate, the more so as she had glimpsed the man Todhunter taking up his reading position immediately below the bloomers. She was convinced he had done it on purpose. Not far from the bloomers hung Mr Todhunter's long pants, such that reached from waist to ankle.

Victoria called down from the bridge. 'Hey, mate.'

Mr Todhunter looked up. 'Do you mean me, Miss Penn?'

'Right you are. Do something for me, eh?'

'Yes, certainly – '

'That lot.' She indicated the washing line. 'See if it's dry yet, eh? Give the drawers a feel, the bloody big ones like they was made for a bloody elephant's arse, right?'

There was no wind to blow her voice away; and her voice was very loud. It could be heard aft of the bridge. Mrs Weder-Ublick clamped her teeth together and rose to her feet. Scarlet in the face, she went below to her cabin. Canon Rampling gave a sad shake of his head. He could see her point in regard to Miss Penn.

In the fore well-deck Mr Todhunter did as he had been asked. More or less, anyway. It would be impolite of him or any man perhaps to judge the state of the washing by a lady's underwear, so he used his own long pants as the yardstick. That word again, or one like it, he reflected. Vulgar, that was, very vulgar. Mr Todhunter had been taught by his old mother to refer to that part of his body, if he had to, as his sit-upon. That was decent as well as descriptive. The washing, he found, was dry. He reported as much to the bridge.

'Thanks, mate,' she yelled down. 'Do us another favour, eh? Get it down for us?'

iv

'Bother take it,' Mr Todhunter said in exasperation and dismay. His bottle of Dr Datchet's Demulcent Drops had fallen from his chest of drawers and lay broken on the deck of his cabin, its priceless contents scattered in all directions and probably now dusty and germ-laden. What a dilemma, for he knew he was going to be in need of them at any moment now. A squall had struck the *Taronga Park* and there was a good deal of commotion on deck, with orders being shouted by the bosun and men trampling about and things banging like drums and Mr Todhunter's cabin was beginning to move about just as though it had by some wicked mischief detached itself from the ship. Up and down it went, sickeningly, the scream of the terrible wind that was driving it along sounding like some crazy orchestra as it twanged through the ship's rigging. Water seemed to be everywhere, even to some degree below decks. A trickle of it entered Mr Todhunter's cabin from beneath the door and ran across the floor, drenching some of the demulcent drops. Mr Todhunter, on hands and knees, scrabbled about for the remainder and thrust them into a pocket. Regaining his feet he placed one of the tablets in his mouth and then took it out again.

The germs. There were bound to be some.

Fears of noxious diseases filled Mr Todhunter's mind. There were so many. Scurvy, Blackwater fever, yellow fever, scarlet fever, cholera, dysentery, typhus. All of them potentially fatal.

Then there was the plague, and Mr Todhunter knew, because he had seen them, that there were rats aboard the *Taronga Park*, and rats, or the lice that dwelt upon them, carried the plague. No medical gentleman aboard, and already germs could have been deposited in Mr Todhunter's mouth. No more would be deposited; seasickness was a far lesser infliction. Mr Todhunter washed out his mouth with water from the water-bottle attached to his wash-stand cabinet, mixing it with some tooth powder as an extra precaution, and spat the result into his basin.

Not far from Mr Todhunter, Mrs Weder-Ublick lay in her bunk, for in such weather it would have been dangerous to do anything else. Her body inert, her mind travelled freely. Not for the first time since learning that Captain Halfhyde had known her naval brother, Mrs Weder-Ublick found her mind going back into past years, as far back as her childhood in a naval family dominated by a father whose ideas of discipline had formed the character of the young Watkiss, a budding tyrant from the days of the perambulator. The family had lived for a while in Southsea, adjacent to the naval port of Portsmouth, the select part, the only part where it was possible for gentry to live. One afternoon the young Watkiss, taken for an outing by nanny, had been left for a moment outside a shop and during this wait an urchin had reared up from the gutter and had smilingly approached the perambulator for a look at what was within. The young Watkiss had promptly raised a wooden monkey on a stick and had brought it down hard on the urchin's head and the urchin had departed roaring out invective. That had been the start of a very difficult life for the young Watkiss' sister, eighteen months older than baby. Her brother had been the leader, never mind her seniority in months, and he had led her into trouble. This trouble was always of her brother's making but invariably she got the blame. When the young Watkiss lit forbidden matches and burned hairy spiders in their harmless webs he always ascribed the act to his sister and was always believed. When he pushed the cat from its position asleep on a high window sill and it landed in the garden, she it was who was deprived of supper for a week.

Brief periods of peace had come when the young Watkiss had gone to his preparatory school and then to the training ship *Britannia* as a cadet in Her Majesty's navy. But on his inevitable return for the holidays or on leave, war broke out again and in redoubled form so that the young Watkiss could make up for time lost. Upon his first leave from the *Britannia* the young Watkiss, now an expert on hammocks and what could be done with them, had found his sister asleep in the family's summer hammock suspended between two garden trees. He had cut the rope with his seaman's knife and his sister had descended with a thump that had almost broken her back. That was the one time the young Watkiss had failed to get away with his crime, since even he could dream up no watertight excuse or alibi. Their father had caned him very hard indeed and had cut off his pocket-money for the remainder of his leave. The young Watkiss had been forced to sell the seaman's knife, a further crime for which he had been severely punished when, on his return to the *Britannia*, he had been unable to produce it for inspection by his term lieutenant. In later years Mrs Weder-Ublick had seen that the harmless hammock had begun the sequence of events that had first turned her brother against her; and her subsequent marriage to what her brother called a Hun had set the seal that had never been broken. For her part, of course, the enmity was equally intense.

She wondered where her brother was now. He might, of course, be anywhere. Her one hope was that never would they meet again. The world was a big place so she considered that to be very unlikely. She ceased the thoughts of the past when the ship gave a very heavy lurch so that she was thrust back upon the bulkhead in a heap of clothing and a great deal of water came from beneath the door, making a surging sound, and kept on coming until it seemed that the bunk must soon be awash. Then the ship righted herself and the water started to run back, or anyway not to increase. Mrs Weder-Ublick sat for a while hunched on her bunk, marooned. Then there was a very bright light followed by an enormous clap of thunder that seemed to shake the ship as though it had been a rat clamped in the jaws of a large dog; then another, and another, a sound of doom coming to a sinful world. Mrs Weder-Ublick, shaking, got down from the bunk and put her feet into the slop of dirty water. She wrenched the cabin door open and emerged, terrified, into the alleyway. She sniffed, lifting her nose high. She believed she smelled burning wood.

Then she saw Mr Tidy.

'What has happened, Mr Tidy?'

'Ship's been strook bah lightning, missus.'

'I thought so! Are we on fire, Mr Tidy?'

'Doan't know like.'

'Then why not *find out*? Is the canon all right?'

'Doan't know that either.'

'For goodness sake do something, Mr Tidy! We may be about to sink!'

Tidy sucked at his teeth. 'Now, doan't go getting theself in a tizzy, missus, 'tain't the first storm to hit a ship at sea and Ah doan't reckon we're going to sink. Ah – ' He broke off as a vast cassocked figure emerged from a cabin. 'Glad you're all reet, Reverend. Ah was joost coming along to see to thee, like.'

'Very thoughtful of you, Tidy, I'm sure. If you – '

'What are you going to *do*?' Mrs Weder-Ublick asked sharply.

'Pray, dear lady. We shall all pray, since there is nothing else we *can* do.' He added, 'But I do feel that perhaps we should offer prayers from the deck. That would be safer, you see. Nearer the lifeboat.'

v

'Getting bloody drenched, they are,' Victoria said, using the voicepipe from Halfhyde's cabin to the bridge. From the port she had seen the three figures, kneeling by the side of a square wooden container in which were stowed cork lifejackets, on the open deck just abaft the lifeboat lying snugly griped-in to the davits. 'Don't know what good they think they're doing, mate.'

'Don't denigrate prayer,' Halfhyde said, his voice coming hollowly down the pipe.

'I don't, mate, not really. But they'll catch their death of cold and that won't help anyone, will it?'

'Let them pray,' Halfhyde said. 'There's no danger anyway . . . but there's nothing wrong with getting a foot in for the future.' He banged down the voice-pipe cover and resumed his stance, braced against the guardrail, facing wind and sea. Already there was a lift of the cloud base and the overall gloom ahead; the squall would blow itself out soon enough. There was still plenty of spume being blown off the wave crests by the tearing wind, but there were no other ships in the vicinity so the comparative lack of visibility was a matter of little concern. The lightning had done some damage but not enough to worry about: the mainmast had been struck and some of the top hamper had come down and had been blown away to starboard. Nothing was left hanging that would prove dangerous to anyone on the deck below and once the squall had passed behind them the carpenter would be sent aloft to make a running repair to the cross-trees and to examine the triatic stay for any fraying of the strands.

Halfhyde turned to look aft. Prayers were still winging their way upwards. Halfhyde thought of all the monks and nuns who throughout the centuries had prayed steadfastly and often in their monasteries and nunneries for the sins of the world, taking it upon themselves to act for universal salvation. It had perhaps done some good; but there was still plenty of sin in the world. And when Canon Rampling had finished there would still be plenty of potential for sin aboard the *Taronga Park*. The men who went down to the sea in ships were not saints and never would be; and many flood-gates would be opened when finally the ship berthed in Valparaiso, one of the world's best-endowed places for sin in the forms of drink and women. In Valparaiso many a shipmaster had lost most of his crew in desertion for the gilded fleshpots and the brothels and had had to go to the boarding-house masters to get together a shanghai-ed substitute crew of helpless drunks who had missed their own ships on sailing, or landlubbers pressed into sea service by the fist, the marline-spike or the gun. Valparaiso, where he was to act as salvation for Admiral Watkiss.

Halfhyde was reflecting on Watkiss when something happened aft by the lifejacket stowage. A sudden gust of wind came and in the same instant the ship plunged heavily to starboard as the bottom lifted to a wave's violent surge. There was movement on the deck, and then a high scream from Mrs Weder-Ublick, and Halfhyde saw Canon Rampling lift into the air like a bat in flight, scrabbling wildly with feet and arms, the wind using his enormous cassock as a sail as his feet slid from under him on the wet, greasy deck, and he went over the side, followed by a released *Book of Common Prayer* that, also caught by the wind, sped ahead of him as he dropped into the ocean.

ELEVEN

'I shall do the nursing,' Mrs Weder-Ublick stated firmly. An ebullient bat had gone overboard, a half-drowned creature had returned in safety. The wind had dropped, presumably in response to recent prayer, and the lifeboat had been got away with all speed under Halfhyde's orders. Obviously, a miracle had occurred; Mrs Weder-Ublick stated that as a fact, and repeated, since no-one appeared to have heard, that she would do the nursing.

Tidy didn't like that. He said, ' 'Tisn't reet. 'Tisn't fitting. In the parish – '

'Oh, what nonsense!' said Admiral Watkiss' sister. 'It is a woman's work, Mr Tidy, and I am going to do it and that's fact, I said it.'

Canon Rampling was borne below to his bunk, gasping and emitting water from his mouth, his hair bedraggled and his clerical collar limp around his neck, reduced to the status of a rag. This semi-cortege was accompanied by Mrs Weder-Ublick and churchwarden Tidy. The cassock had to be removed and the canon put into his nightshirt. This task Mrs Weder-Ublick in fact left to Mr Tidy, quitting the cabin whilst the canon was undressed.

ii

In the residence of the British Minister in Santiago there was much concern. A suave, sallow-faced Chilean had presented the compliments of his President and had been admitted to the presence of the Minister to state that the Commander-in-Chief of the Navy was to be arrested and would answer certain charges of making unauthorized and false reports to Her Britannic Majesty's representative regarding German trading designs that did not in fact exist. The Chilean uttered further: the Admiral Watkiss, he said, making it sound like the name of a ship, was not at his residence and had not been seen by his staff for some forty-eight hours. His personal steward had also vanished.

'Where,' the Chilean demanded ominously, 'is the Admiral Watkiss?'

The Minister did not propose to admit that the Commander-in-Chief had been advised unofficially to make himself scarce pending the arrival in Valparaiso of the *Taronga Park*. He shrugged and said, 'Really, I have not the slightest idea. Admiral Watkiss is not my responsibility. He's a Chilean, after all.'

'Yes, he is a Chilean, Excellency, which makes his crimes those of treason to his adopted state. I ask again, where is the Admiral Watkiss, please?'

The Minister spread his hands wide. 'I can only say what I said before – I've no idea.'

The Chilean, seated, waggled a crossed foot impatiently. 'We believe he is in this residence, Excellency! We believe you hide him, that you consider him to be not what you said he was, a Chilean, but still a British subject.'

'I assure you Admiral Watkiss is not here, señor.'

'My President asks your pardon, Excellency, but I have orders to make a full search of your residence – '

'You have no right to do that, señor. There are, as you and your President know well, international agreements protecting what is in effect British soil, sovereign and inviolable by any – '

'Yes, yes, Excellency.' The Chilean produced an oily smile which became almost a conspiratorial wink. 'But you and I, we are not children, we know that so often the international agreements are eyewash, to be disregarded when it is better so. I shall rephrase my President's demand. I correct: I *ask* – not demand. If you should refuse a request, then we may assume that the Admiral Watkiss is in hiding here. In which case you yourself will be in breach of the agreements, and to have to

report this . . .' He shrugged, his shoulders virtually disappear-
ing down inside his frock coat. 'It would not be good, yes?'

The Minister, on very safe ground vis-à-vis the non-presence
of Admiral Watkiss, appeared to consider then gave in. 'Very
well. Your request is granted, señor – we have nothing to
hide – '

'No admiral?' There was a snigger.

'No admiral, señor.'

'Then all will be well. I should state that there are soldiers
watching all exits from your residence, Excellency, alert for an
escaping admiral.'

The Minister got to his feet and walked across to one of the
big windows, with balconies, looking over the carriage sweep in
front of the building and over the railings beyond. A number of
men in gaudy uniforms lounged about. Many of the jackets had
their buttons undone, one of the soldiers was picking his nose
by the great gates while another urinated against the gate-post,
his rifle lying discarded on the ground. However, no time was
lost in starting the search. The Chilean was angry at the
eventual nil result, his manner being frosty. There was, he said,
a strong possibility that when the Admiral Watkiss was
eventually brought to justice, he would be charged with
desertion. That would attract the death penalty.

iii

The sojourn in the hut had not lasted for long: just the one
night and the following day. Washbrook had made his arrangements for the onward transmission of Admiral Watkiss to
Valparaiso. These were simple, consisting of progress by
shank's pony, a long walk all the way to the port. The distance
would be around seventy miles and since movement would take
place only at night, the journey would take many days.

'Many blasted *nights*, you mean,' Admiral Watkiss said in an
aggrieved tone, 'not days.'

'Yes, sir. Sorry, sir. During the daytime, sir, we shall hide,
see, sir.'

'Where?'

'Wherever we can find to hide, sir.'

'Yes, yes, I suppose that's reasonable, Washbrook.' Leave was later taken of the young woman, whom Watkiss thanked perfunctorily. The stay had not been comfortable and the hurried exit of the pig had not in fact removed all the smell. The straw had been most prickly and contained insects that had caused Admiral Watkiss to pass the night scratching rather than sleeping and breakfast had been green beans, wholesome no doubt but a poor substitute for fried bacon and eggs, kedgeree, toast and marmalade and hot coffee. After gratitude had been expressed, Petty Officer Steward Washbrook had gone behind the hut with the young woman, presumably for his own farewell, and Admiral Watkiss had waited impatiently while giggling and heavy breathing took place. A fairly typical sailor's goodbye, Watkiss supposed, but it smacked of insubordination when it delayed an admiral's progress. He disregarded totally the concept that he could scarcely consider himself an admiral any longer; admirals did not vanish, he knew that, but he had persuaded himself that what he was doing was not vanishing at all, just taking prudent precautions so that Her Majesty in Windsor Castle would not be embarrassed by what the blasted Chileans might do to him if they caught him.

At full dark, and after an eventless day of non-pursuit, and more beans, admiral and steward set out upon the next stage of their flight.

iv

Out at sea, the long days passed. Two more coaling stops, and then the passage of Cape Horn with its long rollers and its buffeting, ceaseless westerly winds that blew around the world's bottom. After Cape Horn, the calm waters of the South Pacific with Puerto Montt ahead and then Valparaiso. As journey's end came nearer, Halfhyde had a number of conferences with Mr Mayhew and Detective Inspector Todhunter. The question of smuggling Watkiss aboard was gone into as to its legal aspect under International Law and Todhunter gave it as his opinion that they would be in breach of the regulations. That was, he said, unless they could do one thing.

'And that is?' Halfhyde asked.

'To bring about the prior arrest of Admiral Watkiss, sir.'

'That makes a difference, Todhunter?'

'As advised by my chief super, sir, yes, it does. Admiral Watkiss will then come under the jurisdiction of British law, sir.' Todhunter gave a cough. 'That is, sir, I stress, according to my chief super. I confess that after much reading, I have been unable to find confirmation in various law and police manuals.'

'I see. And which of your authorities takes precedence in your estimation, Todhunter?'

Todhunter looked puzzled. 'Beg pardon, sir?'

'Which is the most potent, the law books or your chief super?'

Todhunter said promptly, 'Oh, my chief super, sir. A very good police officer, sir. I dare say there are omissions in the manuals, sir, such as would be very quickly pointed out by my chief super were he here with us. My old mother, sir . . . she had a very high opinion of my chief super, very high indeed – '

'Really. I – '

'Oh, yes, sir.' Mr Todhunter would have liked to tell Captain Halfhyde about the tea-party but felt the moment not propitious. 'A very high opinion, sir.'

'Very well, we shall bow to the knowledge of your chief super,' Halfhyde said, concealing a grin. 'It seems to me to be a problem easily enough overcome if we adhere to his dicta. You say the essential pre-requisite is the actual arrest of Admiral Watkiss. Well, surely he can be considered arrested the moment we make contact, can't he?'

'Provided I utter the correct words, sir, yes.'

'Which you can do in an instant?'

'A shade more than an instant, sir.'

'Then that solves that point, Todhunter.'

Todhunter considered for a moment, then said, 'Why, yes, I suppose it does. Yes, you have it, sir.'

'So all we have to do is to find Admiral Watkiss.'

Mayhew entered the discussion. 'I've no doubt he will present himself, Captain Halfhyde. He will have been advised about your ship's arrival – our Minister in Santiago will have seen to that.'

'No doubt. But there may be impediments along the way. There's the German involvement . . . but perhaps more importantly there is Admiral Watkiss himself.'

'But we've just – '

'I know. It should be all plain sailing, Mr Mayhew. But the good Watkiss will like arrest by no man, not even our friend Todhunter. Where – '

'I *am* British, sir,' Todhunter broke in.

'Yes, Mr Todhunter, as British as the London bobby that you are! I still maintain that where Admiral Watkiss is concerned, there's a thousand possible slips between cup and lip – that's all.'

The conference broke up; the major decisions and strategies would have to be left until after arrival in Valparaiso when the lie of the land should become clearer and there might be word from the Minister in Santiago. In the meantime matters were proceeding in Canon Rampling's sick cabin: he had taken his immersion badly and a fever had developed. At Port Stanley in the Falkland Islands a naval surgeon had been summoned from an ancient and stationary battleship and this practitioner had advised that the canon be landed to his care, but Rampling had refused and so had Mrs Weder-Ublick. Shaking his head, the surgeon had provided physic, and poultices for applying to the lungs. Mrs Weder-Ublick had proved an assiduous nurse; she scarcely seemed to leave the canon's bunkside. It was as if she were practising already for her mission work in Chile. She did of course leave from time to time and whenever she did so churchwarden Tidy took over and got his say in. He was very suspicious of Mrs Weder-Ublick's motives.

'Reckon you need to take care, Reverend.'

'I am taking care, or Mrs Weder-Ublick is, Tidy.'

'That's what Ah mean, Reverend. Ah reckon she's too forward like.'

'Oh, nonsense, Tidy, she's a very respectable woman, very respectable.'

'Take care any road.'

Mrs Weder-Ublick, when sitting by his bunk, knitted. When she counted her stitches Canon Rampling closed his eyes in meditation; when the counting took place, Mrs Weder-Ublick was unable, naturally, to talk, and the silences became oases to be looked forward to. Canon Rampling knew very well what was in Tidy's mind, but the churchwarden had no need to be alarmed: Canon Rampling was resolved to maintain his single status, although there was no doubt as to what Mrs Weder-Ublick was manoeuvring towards. She repeated many times that she missed the company of a husband and that support in her mission would be so very, very welcome. And she was a considerate woman, no doubt about that at all. Sometimes she read to him from a sheaf of memoirs left behind by her late husband, memoirs containing a number of facts about the Lutheran church, how unity had been restored between conflicting factions by the general acceptance of the Formula of Concord in the year 1580. There was mention of a number of ecclesiastical authorities, persons such as Dr Eck, and Melanchthon, and Luthardt, Kahnis, Hase, Nitsch and Martensen, plus Hinschius and Friedberg as well as, of course, Luther himself, the founder, the father figure. Canon Rampling said it was all most interesting and when now and again he dozed off was able to ascribe his inattention to his physical weakness. Mrs Weder-Ublick even assisted him in the self-administration of communion, taking it herself also though Canon Rampling was still unsure of the ethics of this; and was aware, too, that Tidy's nose was being put well out of joint over it. There were other ministrations in addition: glasses of water whenever required, and the physic, and the flapping of a handkerchief to stir the sometimes heavy air, and cooling wet linen applied to his brow when the fever shook him. Little things like that.

To be sure, he would miss the solicitude next time he was upon a bed of sickness, which in Chile he well might be. He believed Mrs Weder-Ublick knew this very well indeed. There was an insidiousness about her.

v

'I am very tired, Washbrook. I can go no further.' Admiral Watkiss sank to the bare earth of a field, looking pathetic in the Chilean moonlight. 'I am no longer young.'

116

'Nor me,' Petty Officer Steward Washbrook said with a touch of sourness.

'I hadn't noticed,' Admiral Watkiss said distantly. He stirred angrily; he considered it an impertinence on a steward's part to make any reference to his own age, especially in such a way as to suggest his officer was making excuses. The day after leaving the hut had been sheer torture. Admiral Watkiss had crouched in a ditch some miles north-westward of Santiago and after a while it had begun to rain and there was no shelter to be had other than the placement of Washbrook's body between himself and the angle of the rain, and that wasn't much good. There had been life in the ditch, unpleasant life – field mice, insects of unknown and possibly poisonous origin, the occasional rat that had peered and fled. When the rain had ceased, there was the sun, blinding, scorching, its rays penetrating even Admiral Watkiss' sack which steamed. There had also been hunger; Washbrook, urged out into the open to forage though he had protested that to do so was dangerous, had returned with some nasty-tasting berries and a few wild strawberries that were not quite so bad. They had with them iron rations of a sort provided by the young woman in the hut – beans again, mostly, and the black bread, and some raw vegetables, and a hunk of cooked meat. These were being retained against future emergencies when the hunger pains would grow worse. To live off the countryside, Watkiss said, for as long as possible, was the way to salvation. But when Washbrook was absent on his foraging, Watkiss ate some of the beans.

Washbrook, on his return, complained of a nasty rash on his leg, very sore it was. Without much interest Admiral Watkiss said it must be from the pig. At nightfall they had set out again, emerging from the ditch onto a rough, dusty track lying white beneath the moon. Nothing else had moved on this track and they had made fair progress until it had petered out, which explained something that had been bothering Admiral Watkiss: no pursuit. Since the road led nowhere, it would be presumed that the Commander-in-Chief of the Navy, an officer well used to reading charts and maps in order not to lose himself in strange waters, would not be upon it.

'You're a blasted fool, Washbrook,' Admiral Watkiss said

from his recumbent position: he had sunk to the ground just where the track ran out. 'You should have known the blasted road was a dead end!'

'Wasn't what I were told, sir, by the young woman.'

'Then she's a blasted fool as well. Or you took the wrong road. In any event it's your blasted fault, not mine. What do you propose to do about it, man?'

'I don't know, sir.'

Watkiss waved his arms in the air. 'Oh, balls and bang me arse, Washbrook, what a fine petty officer you make, no damned initiative at all!'

'If so be you 'ad a compass, sir – '

'Well, I haven't a blasted compass, so there. And whose fault is that, may I ask? As a steward of any gumption you should have seen to it that your officer was properly equipped! As God's my judge, Washbrook, I'll have you damn well disrated the moment we reach civilization!'

Washbrook glowered but said nothing. There was no point in exacerbating Admiral Watkiss. Thoughts alone were safe and Petty Officer Steward Washbrook indulged them. Daft old bugger, his thoughts ran, he's in no position to disrate a flea, and never will be again. Not in Chile, anyhow. As for himself, Washbrook had no intention of returning to England, not as Petty Officer Steward Washbrook, that was, and not anywhere near the Queen's ships of war. Once he'd seen the old bugger safely out of Chilean hands, he intended to desert, hide up in Valparaiso for a while, then get himself a berth in a merchant ship under an assumed name. There was safety in that, and a new career; he might get into the liners of the PSNC after a bit, end up as chief steward, in which rank there were any number of perks and fiddles.

In the meantime physical safety was paramount. Washbrook, casting around, used his initiative.

'There be a mountain ahead, sir.'

'Yes, I can see that, thank you, Washbrook.'

'Standing between us and Valparaiso, sir.'

'You think so?'

'Yes, sir. I reckon, sir, we 'ave to climb over it, sir.'

Admiral Watkiss studied the mountain. In truth it was more of a hill, but it was bad enough and it appeared to be in the centre of a whole range of other hills, and it was a long way off to start with. If the going became too rough, Washbrook would have to carry him. With this thought in mind, Watkiss clambered back onto his feet. 'Very well, then,' he said.

They set off. Between themselves and the hill there was a swamp. Admiral Watkiss, in the lead as befitted his status, fell into it. Before Washbrook's startled eyes, he vanished into a great pool of mud.

vi

The search, with police and troops involved, was being co-ordinated by the Commander-in-Chief of the Army, Admiral Watkiss' own opposite number, General Carlos Puga, a porcine man wearing the military equivalent of Admiral Watkiss' gold tassels and epaulettes and medals. He had conferred at some length with the Chief of Police, Colonel Opazo. Opazo said that the capital would be most thoroughly searched and that he would expect the military to cordon the perimeter so far as possible.

General Puga dismissed this as *not* possible. 'The roads, of course – all roads out, they are being and will be watched. But I do not believe Admiral Watkiss will use the roads, Colonel.'

'Then the open country – '

'That also no. I am convinced he is remaining in Santiago as the safest place, some place of concealment that will perhaps be known to the British Minister, whose word I do not trust. So the capture is up to you, you see?'

'I shall do my best, naturally, General. But I do not agree with you. I believe Admiral Watkiss will head for the coast. He is a sailor, and he will attempt to make his getaway by the sea, in a ship.'

General Puga shook his head obstinately. 'That would be too obvious. We would immediately expect that. Santiago must be combed first. Then we shall see.'

Colonel Opazo blew out his cheeks but made no verbal response to what he considered an inanity. The army mind was a stupid one, as porcine and constipated as General Puga's own appearance. The police were different, from a different mould, accustomed to thinking before acting. He would keep his own counsel vis-à-vis General Puga and he would see to it that the coast from Talcahuano to Coquimbo – all of it, including of course the port of Valparaiso – was most closely watched. Being honest with himself, Colonel Opazo did not believe too much in the prospect of success. The British were slippery people, unreliable and untruthful like the Minister, with an extraordinary aptitude for getting themselves out of tight corners. All of which was why it was essential to Colonel Opazo's future that the blame for any failure should be laid at the door of General Puga. And he knew, of course, that General Puga would be harbouring similar designs.

After forty-eight hours of feverish search, Santiago stood empty of Admiral Watkiss. The British Minister had again been questioned, very politely, but still denied any knowledge of the escapee's whereabouts. The help of the German Ambassador was sought by General Puga, aware that his head was approaching the executioner's block. Count Rupert von Gelsenkirchen, aware that the British admiral, or was he Chilean really, had made representations to the British Minister about the German intention to seize the trading advantage from Queen Victoria, was keen to help. The British admiral was a vile person . . . and von Gelsenkirchen preferred to regard him as British, since the British and not the Chileans were the enemy, the wretched race that constantly sought to frustrate the desires of the German Emperor.

He said as much to General Puga: 'The fellow is, after all, British.'

'No, Excellency. He is Chilean.'

'British.'

'Chilean!'

Von Gelsenkirchen blew out his moustache. 'We shall not argue, we shall not disagree. But he is British.'

General Puga left it at that. Seeking help from the German, he needed to be circumspect. But von Gelsenkirchen had little help to offer in any physical sense; he had no troops to deploy, sadly. He would, of course, keep an ear to the ground and report immediately if he heard anything of the British admiral's goings-on.

vii

On firm ground still, Petty Officer Steward Washbrook stayed there. He called out.

'Where are you, sir? Where are you?'

He stared towards the spot where Admiral Watkiss had disappeared. There was a hole, a sort of vortex in the mud, slowly filling up again. There was, in fact, no doubt as to where Admiral Watkiss was; the enquiry was a formality. It seemed unlikely that the admiral would re-appear, but, as was so often the case with Admiral Watkiss, he confounded likelihood. There was a glugging noise, and a sound of sucking, and a foul stench, and the mud itself, apparently, rose a foot in the air.

'You be all right, sir?'

There was an indistinct sound and as the mud began to drain away more of Admiral Watkiss emerged and there was a furious splutter. 'Of course I'm not all right, you blasted fool! Help me out!'

'If I come closer, sir, I'll fall in too, sir.'

'A damn good thing if you did, you're as blasted useless as a whore at a wedding. *Get down on your stomach, man, and reach out to me!*'

With a muttered oath, Washbrook obeyed orders. By the time Admiral Watkiss had been dragged out, both of them were in much the same state of filth. Watkiss, it turned out, had managed to beach himself. His feet had made contact with a kind of rock shelf, as he believed it to be, beneath the swamp. On it had been a structure composed of metal bars in which he had for a while trapped his feet. He believed this to be, perhaps, a discarded bedstead made of brass.

'I see, sir,' Washbrook said. 'What you might call bedrock, sir.'

'Oh, hold your tongue and don't make jokes.'

After an attempt to clean himself off on some scrubby grass and bushes, Admiral Watkiss led on towards the hills.

TWELVE

The outer approaches to Puerto Montt came up to starboard, with Chiloe Island some seven miles off the *Taronga Park*'s bow. On deck stood Mr Todhunter and Mr Mayhew, both conscious that quite soon now their duties might begin. Mr Todhunter was already clutching his Gladstone bag in which there were the documents necessary for the arrest of Admiral Watkiss into British custody, and a letter in his chief super's own hand testifying to Mr Todhunter's identity and rank in the Metropolitan Police Force. In his pocket Mr Mayhew carried something similar signed by Her Majesty's Principal Secretary of State for Foreign Affairs.

Todhunter was of the view that once the ship had entered Reloncavi Bay, on which the township of Puerto Montt lay, there might be news of Admiral Watkiss. 'Something definite, sir.'

'From whom?'

'Why, sir, I don't rightly know . . . but perhaps from the British Minister in Santiago, sir. By means of the overland cable, sir.'

Mayhew pursed his lips, looking to port and starboard at one and the same time. 'I doubt it, Todhunter. Secrecy, you know. Secrecy – that's paramount. In spite of the Foreign Office cypher . . . nobody's to be trusted.'

'That's true, sir, yes. My chief super – he's always – '

'Yes, yes. I'm sure he is, Todhunter. But he's not here now and we must manage on our own.' Mayhew lowered his voice. 'That woman's come up on deck. Mrs Weder-Ublick. Don't turn your head, Todhunter.' He paused. 'I assume you've discovered nothing from her? The German link.' Then he remembered. 'Of course – Funchal. Such a pity.'

'Indeed it was, sir. And since then, or since soon after then anyway, there's been Canon Rampling.'

'Yes.' It had become almost a *cause célèbre*; the ship had buzzed with rumours about the widow and the canon who were now being referred to as the spider and the fly. Mr Mayhew among others had overheard coarse comment from the members of the ship's crew. These, of themselves, had not bothered Mr Mayhew but he was angry that the canon's illness had withdrawn Mrs Weder-Ublick from the sort of conversation, leading conversation, that he had wished to indulge in with her. Canon Rampling, though better now and out of his bunk, had proved a nuisance, unconsciously acting against affairs of state.

From the corner of his eye Mr Mayhew saw Canon Rampling's large head appearing from the hatch leading up from the cabin accommodation. He then saw the head disappear: Canon Rampling had seen Mrs Weder-Ublick. Mayhew gave a sardonic chuckle: if the churchman was to become caught, it would serve him right for being a nuisance.

Victoria was on the bridge with Halfhyde when the ship turned to starboard for the entry to Reloncavi Bay. Although it was, according to the Admiralty Sailing Directions, usual to take a pilot for entry, Halfhyde had decided not to; his ship was small and of shallow enough draft to negotiate the sandbanks and shoals, well marked on the chart. The chief officer was in the eyes of the ship with the starboard anchor veered to the waterline, ready for letting go if required; and the second officer would shortly be sent away in the lifeboat with a party to take soundings ahead of the ship as she moved in at dead slow speed. It was ironic, Halfhyde thought, that the last time he had entered Reloncavi Bay had been under the command of the then Captain Watkiss in the old battleship *Meridian*.

Victoria gave a sudden giggle. Like Mayhew, she had observed the hasty retreat of Canon Rampling down the hatch. 'Poor old bugger,' she said feelingly.

'Who?'

She told him. 'Won't have a bloody chance, mate. That old harridan, she's got her claws in his cassock and she won't ever let go.' She giggled again. 'What if she's got a bun in the oven, eh?'

Halfhyde snorted.

'Yes, I know, past it. Not past trying, though. Don't reckon you ever get to that age. Hope not anyway. But suppose she had got pregnant. Reckon it'd be a toss-up between British and Chilean nationality for the bun. Like your old Watkiss.'

'Who is not to be compared with a bun, Victoria.'

'Some bun, eh!'

Halfhyde said irritably, 'That's enough about buns, Victoria. I need my concentration.' Under Halfhyde's guidance the *Taronga Park* moved inwards for Puerto Montt and the bunkers necessary to take her on to Valparaiso.

ii

From Santiago the orders had gone out; Colonel Opago's orders and General Puga's. Colonel Opago had by now gone behind the general's back: he had sought an interview with the President himself and he had arranged for the Chilean Navy to join the search for their late Commander-in-Chief. The ships, among them those so recently inspected by Admiral Watkiss in Iquique and Valparaiso, were hastily made ready for sea and sent out to patrol the coast between the points decided upon by Colonel Opago. When General Puga's spies informed him of this, he merely shrugged. When Admiral Watkiss was not discovered fleeing from the coast but safe in the perfidious British Minister's care, then Opago would be charged with wasting the country's resources in unnecessary coal for steaming. If on the other hand Opago was proved right, then he, General Puga, would not find it excessively hard to twist the credit round in his own direction.

Before the despatch of the fleet, the ocean cable had been busy between Santiago and London. Using the Foreign Office cypher the British Minister had reported the threatened arrest of Admiral Watkiss and his subsequent disappearance. He reported also that Admiral Watkiss had asked for asylum in the residency but had not been granted it. The arrival of this cable at the Foreign Office caused a conference to be summoned. The Secretary of State for Foreign Affairs took charge. With him was the Secretary of State for Home Affairs and various underlings; and from the Admiralty came the rear-admiral who had given Captain Halfhyde his original instructions in the matter.

'No asylum,' the Foreign Secretary said, tapping a hand on the wood of the long mahogany table.

'No asylum,' the rear-admiral repeated. 'This was as agreed, sir.'

'Yes, I know. But if you remember, Admiral, I made the point some while ago that there is a degree of *Britishness* still about Watkiss – '

'A faded Britishness, and we can't insist on it. That was the whole point of sending this ship, the *Taronga Park*, was it not, sir?'

The Foreign Secretary agreed. 'But actually to ask for asylum and be turned away! I confess I don't like it. Yes, Home Secretary?'

The Home Secretary, who had been looking as if he had an urgent contribution to make, gave a lengthy dissertation on the rules governing nationality. This was somewhat garbled and even vague; such a situation had never arisen before. Admiral Watkiss had appeared to be acting for the British Crown when he had made his report about the German knavery, notwithstanding his current allegiance to Chile, and it was all very involved and difficult.

'Always is with the damned Germans,' the Foreign Secretary said, 'the more so as we have always to bear in mind the close relationship to Her Majesty – '

'There's not much love lost to be truthful.' They all knew that the Prince of Wales, at any rate, loathed his German cousin. The Home Secretary turned to the rear-admiral. 'Admiral, is it not the case that Watkiss still retains his rank of Post Captain in Her Majesty's Navy – on the retired list?'

'That's correct in basis, but whilst holding the appointment of Commander-in-Chief of the Chilean Navy, his rank in the

Royal Navy has been suspended. That is because were he to retain it, certain difficulties could arise between our two countries – '

'Such as has now happened, in fact?'

The rear-admiral nodded. 'Although I would never have believed it possible for even Watkiss to get himself into such a pickle.'

'A division of loyalties . . . so we take it Watkiss is *not* a Post Captain in Her Majesty's fleet?' the Home Secretary asked.

'Yes and no,' the rear-admiral said. 'It appears to be the case that at this moment he is on the run – that *ipso facto* he has relinquished his position as C-in-C. That would appear to restore him to the retired list of the Royal Navy. At any rate, I think he would consider himself so entitled – knowing Watkiss as I do.'

They all looked at one another. If Admiral Watkiss was to be considered a Briton still, and with a British naval rank, then the Minister in Santiago had acted most wrongly even though, as the highly-placed persons knew full well, a general directive had gone out when the trouble in Chile had started to simmer, instructing the Minister, in more diplomatic terms, not to stick his neck out and thus embroil Her Majesty. If on the other hand Watkiss was still C-in-C until he had been arrested and charged and formally relieved of his command, then he had no rank in the British Navy and was not to be regarded as British. In which case the Minister in Santiago had acted with perfect correctness in turning away a fugitive from Chilean justice.

'A difficult situation,' the Foreign Secretary said.

'Most difficult,' the Home Secretary said.

'I call it damned impossible,' the rear-admiral said.

Heads were shaken, mouths pursed. Cigars were lit by permission of the Foreign Secretary and a bell was pushed for sherry. A decision emerged. The Minister in Santiago, the Foreign Secretary said, had merely made a report. No more than that. He had not asked for guidance, had he? He had asked neither for approval nor disapproval.

It was agreed that this was indeed so. It was further agreed that in the circumstances, taking all factors and considerations into full acount, no reply at all need be sent. It was, the Foreign Secretary said with relief, a time for masterly inactivity to be displayed.

When no response whatever reached Santiago, the Minister was not surprised. He had never expected one.

iii

'I believe it's my heart, Washbrook.' On the Valparaiso side of the range of hills Admiral Watkiss, once again, lay flat on the ground, breathing stertorously. 'I've damn well overdone it.'

'But, sir, there's a deal of a way to go yet, sir.'

'Oh, I dare say, you fool, but I'm not fit! I'm very far from well, don't you blasted well understand what I say?'

'Yes, sir, I do, sir, and I'm very sorry to 'ear it, sir.' Petty Officer Steward Washbrook blew his nose to leeward of the Admiral, using the simple sailor's method of squeezing the nostrils together, blowing hard, and then suddenly releasing the nose. He went on, 'Beg pardon, sir, but there's summat we did ought to think about now, sir, seeing you be so bad like.'

'What?'

'Suppose you was to die, sir?'

'Die?' Admiral Watkiss sucked in a horrified breath. 'What a thing to say to your admiral!'

'They said it to Lord Nelson, sir, when – '

'Oh, balls and bang me arse, Washbrook, my situation is not fatal.'

Washbrook persisted; he had to get the old bugger back on his feet for the safety of both of them. The Chileans must surely have picked up some tracks or clues by this time. 'But suppose you was to, sir? Die, like. You'd be buried on Chilean soil, sir. Not British, see, sir. And a Chilean form of service. Candles, sir.'

'Oh, what balls. They'd get the Church of England padre from the Residency.' Watkiss rallied a little and sat up on one elbow. 'You're talking rubbish, Washbrook. They'd bury me, if it came to that which it won't, in the Residency grounds!'

'No, sir, with respect, sir. They turned you away, sir, in life. They'd not accept you dead, sir.'

127

That was possibly true; Admiral Watkiss managed to look pathetic. 'What an appalling lot of bounders they are these days, Washbrook. No longer gentlemen. Counter-jumpers, tradesmen, time-servers! Every damn one of them needs flogging round the fleet.'

'Yes, sir,' Washbrook agreed pacifically, 'but they 'as the upper hand though I don't like to say it to you, sir, you 'oo are a proper gennelman like.'

'Yes . . .'

'Always considerate like, sir, and fair.'

'Yes.'

'Treats a man decent, sir.'

'Yes, I've always made a point of that, Washbrook. I trust you've never taken it personally when I've sworn at you. It was never meant, you realize. It's those blasted dagoes I swear at. I can't damn well stand foreign buggers, Washbrook.' Admiral Watkiss was sounding really pathetic now. 'They're not *British* and they have no blasted standards. They all tell lies and are most untrustworthy. Half of them don't wash, either.'

'Yes, sir, that's the truth of it, sir.' Petty Officer Steward Washbrook knew his man and knew too that he had now got him where he wanted him. 'All that, sir, is why I don't want to see your body, sir, dug down into Chilean ground and left there for ever like, and all them dagoes treading – '

'Oh, hold your tongue, Washbrook, do! I'm *much* better now. I simply needed the rest, there was no need to make quite so much of it. Don't just damn well stand there, you fool, pull me up.'

They set off again. Well clear now of Santiago, they moved, taking great care, largely by daylight, not waiting for nightfall. The whole area seemed totally without any human presence, and cover, once away from the bare hillside, was very adequate. After a couple of hours march a halt was called for food, and they broached the rations provided by the young woman in Santiago. They drank fresh water from a brook, upstream of where some cows were also drinking amid trodden mud, Admiral Watkiss pronouncing that since the cows were all right the water was safe for humans. They slept for a while in the

128

shade of some trees and then, refreshed, moved on again. Next day they came upon a lonely hovel, an apology for a farmhouse, occupied by an old man and a mangy dog. The old man had no teeth and grinned and chewed at their approach. Washbrook had picked up enough Spanish to be able to converse a little.

'What does he say?' Watkiss asked impatiently.

' 'E says, sir, we're very dirty. All that mud, sir.'

'No dirtier than him – no, don't tell him that, Washbrook, one has to be tactful, something persons of your sort don't understand.' Watkiss sighed. 'Ask him if anybody has come this way recently.'

Washbrook did so; the answer was no. Nobody, it seemed, ever did come, which suited the old man and the dog well enough. Watkiss said, 'That means we're in the clear so far. Ask him how far off the coast we are.'

'Off Valp – '

'No, no, no, you fool!' Admiral Watkiss danced up and down. 'Don't mention that place, one can't be too careful in case someone *does* come. Just the coast.'

'But, sir, the coast's long and – '

'Oh, don't argue with me, Washbrook, I know what coasts are. Just do as I say.'

'Yes, sir.' It transpired that the coast, or some of it, was about thirty miles westward. 'Still a long way to go, sir.'

'Yes. I think we can rest first. Ask him if he can accommodate us. I have no objection to paying him a small sum.'

'I wouldn't tell him that, sir, if I was you, sir – '

'Why not?'

Washbrook drew a hand across his throat, suggestively. 'If he sees money, sir, he'll wait till we're asleep and then – '

'Oh, all right, all right, we have no money. Certainly I've heard it said that these appalling dagoes are quite hospitable to – to penniless wayfarers. Go on, ask him.'

Assent was given; straw would be available, Washbrook interpreted. They went inside the hovel. There was no pig but otherwise it was much the same as the hovel of the young woman. Both footsore and weary, they fell asleep quickly. Watkiss woke after some hours to find that the old man was sharing the straw, an appalling and alarming thought. He heaved himself away from the close proximity and when he did so there was a deep growl. He was in bed with the dog as well.

THIRTEEN

Mrs Weder-Ublick wished to go ashore in Puerto Montt.

'I should see these small ports when I have the chance, Canon,' she said. 'No doubt very different from what I shall find in Valparaiso, don't you think?'

'Oh, undoubtedly, dear lady, undoubtedly. A different sort of people, you know, less cosmopolitan I dare say.' Puerto Montt was very small indeed, looking from the *Taronga Park*'s decks not much better than an African fishing village. It was because of this that Mrs Weder-Ublick's missionary fervour had surfaced so insistently; she was indeed very insistent also that the canon should accompany her. Canon Rampling murmured that he really ought to – er. For the life of him, thus caught, he couldn't think of anything he had to do.

'Nonsense, Canon!' Mrs Weder-Ublick was being a shade flirtatious; if she had had a fan in her hand, she would have brushed his cheek with it in a maidenly gesture. 'You're just being bashful, which is silly. You know how much I have come to rely on you. Please do come.'

'Yes, well. Yes, dear lady.' There was no escape. Tidy, lately very withdrawn, was being obtuse. No help there; Tidy was leaving his reverend to it. The conversation, however, was overheard from behind a bell-mouthed ventilator by Mr Mayhew, who at once sought out the detective inspector, who was below.

'You're going ashore, Todhunter.'

'Really, sir, I've no wish – '

'You're going ashore. That's an order. In the boat with Mrs Weder-Ublick and – '

131

'But, sir!' Todhunter wrung his hands in dismay. 'I can't possibly, not after Funchal, I – '

'That is precisely the point, Todhunter. You're going to *say* you're going ashore – so that Mrs Weder-Ublick remains aboard. You'll remember she said most firmly that if you went ashore anywhere, then she would not.'

'Yes, sir, but – '

'Listen, Todhunter.' Mayhew put his lips close to Todhunter's ear. 'I don't want Mrs Weder-Ublick to set foot on the shore. The German link – and there is a German vessel in the port. I have seen it. I shall not take the risk of a possible meeting out of my hearing.'

'But you might pick up a further clue, sir, might you not?'

'Not if I'm out of hearing, Todhunter.'

'Ah – well, no.'

'And I am adamant. You'll announce you're going ashore. Quickly, man!'

Obedient though dismayed, Todhunter scuttled up on the deck, clutching his bowler hat, for there was a breeze coming off the land. He approached Canon Rampling. 'Good morning, sir. Perhaps you can tell me what time Captain Halfhyde proposes to lower the boat so that we can go ashore?'

Before Rampling could reply Mrs Weder-Ublick addressed a question to him. 'Is this person going in the boat, Canon?'

'It appears – '

'Yes, ma'am,' Todhunter said, lifting his bowler hat but casting his eyes down towards the deck.

'Then I am *not*!' Mrs Weder-Ublick said explosively. She turned her back on both men, gathered up her serge skirt, and went below. Mr Todhunter reported later to Mr Mayhew that the canon had seemed greatly relieved and had almost bestowed a wink on him as the bearer of excellent news, a favour that Mr Todhunter construed as being perhaps a sign that he had been forgiven by the church at any rate, which was a very great happiness to him, for his old mother (and his chief super) had always set much store upon being in good standing with the church.

But Mr Todhunter, unwillingly, had to go ashore now,

having said that was his intention. A lonely, non-seafaring figure in the boat with the brawny sailors, he went. The boat had gone a matter of fifty yards from the *Taronga Park* when there was a shout from the bridge and the boat was pulled back towards the accommodation ladder. Miss Penn also wished to go ashore to make some purchases. In a white dress with a very full skirt she sat in the sternsheets with the detective inspector. Scent wafted into Todhunter's nostrils and, not liking to sit too near a young woman, he shifted a little.

She giggled. 'What's up, eh, mate? Contamination?'

'Oh no, indeed not, Miss Penn.'

'I'll bet! You needn't worry, though. I'll keep me distance for the sake of your virginity, mate.'

Mr Todhunter went a very deep red and didn't know where to look. What a hussy – and the sailors had obviously overheard, they could scarcely help it. There were grins and muttered remarks which fortunately Todhunter didn't catch. He sat frigid, as the woman chattered the whole way to the shore, all about nothing he thought; she was utterly brainless and frivolous and her sheer brazenness took away the breath. She seemed to care not one jot what people thought. Nevertheless, she was attractive, Todhunter realized. There was almost something engaging about her very giggle.

She was looking at him now. 'Never thought of getting married, did you, mate?'

'No. Never. You see, I had my old mother to think of, Miss Penn.'

'She wouldn't have approved, eh?'

'I fear not. She was very dependent upon me, her only son.'

'Kicked the bucket now, hasn't she?'

Mr Todhunter gasped with outraged astonishment, aghast that anyone should speak thus of his old mother, a personal thing. He brought out a large handkerchief and mopped at his face, unable to speak, to make any response at all to such an appalling utterance. Miss Penn seemed to understand that she had overstepped the mark. She apologized. 'Sorry, mate, didn't mean to upset you. Fond of her, were you?'

'Yes, very.'

'Sorry again, mate. I'm a bit of a bugger like that, can't control me tongue. I'll stop, right?'

Todhunter nodded, still speechless. The boat was pulled on for the shore, going past the German vessel spoken of by Mr Mayhew. It was a warship, a cruiser Todhunter believed it would be called. There were many guns, and the flag of the German Emperor was flaunted at the jackstaff. German sailors peered from the decks which they were washing down with hoses, or from guns that they were engaged in cleaning by the look of it. German petty officers roared in harsh voices, bellowing orders and looking angry. As they passed by, Mr Todhunter was very conscious of that German link that Mr Mayhew so strongly suspected – wrongly suspected still, in Todhunter's view. However, there was something sinister, something menacing about the very appearance of the German cruiser that made Todhunter glad when they had moved on and left it astern.

In a silence unusual for Miss Penn, she and Mr Todhunter reached a broken-down jetty and disembarked. The boat was pulled away again, back to the *Taronga Park*; it would return for them, the coxswain said, in two hours' time as ordered by Captain Halfhyde.

Victoria broke the icy silence. 'Where you going to, mate?'

'Merely a look round, Miss Penn, that's all.'

'Sight-seeing, eh?'

'Broadening the mind.'

'Bloody needs it and all – sorry. Me again, don't take any notice.' She giggled and suddenly seized his arm. 'There's a bar. Reckon I c'd do with a beer. How about you, eh?'

'Oh no, I – '

'C'mon, be a devil, why not?' Another giggle. 'Look, we're half-way to bloody Sydney and I feel me Waltzing Matildas stirring. Look as though you c'd do with a drink an' all.'

It was, in truth, a very hot day and the blue serge suit was heavy, the starched collar and cuffs of his shirt were limp and sticky. Mr Todhunter opened his purse and peered inside, cogitating. Detective inspectors of the Metropolitan Police Force were not paid a princely sum and his old mother had always preached the twin virtues of sobriety and thrift. However . . . it *was* a hot day.

Victoria became impatient. There was a mean look about the way in which the policeman examined his purse. She said, 'Sod the expense, mate, buy the cat a goldfish, why not?'

Mr Todhunter suffered another sense of shock. Such language! And cat. A very expressive epithet for Miss Penn. They entered the bar. The interior was dim and, like the German cruiser, somehow sinister, but Victoria didn't seem worried. No doubt she was accustomed, Todhunter thought, to the low taverns of Sydney, which he had always understood to be a dangerous and wicked place where evil ruled, at any rate in the dockland areas.

ii

'Valparaiso ahead, sir, I do believe, sir. That's what I calls a stroke o' real luck, sir!'

'Nonsense, it's simply good navigation on my part, Washbrook. I never doubted we should arrive at this spot.'

'No, sir, o' course not, sir.'

'We must now consider what to do next,' Admiral Watkiss said. It was some while now since they had left the hovel with the old man and the dog, but there were still fleas to be scratched away. They were now very thirsty; there had been no more streams and by that same token they were both dirtier than ever, for no washing had been possible, which partly accounted for the continued presence of the fleas. 'God damn that blasted dog! What do you think, Washbrook?'

'About the dog, sir?'

Watkiss waved his arms in the air. 'Not about the dog! About how we should proceed.'

'Well, sir, I'd say cautious like, sir.'

'Oh, balls, Washbrook, there's nothing like taking the bull by the horns. It's always been my principle. March ahead smartly, look as though you're going somewhere, and no-one questions you.'

Washbrook thought, full of bullshit. But bullshit did have a way of working out, no doubt about it. He'd used it himself often enough before now. Maybe the old bugger was right. He looked around. For the last stretch they had walked through most of the night, with short rest periods, and now it was full daylight and a nice, fine day at that. The outskirts of Valparaiso beckoned Watkiss strongly, for once in the teeming crowds of the big port they would be sure to find a degree at least of safety even though the Chileans would very likely be concentrating their efforts there. Washbrook felt obliged to point this bit out to his superior officer.

'Oh, I know, I know, Washbrook, it's obvious enough and I'm not a fool. But I've every reason to know that the blasted Chileans are quite useless – lazy – inefficient. They have no intelligence in the British sense, none at all. I feel quite confident of my future, Washbrook. All we have to do is to make contact with the *Taronga Park* when she enters.'

'Yes, sir. Should be quite easy like, sir.'

'Which isn't to say, of course, that we must cast care entirely to the winds, Washbrook. We must preserve our anonymity.'

'Yes, sir – '

'By which I mean, we do not make ourselves obvious. We do not *intrude* ourselves. If there is trouble – say, a fracas in the street, not unlikely with dagoes, then we avoid it. We turn the other cheek, Washbrook, do you understand?'

Washbrook nodded. 'I reckon I do, sir. What if them natives insult us like, sir?'

Watkiss said energetically, 'We damn well tell them we're *British*, Washbrook, and expect to be treated with courtesy and blasted respect!'

iii

Beer had been ordered and had been thrust into Mr Todhunter's hand by a large Chilean with a heavy black moustache and a filthy apron. Todhunter carried the glasses back to where Miss Penn sat at a table exchanging eyes with a group of uniformed seamen nearby.

She took the glass. 'Thanks, mate.' She drank almost half, Todhunter noticed with awe, in a single draught. Setting the glass down, she wiped the back of a hand across her lips. Mr

136

Todhunter, whose manners were good, wiped his own with his handkerchief, somewhat obviously.

'Sissy,' she said, staring. 'Anyway, thanks again. Reckon I bloody needed that. Know something, do you?' She leaned across intimately and Todhunter drew back a shade. 'That bunch. They're Germans.'

'So I see.'

'Speak German, do you, eh?'

Mr Todhunter said he did not; nevertheless, he listened to the seamen's conversation as a simple matter of routine. In the Metropolitan Police Force one always listened because you never knew what you might pick up. Even when in happier days on an outing with his old mother he had listened to conversations and now and again had by the sheerest chance picked up vital information that had led to the solving of crimes. Having trained himself to listen through his old mother's conversation, he was now able to listen through the inconsequential chatter of Miss Penn; but was forced to quieten her when at one moment he heard what he believed to be a word of English. He laid a hand on Miss Penn's wrist. 'One moment, Miss.'

'Eh?'

'A moment's silence. If you please.'

'Oh. Being the dick now, are we? Listening Tom. What's up, eh?'

Mr Todhunter sighed and explained. But it was too late now. She said, 'Forget it, mate, and how about another beer, eh?'

Sighing again, Mr Todhunter went to the bar. Perhaps the beer could go down to expenses; he was, after all, pursuing his duty and truth to tell it would not be the first time his chief super had passed expenses that included visits to places selling intoxicating liquors. He could report an attempt to glean information at any rate . . .

iv

Entry was made to Valparaiso, entry without incident. Admiral Watkiss and his steward walked in from the surrounding country, past hovels similar to those in Santiago, making towards the dock area where they could mingle with seafarers of all nationalities, rough men who would ask no questions lest questions be asked of themselves. Valparaiso was a wild and dangerous place, like many other ports around the world, and wild and dangerous men lurked in it as Admiral Watkiss knew – you had only, he thought with a sniff of disdain, to look at the men of the Chilean Navy. The city was filled with murderers, ship deserters, spies, confidence tricksters, dishonest pedlars of every description. But today, as it happened, the place seemed to be *en fête*. Crowds surged about, the women gaily dressed, laughing and chattering. Admiral Watkiss found himself borne along on a kind of tide, willy-nilly, Petty Officer Steward Washbrook keeping close astern.

'What's going on, Washbrook?'

'I couldn't rightly say, sir. Kind o' celebration, sir. Maybe it's to do with one o' them saints, sir.'

'Oh, yes, a saint's day, I suppose, you may be right. Get in front of me.'

'Sir?'

'I said, *get in front of me*. Not behind like a blasted nursemaid. Act as a ram and keep the way clear for me.'

'Aye, aye, sir.' Washbrook shifted to the front and they went on, pushing through the mob as best they could. After a while there was music, and a procession appeared ahead, a number of priests, Watkiss took them to be, wearing frilly white surplices and in some cases curious headgear – birettas, Admiral Watkiss thought they were called. Some of them carried effigies on poles, and there were a number of small boys, also wearing surplices, at the tail end of the procession. Flowers were being cast by the multitude and there was a strong smell of incense. As the two British seafarers pushed on, and the procession began to straggle and extend its length, Admiral Watkiss found himself part of it, moving along between a group of small boys and two elderly priests with what he considered evil expressions. One was wearing sandals, the other, incongruously, a very heavy pair of brown boots that could have come from military stores. Some of the cast flowers landed upon Admiral Watkiss.

'Washbrook!'

'Sir?'

'Move off to the left. At once.'

As Washbrook attempted to obey the order, more priests moved up and he was pushed aside.

'Oh, for God's sake, you blasted fool, go the *other* way, then!' This time the pressure of priests was from the right. There seemed to be no escape and Watkiss grew frantic. 'Balls and bang me arse, man, use your blasted initiative and get me out of this blasted skylark!'

'How, sir?'

'Oh, just stop! Let the buggers go past!'

Washbrook stopped and Watkiss cannoned into his back. The ploy succeeded: priests and small boys and effigies surged past on the wafts of incense and after a while Watkiss found himself back with the joyous throngs of lay spectators. For the sake of peace and quiet he detoured into a side street, a narrow way of evil-smelling dwellings with refuse piled against the walls. This side street, or alley, led by devious twists into a square where there were more crowds and some of the dishonest pedlars that had come earlier into Watkiss' mind, persons selling all manner of wares from cheap trinkets of jewellery to articles of sea apparel, probably filched from equally dishonest bosuns responsible for ships' gear. One of the pedlars, to Watkiss' astonishment, was calling out his wares in English.

'Very curious, Washbrook.'

Washbrook thought so too; then they realized that the pedlar's audience was composed of British seamen. 'From ships in the port, Washbrook! How very fortunate! We may get word of the *Taronga Park* – and in any event they may provide sanctuary afloat.'

They stopped, hopefully. Admiral Watkiss, surrounded by British persons, however common, felt much more at home. They listened; the pedlar was a seller of panaceas, cure-alls that might sell to seamen about to sail in ships without medical men aboard. A bottle was held aloft; it contained a greenish-yellow liquid, clear and bright in the sun, and the pedlar was extolling its virtues.

'Roll up, roll up, me lucky lads! This could be the day you'll never regret, the day you bought good 'ealth! Come along now, come and buy. Doctor Mallett what practises in Liverpool, 'as invented this 'ere potent potion, 1/3d the bottle in real money . . . cures coughs, colds, sore 'oles, and pimples on the dick!'

'Sounds 'andy, sir,' Washbrook said, much impressed. 'Might cure me pig rash, sir.'

'What nonsense, don't be a fool, Washbrook.'

'No, sir.'

'Some people are very gullible. I doubt if the stuff's much use, too wide in its application I fancy.'

Washbrook had an idea. 'If I was to buy a bottle, sir, I might engage the vendor in conversation like, sir.'

'What for?'

'Why, sir, to find things out like.'

Watkiss pursed his lips. 'Probe the situation? Yes, I suppose there are possibilities, Washbrook. But I shall not waste the money – 1/3d is expensive. We shall stay with the crowd and approach the man when he has sold his stock. He certainly may be of some use.'

v

Two hours was quite a long time and during it much beer could be drunk, and was. Victoria was persuasive and Mr Todhunter had felt his resolution slipping away. The situation was, to him, a unique one – to be sitting in a dockside bar surrounded by German sailors, in the close company of a woman. However the woman might be lacking in morals, she was a woman and she certainly wasn't Mr Todhunter's old mother, very far from it. His old mother had never . . . but no, he mustn't ever even think of comparing the two. Comparison was not possible, anyway.

The beer, specially brewed for the seaports, was strong and Mr Todhunter was unaccustomed to it. Victoria surveyed him with a glint of wickedness in her eye. Do him good to get blotto, she thought, de-fossilize the poor bloke, though he wouldn't appreciate it when he sobered up. Mr Todhunter talked quite a lot as the alcohol did its insidious work, all about his adventures in the Metropolitan Police Force and how he'd been commended once for pursuing a hansom cab on a bicycle and upon overtaking it by superhuman effort had arrested the occupant, later found guilty of procuring young women for immoral purposes. So loosened was his tongue that Mr Todhunter even admitted to having once acted as guinea-pig in the pursuance of his duty, allowing himself to be picked up by a young woman whose trade had been obvious. He described the sordid scene he had been led to in an upstairs room in Soho and how he had then pounced, forcing the young woman to release the name of her pimp.

'Before you'd taken advantage, eh? Or after?'

'I did not,' Mr Todhunter said with immense dignity, 'take advantage, Miss.'

'Bloody fool, eh?'

'Dear me, no! I would never – ' Mr Todhunter's voice trailed away; already he was beginning to lose his thread. He veered onto his old mother, becoming maudlin about the happy past. After some minutes of this Victoria became restless; and, since the German sailors, also filled with beer, had started to sing patriotic songs, she suggested she and Mr Todhunter might do likewise.

'Show the flag, mate, why bloody not?' She started on 'Waltzing Matilda', fairly bellowing it out, with Todhunter making an attempt to join in though he was unsure of all the words. She suggested 'God Save the Queen'. Todhunter agreed whole-heartedly: he knew those words very well indeed and it might do the Germans good to listen. The words came out strongly and the German song, 'Deutschland Uber Alles', currently being sung, came to an abrupt stop and one of the Germans approached Mr Todhunter's table, bent down, and hoisted him up by his neck, half strangling him so that his protest was lost in a terrified gurgle.

'Pig Englander,' the German said, more or less in English.

Mr Todhunter gurgled again, but was released when Miss Penn drew the hatpin from her hat and pushed it a little way into the German's thigh.

'Bullying bugger,' she said calmly. 'Attacking a little bloke like that, you ought to be bloody ashamed of yourself, mate.'

The German, furious, waved big hands like hams. He said, 'To sing of your Queen Victoria, it is insulting. Ze small pig, 'e intended ze insult to my Emperor.'

'No he bloody didn't, mate, it's just your bloody German mentality, that's all.'

The German immediately made another rush at Mr Todhunter, who was thrown violently against a wall, where on impact he slid to the floor in a heap. After that all the Germans went mad, the Chilean bartender was attacked, the bar itself smashed up, chairs and tables flying in all directions. But succour was at hand: the two hours were up and the boat from the *Taronga Park* had come alongside the ramshackle jetty. A fight was a fight, and the British seamen spat on their hands and joined in to add to the rumpus. German heads were banged together, hard; and Mr Todhunter was collected up and borne to the boat, with an undamaged Miss Penn bringing up the rear. The Germans had behaved as gentlemen towards her. But she was somewhat fearful of what St Vincent Halfhyde would say upon her return aboard with the sorry-looking detective inspector.

FOURTEEN

In Valparaiso the seamen, not all of whom were in fact British –
there were, Admiral Watkiss believed, some Huns among
them, persons in front of whom it would be unsafe to speak
freely – were very gullible. The pedlar's panacea went like hot
cakes and so did much of the other stock, including the cheap
jewellery, no doubt to be taken home to wives and sweethearts.
Admiral Watkiss conferred with his steward: an approach
would be made to the pedlar, about whose nationality there
was no doubt at all, once his customers had departed.

'Be very careful, Washbrook. Remember, my name's not to
be mentioned, nor is my rank of course.'

'No, sir. 'Oo shall I say you are, sir?'

'Oh, something anonymous. Use your head, Washbrook.'

'Yes, sir.' The steward pondered. 'With respect, sir, shall I
just say you're my mate like, sir, like I did to the young woman
in Santiago, sir?'

'Oh, very well,' Admiral Watkiss said huffily. They waited
while the throng thinned. Watkiss didn't like the idea of his
forthcoming role but knew it was better for Washbrook to do
the talking and bargaining, if there should be bargaining to be
done; Washbrook was of the same class as the pedlar and a
man-to-man approach could be adopted, with Watkiss himself
keeping in the background so far as possible. In the meantime
he kept a sharp lookout for anyone in Chilean uniform, but the
only police and soldiers that he saw seemed to be caught up in
the prevailing festive spirit, many of them being bedecked with
flowers and one policeman at any rate being more concerned
with a young woman who was dragging him by the arm

towards a doorway than with conscientious thoughts of arrest and the performance of duty . . . Admiral Watkiss became aware that Washbrook was being addressed by the pedlar.

'Anything you want to buy, sir? Last offers, all going cheap, clear me stock, sir.'

Washbrook looked flattered at being addressed as sir; Watkiss hoped it would not go to his head. But Washbrook surprised him by saying to the pedlar, 'No call for the sir, mate. Got a bottle o' that medicine left, 'ave you?'

'Sorry, all gone.' The pedlar was busily stuffing his unsold stock into a sack. When he started dismantling his rostrum, Washbrook offered his assistance and whilst so doing asked casually if the pedlar happened to have any news of the arrival of the *Taronga Park* in the port. The pedlar had not, but asked, 'You joining her, are you?'

'Yes. Me and me mate.' Washbrook had the wit to try another tack. 'Don't 'appen to know anywhere we can doss till the *Taronga Park* comes in, do you, eh?'

'Tried the Sally Army?'

'Full up,' Washbrook said.

'I might know somewhere,' the pedlar said off-handedly.

Washbrook understood. 'Hang on,' he said. 'I'll 'ave a word with Ad – with me mate.' He approached Watkiss, waiting in the rear. Speaking in a low voice Washbrook explained the position. Watkiss brought out his purse and handed over yet another gold *peso* coin. This coin was transferred to the pedlar's palm. The pedlar said, 'There's an old bloke, used to be in the British Navy. Got a room what 'e lets out. Just you follow me.'

ii

While Victoria and Todhunter had been ashore in Puerto Montt, Halfhyde had had a visitor: Canon Rampling. 'If I might have a word, Captain? Very privately.'

'By all means, Canon.'

'Thank you so much.' Rampling lowered his bulk into a chair. 'I'll come straight to the point – you're a busy man, I know.' He gave a cough. 'It's Mrs Weder-Ublick.' Another cough; he had begun to sweat freely, more than the

144

temperature seemed to warrant. 'A personal matter, Captain Halfhyde. Personal, very. Mrs Weder-Ublick is a very forceful lady.'

'Like her brother.'

'Yes, indeed, very like. As you know, she intends taking up missionary work among the South American Indians.'

'Yes.'

'And I have my cousin to consider.'

'I'm afraid I don't see the connection, Canon,' Halfhyde said, concealing the glint of amusement in his eyes. 'Perhaps you'll explain?'

'Yes.' Suddenly Rampling lowered his head into his hands and began to shake all over. 'I am being subjected to pressure, Captain Halfhyde. I am being forced against my will.'

'Into marriage, Canon? Is that it?'

Rampling looked up. 'You've guessed?' He seemed surprised.

'It has not been hard,' Halfhyde said.

'I never realized . . . yes, I fear marriage looms. Not as an immediate prospect, but as an eventual one which I would not be able to avoid.'

'And the pressure, the forcing, Canon?'

'Mrs Weder-Ublick has talked a great deal about my duty as a churchman. I may, she says, be retired, but cannot ever evade God's service and His call. With that I cannot, of course, disagree.'

'Nor with Mrs Weder-Ublick?'

Rampling, sounding almost savage, said, 'She will not brook disagreement, Captain Halfhyde! She insists that God has called me – '

'And has He?'

'No, not directly. If the call exists, it has not reached me in person, only through the medium of Mrs Weder-Ublick – '

'And your cousin? Have you spoken to Mrs Weder-Oblick of him, and his needs?'

'Oh, yes, indeed I have, but Mrs Weder-Ublick insists that the greater call is to the South American Indians. She insists that my cousin is but one old man, while there are many South American Indians.'

'True, of course.'

'I know,' Canon Rampling said sadly. 'Perhaps I am being selfish. But the fact is I have no feelings towards the South American Indians. I have tried to care but I have failed. And now I fear I am being put out of favour with the Almighty. By resisting the call, you see.'

'But you said it hadn't reached you, Canon.'

'Mrs Weder-Ublick insists that it has, through her.'

'A very tenuous connection, Canon. I think you should await something more positive, before blaming yourself in any way.'

Canon Rampling's bull-like head nodded. 'That is what I would wish to do, certainly. But Mrs Weder-Ublick . . .' His voice tailed off for a moment, then he looked up at Halfhyde and said, 'Since I have no living, Captain, I have no bishop. In a sense, I come to you as my bishop.'

'A poor substitute,' Halfhyde murmured. 'I fear the House of Lords will never see me as one of their spiritual peers, Canon.'

'Then I come to you as a man of the world,' Rampling said. 'I come to you for a man of the world's advice. And perhaps help also.'

'In what way?'

For an instant Canon Rampling bared his teeth. He said, 'I cannot abide that woman, Captain Halfhyde. I simply cannot! At the same time, neither can I accept the thought, the possible thought, of failing deliberately to hear God's call in aid of the South American Indians. I need, shall we say, help from an unecclesiastical source – '

'Someone *not* a bishop?'

'I believe so, yes. My mind is so confused on the point, thanks to constant proddings from Mrs Weder-Ublick – '

'You are asking for a stratagem, perhaps, to drive a wedge between you and Mrs Weder-Ublick – is that it?'

'Bluntly put, Captain. But – yes. Oh, yes! And to that end I have a suggestion to make, and it is this. If Mrs Weder-Ublick and I leave the ship together in Valparaiso, then I fear it will be too late. I shall never rid myself of the woman. She intends travelling with me . . . her route to her mission and mine to my cousin are broadly one and the same, unfortunately.' Rampling

146

leaned forward in an attitude of beseechment. 'If you were able by some stratagem, as you said, to keep Mrs Weder-Ublick aboard ship until I have left, I may yet find salvation.'

'Will she let you leave without her?' Halfhyde asked.

'I shall merely go. Willy-nilly, Captain Halfhyde! I have the strength for that, I believe. What do you say?'

Halfhyde paced his cabin for a while, deep in thought. Something was already emerging and after his cogitation he faced Canon Rampling and said, 'I doubt if I can keep the lady aboard, Canon. But let us approach the matter from the opposite direction, shall we? Suppose I were to arrange for Mrs Weder-Ublick to leave the ship before you do? Would that suffice?'

'Yes, but how – '

'You're aware that Admiral Watkiss is her brother. Use can be made of Admiral Watkiss, I fancy. Leave it to me, Canon, and put your mind at rest. Before our arrival at Valparaiso, I shall have words of my own with Mrs Weder-Ublick.'

iii

Mr Todhunter had been assisted out of the lifeboat and up the accommodation-ladder. Victoria followed, aware of Halfhyde looking down from the deck outside his cabin. By mischance Mr Mayhew was at the head of the ladder.

'Wotcha, mate,' Victoria said. Ahead of her, Mr Todhunter sprawled on the deck, having caught his foot on a ringbolt. Two seamen lifted him up.

'Pardon me,' he said, and belched. The beer fumes were strong and Mr Mayhew stepped back a pace. He was looking very angry. 'I . . . wash overcome. By Germansh.'

'*Germans?*'

'Un . . . unruly men, sir.'

Mr Mayhew sniffed the air. 'Not only Germans overcame you, I fancy. This is disgraceful, Todhunter! I suggest you go below, and remain there until you are better. Perhaps Miss Penn would attend to your injuries.'

'Too right, I will,' Victoria said. 'And don't blame the little bloke. I reckon it was me own bloody fault as usual. Can't be bloody trusted, I can't.' She sounded quite cheerful about it. As Mr Todhunter was assisted along the deck and down the ladder to his bunk, she followed behind, detouring towards the saloon to find the steward who would have charge of the ship's medical bag containing bandages and ointments. Mr Todhunter, now feeling dreadfully ill and confused, lay down upon his bunk. He groaned. Later, as the beer drained away into hangover and remembrance, he knew he had let his chief super down badly and if his misdemeanour should be reported back to the Yard he would be a finished copper. Women and drink, the twin downfalls that beset man in his wicked frailty.

iv

The pedlar, as good as his word or the feel of the gold *peso* in his pocket, had led them to a narrow building in the usual dog-infested, smelly alley for which Valparaiso was notorious in its sleazier quarters, those used by the seamen off the many ships in the port, ships both sail and steam and of many nationalities. Admiral Watkiss, shaking off the attentions of the scavenging dogs, was taken through a doorway into a long passage and thence into a dark room at the end, a room the single window of which was more than half obscured from the outside by a proliferating plant, green and thick-stemmed. As his eye penetrated the gloom he became aware of a figure seated in a vast arm-chair set in a corner of the room. From behind Admiral Watkiss the pedlar called a greeting, which was answered in a quavery voice. 'What be this, then?'

'Two sailors waiting for a boat,' the pedlar said. 'Want a doss down, they do.'

'Who be they?' the quavery voice answered. By this time Admiral Watkiss was better able to see the speaker; the pedlar had referred to him as old, and old he most certainly was. Well past ninety years of age, Watkiss guessed. The face was wizened to the point of a resemblance to parchment, at least where it was visible: the old man wore a long white beard, tobacco-stained in parts. When he lifted a hand it was like that of a skeleton. He repeated his question. 'Who be ee?'

Admiral Watkiss felt it incumbent upon him to answer since

148

the old man's eye was upon him, and Washbrook was remaining silent. 'A seaman,' he said. 'My name is Smith.'

There was a silence, then the old man said, 'You be no seaman, zur.'

'I beg your – '

'You be a gentleman, zur. There be no mistaking the voice of a *gentleman*, zur.'

'Oh, very well, then I'm a gentleman seaman. Are you able to let me and my – my friend have accommodation, or are you not?'

'There you be, zur,' the voice said triumphantly. 'You say accommodation, not doss. And there's no call, zur, none at all, to be hoity-toity. Not even though you be a gentleman, zur. I'm proud to welcome a gentleman to my abode, zur, you may be sure.'

'Well, thank you.' Admiral Watkiss wished the old fool would stop going on about his being a gentleman; it might give the pedlar ideas, and pedlars were never honest men. 'I'm told you were once in the Navy. The *British* Navy.'

'Aye, zur, that be perfectly true. Bosun I were, zur. As ee should know well, zur.' There was a senile-sounding cackle of amusement. 'Don't ee recognize me, zur?'

'No, I do not!' Admiral Watkiss snapped. 'Really, I'm – '

'Upon the Yangtse River, zur, we met last. When ee commanded a river gunboat flotilla, zur, in that there China. I showed ee the Street of the Prostitutes, zur, when we passed through Chungking. All flooded, it were. I had a young lady in them happy days, zur, name o' . . . why, dang me, zur, if I haven't gone and forgot the young lady's name. Chinee, she were . . .'

Remembrance had come back to Watkiss in a flash of fear. He made an attempt to bring the old man's talk to a stop, but there was no stopping him. His name, he said, was Mr Bodmin. He insisted on the 'Mister' because as a warrant officer he was entitled to it. He had first known Captain Watkiss when he had been young Mr Midshipman Watkiss. 'As snotty-nosed a young bugger as ever I did see, zur, begging your pardon o' course, zur. I was a leading seaman, then, and I learned ee a thing or two.'

149

'I – '

'*Captain* Watkiss you be on the Yangtse. And now you be the Commander-in-Chief o' the Chilean – '

'Washbrook!'

'Yes, sir?'

'*Seize that blasted pedlar!*' Admiral Watkiss, now very much at risk of being reported to the Chilean police, turned as he spoke. But already it was too late. Through the poor visibility of the long passage Admiral Watkiss saw his steward making an attempt to obey orders and then fall to the floor with a sharp cry of pain. The pedlar was seen emerging from the end of the passage into the alleyway, a flurry of arms and fast-moving legs. Admiral Watkiss bounced up and down in fury. 'Oh, you blasted fool, Washbrook! Now I'm damn well done for, d'you hear? Done for and it's all your blasted fault!'

As the steward pulled himself together and rose, the quaver came again from the rear. 'Ee be safe enough here, zur. I be a loyal subject of Her Majesty. O' course, I did hear ee was being searched for, zur. Never did I expect ee'd turn up here, zur, seeking asylum, zur.'

'It was quite fortuitous – '

'And who be the other gentleman, zur?'

'Not a gentleman, Mr Bodmin, my steward. Petty Officer Steward Washbrook, and damn useless – '

There was another cackle, a scornful one. 'Petty Officer Steward, did ee say, zur?'

'Yes – '

'Well, now, I never 'eard the like of that, zur, never in all my born days. Ee know what we used to call 'em, zur?'

'Yes, I do, po bosuns. But never mind that. The question is, what do we do now?'

'Stay here, zur, where ee be safe.'

'I don't know so much about that. That blasted man, that pedlar, he'll go for the police you may be sure!'

'I'll not let the buggers enter, zur. I be strong still.' The withered arm and skeletonic hand were lifted in what appeared to be an attempt to flex a long departed muscle.

'You may find your strength is not quite up to it, Mr

Bodmin.' A nasty thought occurred to Watkiss. 'Tell me – has a reward been offered?'

'For ee, zur? Yes, it has, zur. Ten thousand *pesos*, zur, if ee be taken alive.'

'Alive only?'

'Yes, zur. They don't want ee *dead*, zur.' Mr Bodmin sounded surprised.

'Well, I suppose that's something to be thankful for at all events. Washbrook?'

'Yes, sir.'

'We must leave at once, Washbrook, immediately. We must hide again. If only that blasted Halfhyde would make haste!' Admiral Watkiss turned to the old bosun. 'Thank you for your offer, Mr Bodmin. It's appreciated but it's not good enough.' He paused. 'Of course, you'll not give me away to the damned dagoes.'

'No, zur, I be loyal like I said, zur. God Save the Queen, zur.'

'Yes, God Save the Queen,' Watkiss said in a pre-occupied tone, and turned to push Petty Officer Steward Washbrook along the passage. As they went Washbrook said something about the Chilcans being likely to arrest Mr Bodmin on a charge of assisting the escape of a criminal.

'I am not a criminal, Washbrook, and Mr Bodmin is loyal, as he said. He'll not mind. Men of his calibre, Washbrook, are prepared to suffer for their country.'

Unremarked save by dogs and dagoes, they hurried from the vicinity. Admiral Watkiss intended trying the Salvation Army, whose Valparaiso citadel might or might not be full up. Even if it was, they could scarcely refuse refuge to a fugitive. After all, they called themselves a church. If Washbrook hadn't been such a blasted fool, they would have gone there straight away. Then they would have been perfectly safe, their anonymity preserved in the equivalent of the confessional's integrity. They put on speed towards the dock area, down by the familiarity of ships and the sea, the great, wide ocean that connected them with Great Britain and Her Majesty's authority, away from smelly dagoes. But luck, having so far smiled upon them, now decided to frown.

The dishonest pedlar had wasted no time. He had in fact been lucky in coming upon a military patrol not far away in the direction opposite that taken by Admiral Watkiss and his steward. The pursuit came from the rear. It was accompanied by the pedlar himself, anxious about his ten thousand *pesos*. The point of a bayonet was thrust into Admiral Watkiss from behind, and he turned in a panic.

'You are the Admiral Watkiss?'

'No, I'm blasted well not! I'm a – a seaman.'

'The Admiral Watkiss is a seaman also?'

'Oh, yes. But I am not he.' Watkiss thought desperately and came up with the first name that occurred to him. 'My name is Washbrook,' he said, and at once realized his terrible error. Petty Officer Steward Washbrook would also be upon the wanted list.

FIFTEEN

The *Taronga Park* was to take her bunkers early the next morning and on completion would sail at once for Valparaiso. After his talk with Canon Rampling, and after Mr Todhunter and Victoria had returned aboard, Halfhyde was approached by Mrs Weder-Ublick with a complaint about the policeman.

'Inebriated, Captain Halfhyde. A deplorable sight. The wretched man came out from his cabin and was sick upon the deck outside my own cabin.'

'I'm very sorry, Mrs Weder-Ublick.'

'Well, I don't think that's good enough and that's fact, I said it.' Mrs Weder-Ublick, in moments of stress, tended to forget her earlier resolution not to make further use of her brother's phrase. 'I *insist* that he be put ashore here in this place. To voyage on with – '

'I'm sorry, Mrs Weder-Ublick. That's quite impossible, I assure you – '

'But I said I insist – '

'Mr Todhunter is a policeman in pursuit of his duty, Mrs Weder-Ublick, and you are in no position to insist. And as for me, my hands are tied in the matter. Mr Todhunter must voyage on to Valparaiso and that, I'm afraid, is the end of the matter.'

'Not quite, Captain Halfhyde.' Mrs Weder-Ublick's face had reddened in the true Watkiss manner and if she had had a telescope, Halfhyde knew she would have flourished it. 'Not quite the end. If Mr Todhunter is to travel on to Valparaiso, then I shall *not*. I shall leave the ship here in this place and go overland to Valparaiso. And I shall naturally expect the balance of my passage money to be repaid to me before I leave.'

Matters were going the way of Canon Rampling, it seemed: the cleric would be much relieved – he would surely be able in the circumstances to resist Mrs Weder-Ublick's blandishments if she left quickly and on the wave of her temper. That, in any case, would be up to him. Nevertheless, Halfhyde felt obliged to point out to a lady that the land route to Valparaiso had its discomforts. The coach, he said, would be primitive, and the horses, changed at intervals, moved but slowly and the wayside hostelries would be primitive too.

'No worse than that inebriated man.' Mrs Weder-Ublick was not going to speak of the Funchal incident but Halfhyde knew it was much in her mind. 'Besides, I think you under-estimate me, Captain Halfhyde. You know very well that I am offering myself to the South American Indians. I am ready for discomfort and even perhaps danger.' She played her trump card. 'I shall also expect Canon Rampling to leave the ship with me. He will be protection enough.'

'Ah. Suppose the canon doesn't wish to leave the ship here?'

'He *will* wish,' Mrs Weder-Ublick stated. 'But even if he did not, then I should go alone. I am no silly young woman, Captain Halfhyde.'

When Mrs Weder-Ublick, her mind made up, left his cabin, Halfhyde sent his steward down with a message scrawled on a piece of paper for Canon Rampling. The canon would be well advised to invent an illness, such as would prevent any possibility of his leaving the ship at Puerto Montt. It would then be unnecessary for Halfhyde to make use of his original stratagem involving Admiral Watkiss, a stratagem that he had not yet put in full to Canon Rampling.

ii

Admiral Watkiss, with Petty Officer Steward Washbrook, was marched ahead of the rifles and bayonets, through the hot, dirty streets of Valparaiso towards the local headquarters of Colonel Opago's police. There he was interrogated like any common criminal, by a person of low rank.

'You are by name Washbrook.'

'No, no, there's been a mistake – '

'You gave your name as Washbrook.'

'Did I?'

'Yes.'

'That was where the mistake lay, don't you see!'

The interrogating eyes were hard, though Watkiss fancied he caught a glimmer of humour, cruel humour. 'You are mistaken about your own name, Washbrook?'

'I think I must have been, yes.' Admiral Watkiss believed he might after all get away with it, all Chileans were very stupid and he thought he might baffle them. Certainly he believed he had not been actually recognized; he was very dusty, covered in a layer of dried mud and he still wore his sack and the canvas trousers – it would be hard to recognize an admiral undoubtedly, and the stupidity helped. The Chileans could have pounced on the wrong man. 'I dare say I was getting muddled, don't you know. The sun.'

'Ah, the sun. Yes. It is so strong for the weak English. But in spite of the sun we believe you to be who you said you were – Washbrook. And the other person, whom you are shielding, is the Admiral Watkiss, lately Commander-in-Chief of the Navy and wanted in Santiago.'

iii

They had deliberately misunderstood, of course – Admiral Watkiss knew that; it explained the odd look in the eye of the interrogator. It was just like blasted foreigners! When Admiral Watkiss reached Santiago he would have their balls for breakfast, or see to it that their superiors did. In the meantime he was in dire straits, confined in a cell, one of a line of similar cells divided by bars like cages and with a warder making frequent checks on the prisoners, of which there were very many. Watkiss shared his cell with six other men, two of whom lay huddled on the floor surrounded by vomit. The other four looked at him silently from recumbent positions. A large chamber pot stood in the centre of the cell. After a while one of his companions spoke to him in Spanish but Watkiss didn't understand a word of the patois of common persons and maintained a frigid silence until the man, leaping to his feet and

155

seeming to go into some kind of frenzy, seized him by the throat and shook him. When Admiral Watkiss managed to gasp out that he was British, the man let go and spat upon him. This action was applauded by the inmates of the adjoining cell, female persons who had the aspect of prostitutes of the very lowest sort and who seemed to have command of foul words in English, no doubt picked up from seafarers who had made use of their services. These words were addressed to Admiral Watkiss, who turned his back. When he did that they yelled further obscenities, confirming Watkiss in his opinion of foreigners.

After some hours, during which Admiral Watkiss' demands that the British Consul be sent for were totally ignored, communal food was brought in a large earthenware dish. It was soup, in which vague things floated, vegetables and pieces of very doubtful meat. With his health in mind, and not wishing to share the spoon in any case, Admiral Watkiss ate nothing. There was also water in a jug, but it smelled most unpleasant and this he rejected also. When one of the drunken persons recovered a little and lurched to his feet he stumbled against Admiral Watkiss, who staggered back against the bars on the prostitutes' side. Lewd laughter assailed him. He thrust himself away in horror. When, exhausted and repulsed, he dropped down upon the floor, a large thing like a slug crept onto his arm. Or it might have been a leech.

It was all the more galling because it could be assumed that the blasted Chileans' perverted sense of humour had projected them into treating Washbrook as though he were Admiral Watkiss; he would be living in comparative luxury as befitted any admiral, even a disgraced and arrested one. Even the dagoes treated gentlemen, or those they pretended were gentlemen, in a different way from common people. One thought kept Watkiss going: this would not last – it couldn't, obviously; when the British Minister learned of his treatment, then the blasted dagoes would laugh on the other side of their faces. So would Petty Officer Steward Washbrook.

iv

That night, Canon Rampling conveniently and mendaciously went down with a sickness. Malaria, he announced it to be, a recurrent malady first caught during his chaplaincy with the British Fleet. It was a handy sickness, for all the supposed patient had to do was to induce much sweat, not difficult below decks in the *Taronga Park*, and shiver, and from time to time clack his teeth together. Canon Rampling put on an impressive performance; and all seemed well at first. Fate, however, stepped in. Mrs Weder-Ublick came again to Halfhyde's cabin.

'Canon Rampling is most unwell, Captain Halfhyde, and won't be able to leave with me tomorrow.'

Halfhyde nodded. 'It would be unwise, certainly. It's very unfortunate . . . but I understood you to say you'd leave notwithstanding?'

'Yes, I did. But I've changed my mind. One must have charity, and not only towards the South American Indians. Canon Rampling has been a most attentive companion throughout the voyage from London, Captain Halfhyde, and we have become good friends. I don't feel I can leave him now.'

'Oh, he'll be well cared for, Mrs Weder-Ublick, you – '

'Oh, yes! Well cared for, by a book called, I understand, *The Ship Captain's Medical Guide*, and a steward whose clothing and habits are not as clean as they might be. Frankly, I don't find that good enough, and I intend to remain on board your ship and leave with the canon at Valparaiso.'

'And Mr Todhunter?'

'I suppose he'll have to be endured, Captain Halfhyde.'

'He will indeed.' Halfhyde paced his cabin; he held no particular brief for Rampling's future happiness and peace of mind, but he would wish Mrs Weder-Ublick onto no-one at all. Canon Rampling would be a broken man within a month. And Puerto Montt was as good a place as any to break a romance in two. Mrs Weder-Ublick had already said she was prepared for the nightmare of the coach to Valparaiso. Very well: she would be urged upon her way. The presence of the Peeping Tom of Funchal, the drunken Detective Inspector Todhunter, was not threat enough, it seemed, to relieve the ship of Mrs Weder-

Ublick; but a greater threat could lurk. Hatred was a potent emotion; and now Halfhyde employed his stratagem. Mrs Weder-Ublick would in any case be sure to dig out the facts soon enough.

He said, 'I believe the time has come to be frank with you, Mrs Weder-Ublick.'

'Really. In what way?'

'I have to speak again of your brother. He – '

The face was truculent. 'What, pray, has my brother to do with you, Captain Halfhyde?'

'A very great deal, unfortunately. You are, I imagine, unaware that he is now Admiral Watkiss. Admiral Watkiss of the Chilean Navy.'

Mrs Weder-Ublick started. '*What* did you say, Captain Halfhyde?'

Halfhyde repeated what he had said. Mrs Weder-Ublick stared uncomprehendingly, seeming flabbergasted that the tiresome brother could have achieved flag rank in anybody's navy. 'I do *not* believe it,' she stated flatly. 'I simply do not. My brother *always* held such strong views about foreigners. The fact that I myself was married to a German . . . my brother was quite appallingly rude. No, it quite fails to check, Captain Halfhyde, and I think you must be mistaken, that it is some other Admiral Watkiss. For years now I have thought it likely my brother was dead. I believe I have told you that.'

'He is far from that, Mrs Weder-Ublick, I assure you absolutely. And he is expected to board my ship in Valparaiso.'

'Board your ship? Are you quite serious?'

'Entirely so, Mrs Weder-Ublick. He will be waiting in Valparaiso, which we shall reach in a little under three days' time. So, you see, you and your brother will be reunited – '

'Never!' Mrs Weder-Ublick's face had gone a deep purple, a dangerous colour, and she had begun to shake throughout her body. Halfhyde feared apoplexy. 'My brother is a *vile* man, Captain Halfhyde, who brought a great deal of sorrow to me and my late husband. I cannot tell you how much I suffered even as a child, a despised girl. I cannot tell you of his cruelties . . .' For a while she sat in silence, an inward look of hate in her eyes as she recalled the hideous past; then she went back on her last statement and began, in a torrent of words, to tell Halfhyde of her brother's cruelties. The story of the innocent spiders came out along with much else. The story of the cut hammock emerged, together with its aftermath that had set the final seal on a brother and sister's mutual hatred.

Halfhyde, when he was able to get a word in, uttered the hope that the reunion would prove hatred to be in the past.

'No, no,' Mrs Weder-Ublick said. 'I could not stand a meeting with my brother. It would be quite impossible, Captain Halfhyde, quite impossible.'

'Then – '

'It is fortunate that I had already made up my mind to leave the ship here in this place. That is what I shall do.'

'And Canon Rampling?'

'I shall arrange to see him again in Valparaiso. But not aboard the ship.'

It should not be difficult, Halfhyde thought, for Rampling to leave for his cousin's side immediately after arrival.

v

While Halfhyde had been engaged with Mrs Weder-Ublick a boat had come off shore, a small steamboat belching thick black smoke across Reloncavi Bay, and had approached the *Taronga Park*'s accommodation ladder. A grimy person in a colourful uniform – that, as it transpired, of the posts and telegraphs – had come aboard and enquired for Mr Mayhew. A cable from Santiago was produced, handed over and signed for. Mr Mayhew went to his cabin and tore open the envelope. The message was in the Foreign Office cypher, to which Mr Mayhew had the key. Laboriously he broke down the cypher into plain language and then, giving a gasp of near despair, approached the bunkside of his cabin companion. 'Todhunter!'

The reply was indistinct. Mr Mayhew shook the inert body, swearing viciously. 'For God's sake, man, wake up and listen! I have news of the greatest urgency and importance.'

Todhunter opened an eye and groaned. 'Wh-what is it, Mr Mayhew, sir?'

Mayhew almost bawled the message in Todhunter's ear. Just outside the cabin air blew down from a ventilator the bell mouth of which stood upon the upper deck near the davits of the lifeboat. Happening to pass by, Victoria heard Mayhew's urgent voice, loud and clear, and she made at once for Halfhyde's cabin. Reaching it before Mrs Weder-Ublick had departed, she was unable to contain her news.

'The old bloke,' she said. 'He's been bloody arrested, mate! That Admiral Watkiss, they've shoved him in a cell in bloody Valparaiso. I reckon he c'd bloody swing!'

vi

Admiral Watkiss had been right: his ordeal came to an end the next day, after a night of utter torment during which many more fleas had bitten him together with lice, and his face and torso had been scratched to ribbons where the fiendish creatures had dug in. From time to time the nearby prostitutes had woken to scream abuse at the night guard, who had screamed back at them. Breakfast, like the previous earthenware-potted meal, had been forsworn and Watkiss was very hungry and thirsty. Much humiliated by his shabby treatment, he was almost in a state of frenzy when, after the breakfast pot had been removed, he was sent for to be addressed by a uniformed and tasselled person in the police office.

'We offer much apology, señor. We admit a grave mistake. We now know that you are the Admiral Watkiss.'

'You do, do you?' Admiral Watkiss simmered down but was non-committal; it still might be a ruse, they still might not know his identity for certain and he must play his cards with care even though the Chileans now seemed prepared to grovel. What with everything he was feeling a confusion in his own mind now. 'I can't say I agree with you, but still. I'm certainly not Washbrook, as I think I told you yesterday. I admitted a mistake in my identity, quite clearly.'

'Yes, yes, we understood fully – '

'What is to happen to me? I have a right to know.' Admiral Watkiss scratched. 'And I say again, I demand the presence of the British Consul.'

The tasselled man said, 'The British Consul is not concerned with Chilean subjects, señor.'

'Oh, nonsense, I'm not – ' Admiral Watkiss bit off a possible indiscretion: better not to say too much. He must wait, and see more precisely how the land lay. He went on, 'In any case, kindly tell me what is to happen next in this ridiculous charade.'

'This I am about to do, señor. You are to be taken to Santiago by the train later, to be interviewed by the Minister of Marine.'

'I see. And in the meantime? Am I to be returned to that stinking cell?'

The man shook his head. 'No, no – we have admitted a sad mistake, señor. You will be placed where you will have comfort and privacy.'

'So I should damn well think!' Watkiss said indignantly. 'And the other man, Washbrook?'

'He will be removed from comfort and go to the cell.'

'Good,' Admiral Watkiss said vengefully.

vii

With her bunkers aboard, the *Taronga Park* steamed out from Reloncavi Bay and Halfhyde set his course northerly, up the coast of Chile for Valparaiso. With the ship went, after all, Mrs Weder-Ublick, who, to the dismay of Canon Rampling who would now need to malinger for at least three more days, had had a change of heart. Victoria Penn had put her foot right in it with her announcement of the arrest of Admiral Watkiss: Mrs Weder-Ublick had seemed, curiously, stunned by the news. She had gone down the ladder to the upper deck and could be seen walking up and down, muttering to herself. Then Mr Mayhew had come on deck intending to make his report to Halfhyde, but had been seized upon, and there had been a lengthy conversation between them, during the course of which Mrs Weder-Ublick had shed tears. The ubiquitous Miss Penn, ears a-flap, had reported to Halfhyde that Mayhew had thought it unlikely that the brother would swing, but there was no doubt about it he was in the most serious trouble and one never knew with South Americans: yes, the death penalty was

not unknown for treason and espionage, certainly not unknown, but in Mayhew's view the British Government would
step in and exert its influence to have the sentence, if sentence
there was to be, commuted to life imprisonment. The great
difficulty was, the Foreign Office man said, that the British
Government might not have much influence left in a situation
where the Germans were doing their best to oust British trading
interests and to bring about the banning of British ships in
Chilean ports, a process said to be welcome to the Chilean
Government. And yes, Admiral Watkiss was, it had to be
admitted, on a sticky wicket. It was likely that his sister might
be a welcome visitor, all wounds healed in the face of adversity.
And, perhaps, death by shooting rather than swinging, Mr
Mayhew surmised.

Mrs Weder-Ublick had gone again to Halfhyde's cabin. Her
brother was the last of the Watkisses. He was, when all was said
and done, her last kith and kin. Blood, she said, was thicker
than water. To forgive was divine. Duty must be done to a
mother who had gone before, and had been devoted to the little
Watkiss, however naughty and unpleasant he had been. Mrs
Weder-Ublick would do her duty as she had always done it,
and the South American Indians would have to wait a little
longer. She would sail on with the *Taronga Park*, and during the
voyage to the north she would seek assurance and prayer from
Canon Rampling who was such a comfort. She would bring
together in her person the joint comforts and supplications of
both the Lutheran Church and the Church of England, Canon
Rampling being the mediator. And she understood that
malaria was in no way catching.

SIXTEEN

'Oh, very well, dear lady, let us pray again.'

Canon Rampling sighed, then intoned – again – the words of a special prayer for Admiral Watkiss, beseeching the Almighty to look with compassion upon an admittedly tiresome man who had done much that was wrong in the past and had been overbearing and rude. Mrs Weder-Ublick had insisted on the truth being offered to God; to attempt to whitewash her brother would be an insult and in any case unavailing, as Canon Rampling had agreed. Aloft, all was known and no wool could ever be pulled. They had now to rely on mercy alone, and hope that even now in his extremity Admiral Watkiss was not piling up further sins of arrogance and pettishness.

Mr Mayhew had told Mrs Weder-Ublick all the facts of the *Taronga Park*'s mission and she was, of course, now aware that her brother faced those charges of espionage and of disloyalty to the Chilean State. Thus Canon Rampling, kneeling with Mrs Weder-Ublick by her bunk, besought God's mercy on a man who did not know where his loyalties lay, a man pulled two ways at once.

'A mind split, O Lord, knowing not whither it should go.'

'Rubbish,' Mrs Weder-Ublick said.

Rampling was startled. 'I beg your pardon, dear lady?'

'I said rubbish. My brother is certainly not pulled two ways at once and his mind is not split. He is British through and through and his loyalties will be to Her Majesty. That is why the British government must be made to act.'

'Yes, yes.' Canon Rampling paused, then twitched a little, feeling cramp in his right calf. 'Shall we continue with our prayers, dear lady?'

'Yes. And I shall go myself to Santiago for words with the British Minister or ambassador or whatever he is.'

Canon Rampling gave another sigh. The Almighty asked for total trust and would not be prepared to play second fiddle to the British Minister in Santiago. On the other hand, it was said that the Almighty helped those who helped themselves so perhaps Mrs Weder-Ublick was right after all, who could tell? As for himself, he had done his best. But Mrs Weder-Ublick did not seem to be concentrating wholly upon prayer and when he came to a convenient breaking-off point Canon Rampling invoked his malaria and said he must rest.

ii

The train journey to Santiago was hot and not very comfortable, though Admiral Watkiss had been accorded a first class carriage while Petty Officer Steward Washbrook travelled, as was right and proper, in something akin to a cattle truck, bare and rattling. Both of them were naturally under strong guard: a naval escort rather than a police one. Each was surrounded by four seamen, armed with rifles and bayonets, Admiral Watkiss' escort commanded by a lieutenant, Washbrook's by a petty officer. Admiral Watkiss sat slumped in a corner of the carriage refusing to speak. He was well aware that his escorting officer would be under orders to take note of anything he might say, so he didn't say it.

Petty Officer Steward Washbrook was more forthcoming, seeing it to be in his interest to co-operate with the Chileans and not being much subject to thoughts of loyalty. The old bugger had asked for it and now he'd got it. The trouble was, he'd gone and brought him, Washbrook, down with him.

He answered all questions readily.

'He has said disloyal things, the Admiral Watkiss?'

'Never said a loyal one 'e 'asn't. Not about you lot. Dagoes 'e calls you.'

'Yes. Not a good master?'

'No. Mean as sin. When we was up country once, I 'ad to use 'is bath water after 'im.' Petty Officer Steward Washbrook glanced aside to see how his escort took that one, but saw that it

164

didn't register, perhaps because even second-use bath water would probably be considered a luxury in Chilean circles. He tried to think up something more telling but before he had got there the petty officer of the escort had moved on to other sayings of the Admiral Watkiss. Had the Admiral Watkiss, he asked, given any evidence of having transmitted information to the British?

'Eh?'

'Has the Admiral Watkiss acted as a spy?'

'Oh. Yes, I reckon 'e 'as. I over'eard 'im talking to a bloke from the Residency.'

'About what?'

'Germans.'

'Ah. Germans. Yes?'

Washbrook lifted a hand to scratch his neck where a flea had bitten. But he withdrew the hand when his action was misconstrued and a rifle was held closer to his chest. He said, 'I dunno as I caught much like. Except Watkiss called 'em 'Uns and square'eads. There was something about trade . . . I dunno.'

'Trade, yes?'

'Yes, I just said.'

'Please to go on?'

'I dunno. Over me 'ead it was, see. But 'e went on a lot about blasted 'Uns having the cheek to try to interfere with 'Er Majesty's rights, and blasted Chileans conniving like, 'oo did they think they were 'e said.'

iii

Aboard the *Taronga Park* now not far off Valparaiso, Halfhyde called a council of war in his cabin.

'Not war, Captain,' Mr Mayhew said, drawing in his sallow cheeks.

'A figure of speech only, Mr Mayhew.'

'I'm glad to hear that. War is certainly not desired by Her Majesty's Government. My mission – '

'We all know your mission, Mr Mayhew. Diplomatic means – but also if necessary the cutting-out of Admiral Watkiss for arrest by Todhunter. But suppose we find Admiral Watkiss so deeply in the mire that he cannot be cut out by peaceful means – by persuasion of the Chilean authorities, which I understand is what your mission is directed towards?'

'Yes, that is so.'

'It may become necessary to bring him out by force. Since we have no force, we may have to await warships from England – '

'I have already said, Captain, that war is not to be considered. Warships mean war. There will be no warships. We stand or fall by persuasion and that is final.'

'You mean Admiral Watkiss may have to be sacrificed?'

'No. No, I do not mean that. There will be no question of sacrifice, I assure you.'

'But Watkiss will be left in Chilean hands, rather than risk a show of force?'

'That,' Mr Mayhew said stiffly, 'is a crude way of putting it, Captain Halfhyde, very crude.'

'Admiral Watkiss is likely to find it cruder I fancy.'

'He is on, shall we say, the sticky end by his own fault.'

'Because of his loyalty to the Crown, Mr Mayhew. Admiral Watkiss and I have been shipmates in the past. I admit we've had many disagreements. I admit Admiral Watkiss is a difficult man, not to say impossible. I admit his arrogance. But I am as British as he, Mr Mayhew, and I do not propose to leave him to the mercy of the Chilean authorities when, according to his lights, however curious they may be, he has done his best for our British interest.'

'I see.' Mr Mayhew's tone was calm but cold, like a Foreign Office corridor in winter. 'What, may one ask, do you propose to do?'

Halfhyde gave a short laugh. 'We shall see. I have no force, but a stratagem will come. For what it's worth, we have Mrs Weder-Ublick. A forceful woman who could wear down mountains, and I – '

'I scarcely see her relevance now,' Mayhew said impatiently. 'I believe the most potent weapon we have is Mr Todhunter. I advise that matters remain in his hands, at least to begin with. What do you say, Todhunter?'

Mr Todhunter, flattered at the reference to the most potent weapon, eased his neck away from the sticky limpness of his starched white collar and said that yes, he did agree most fully. He opened his Gladstone bag and produced papers, the shells as it were for the most potent weapon. He flourished them, then looked at them more closely.

'Oh, beg pardon,' he said, and stuffed them back. 'Wrong lot, gentlemen.' Halfhyde caught a glimpse of a heading, HOW TO OBVIATE THE NOXIOUS EFFECTS OF BEE STINGS UPON THE PERSON. Mr Todhunter tried again and was successful. There was a treatise on International Law, another on Espionage, another on The Proper Conduct of Police Officers on Attachment for Foreign Office Duties, another on When a Police Officer Should Refrain From Making an Arrest and another that seemed to have to do with the Conduct of Police Officers When Out of Their Jurisdiction Area.

'A formidable armoury, Todhunter,' Halfhyde said.

'Oh yes, sir, and all approved of by my chief super. I feel sure of my ground, sir.'

'Having read it all up?'

'Yes, indeed, sir, I have burned the midnight oil as they say. My chief super has always impressed – '

'I'm sure he has. You believe you can arrange the handing over of Admiral Watkiss without resort to war?' Halfhyde asked, casting a glance at Mr Mayhew as he said the word 'war'.

'Oh yes, sir, with the help, however distant it may be, sir, of my chief super. I may say, sir, he has never failed yet to bring a case to a satisfactory conclusion.'

Halfhyde said, 'Good! But he's never come up against Admiral Watkiss before. You, of course, have.'

'Yes, sir. And if I may say so, that's my one great worry. The gentleman is unpredictable, sir. He may act in such a way as to cast down his own wicket, so to speak.'

'Possible, but unlikely. Admiral Watkiss has always been very adept at guarding his own wicket as matters approach a climax. It is other people's wickets that find themselves cast down, something worth bearing in mind, I fancy.'

'Oh yes, indeed, sir.'

'Anyway, I'm sure your chief super will have covered the point.'

'Oh yes, sir. I did put it to him that Admiral Watkiss had that quality of unpredictability.'

'And his reaction?'

Todhunter pursed his lips. 'Somewhat imprecise, I fear. He gave me to understand that should Admiral Watkiss be so foolish as to commit himself unnecessarily – '

'Fly into a tantrum, you mean, and insult the Chileans?'

'Well – yes, sir. If that took place, my chief super said he'd be best left to stew in his own juice. Mind you,' Mr Todhunter added hastily, 'that was said in such a way as not to be taken seriously. It was never an order in writing.'

'Quite.'

'But my chief super did say, and indeed has always said, that no man can do better than his best. I shall do my best you may be sure.'

'Best foot forward?' Halfhyde said with a straight face.

'You take the words right from my chief super's mouth, sir.'

iv

The initial interview with the Chilean Minister of Marine took place in an ornate chamber in the House of Congress, General Puga and Colonel Opago both being present at their own requests, since each had to watch his own position in the matter of the pursuit and subsequent arrest of the naval Commander-in-Chief; and Colonel Opago was determined to take all the credit for himself, as it had been to the police that the pedlar in Valparaiso had reported his sighting of the quarry.

Admiral Watkiss seethed under a number of what he considered stupid questions about his past.

'Yes, yes, yes. Yes, I was and am a Post Captain of the Royal Navy. You know very well that I was and am.'

'It is necessary,' the Minister of Marine said, 'for the purposes of the law, to establish formally beyond doubt that you are the Admiral Watkiss and – '

'Oh, what nonsense! I've already admitted – and you damn well know – '

'Yes. Well, we shall let the point pass.' Papers were rustled and the Minister of Marine went on, 'More recently you were the Commander-in-Chief of the Brazilian Navy.'

'Yes,' Watkiss said sulkily. 'I prefer to forget that, I must say. They were a dishonest lot, you know. I believe you are aware of the details, Minister.'

'Yes.' A document was lifted and scrutinized. 'You became involved with the construction of a German base – '

'I damn well saw to it that – '

'Yes. You were opposed to the German plans, of which your then masters approved. As a result you were suspended from your duty – '

'Yes, and when I was finally vindicated, the buggers refused me my back pay. Whereupon I resigned.' Admiral Watkiss heaved with anger at his past injustices. 'I would have gone back to England, but – but I didn't.'

'Why not, Admiral?'

'I consider that none of your business, Minister.'

The Minister shrugged and gave what Watkiss thought an oily smile. 'Well, we know the answer, of course. You were not required in England. There would have been no employment for you.' He leaned across the table and pointed a quill pen towards his victim. 'The British Admiralty was not desirous of seeing you back in England, Admiral. Which leads me to say this: we doubt your assertion that you *are still* a Post Captain in the British Fleet. We believe you not to be so, and we await confirmation of this from your British Minister here in Santiago.'

Watkiss shook a fist in the air. He was speechless; he was about to be cast to the Chilean wolves, left friendless in a hostile land, deserted by his own countrymen, even, perhaps, by Her Majesty. He had always known that in the Admiralty dwelt a bunch of pimply clerks and time-servers plus landbound admirals seeking to feather their own nests towards retirement, wily persons ever ready to walk back on their own orders when it suited them to cast blame for their own lack of efficiency upon seagoing officers. He knew this in an abstract sense; but now he was faced with the reality. What a despicable bunch they were to be sure!

The Minister of Marine was going on: he, Watkiss, had come up against the Germans in Brazil. Now, in Chile, he was opposing them once again and in so doing was opposing his Chilean masters as he had opposed his former masters in Brazil. It was a long record of disloyalty; and this time it was worse because he had been engaged in espionage.

Admiral Watkiss seethed. 'I did not engage in espionage! I merely listened, that's all!'

'According to the testimony of Petty Officer Steward Washbrook – '

'I refuse absolutely to be *testified* against by my blasted steward! If you can sink so blasted *low* as to take the word of a blasted steward before that of an admiral, then all I can say is, you're all blasted *scum*, and that's fact, I said it!'

Seething to a stop, Admiral Watkiss sat back with his arms folded across his chest, the head of the tattooed snake appearing from beneath the cuff of the uniform jacket that he had been permitted to change into from his sack upon return to Santiago. The Minister of Marine seemed unperturbed by the outburst, merely drawing Watkiss' attention to his surroundings: the ornate furnishing, the portraits in oils of distinguished Chilean politicians and generals, the simple dignity and quietness of the chamber. 'There is the contrast, Admiral. You show little dignity to match your surroundings. You do not appear as an ornament to your country of birth, and that is a pity.' He raised his voice to address a civilian standing by the great door at the end of the room. 'Call Count von Gelsenkirchen.'

v

In Valparaiso a further cable in Foreign Office cypher had awaited Mr Mayhew's arrival aboard the *Taronga Park*. When decyphered this cable revealed that Admiral Watkiss had been formally charged with his alleged crimes and was being held incommunicado in his official residence. He had been suspended from his duty as Commander-in-Chief pending his trial, which was not expected to take place for possibly two months. In the meantime the British Minister in Santiago had been in touch frequently by the cable with the Admiralty and Foreign Office in London. It appeared to be the view that since Admiral Watkiss was in suspension he could be considered as being temporarily restored to his position on the retired list of Her Majesty's Navy.

'You mean, sir, he's British again?' Todhunter asked.

'Ah – I don't know that that's entirely clear. I think we may say that he's never actually relinquished his British nationality . . . so I imagine to that extent yes, he is British. But not *again*, if you follow, Todhunter.'

'Yes, I do follow, sir. Does it make a difference, then?'

Mayhew's answer was, like the Foreign Office dictum, very cautious. 'Perhaps, and again perhaps not. We shall see, no doubt. Yes, we shall see. But I gather from the way the British Minister summarizes London's instructions, that the possible fact of Admiral Watkiss being able to consider himself back on the retired list and thus a British post captain, is not to be unduly stressed.'

Todhunter looked puzzled. 'Not unduly stressed to whom, sir?'

'As to that, I can't be precise, Todhunter.' Mr Mayhew placed his finger-tips together and looked sagely over the tops of them. 'If I were asked to guess, and it would be no more than that, I would venture to say not unduly stressed to the Chilean authorities . . . perhaps. Perhaps not.'

'Perhaps not to Admiral Watkiss himself, sir?'

'Perhaps, yes.'

'Why would that be, sir, do you think?'

'I really don't know. Perhaps because the knowledge, the *positive* knowledge that London was considering him to be a post captain of the Royal Navy might make him . . . er, more forthcoming in his demands upon the Crown – but I can't say, of course, and I'm not be quoted on that, Todhunter.'

'Oh no, sir, indeed not.' Todhunter hesitated. His chief super was a fair man and gave every crook a full hearing. 'I do think, sir, that's a trifle hard. To deny the admiral his rights like. After all, if it is *positive* – '

'Ah, but it isn't, you see! Not wholly positive. More persons have yet to be consulted, including the First Sea Lord and indeed the Board of Admiralty itself. It's no light matter, Todhunter, indeed it's very serious. Not just a question of a good deal of unpleasantness with the Chileans, whom Her Majesty does not wish to upset, as you know. There is the question of money, and that could bring in the Treasury.'

'Money, sir?'

Mayhew nodded. 'If Admiral Watkiss is restored to the retired list he will become entitled to the retired pay of his rank, a not inconsiderable annual sum. I would surmise that there is fear in some quarters that being Admiral, or Captain, Watkiss, he might find a way of establishing an argument for his having never been legally removed from the list. In which case his entitlement to a very great deal of back pay would become involved.'

'Yes, I see, sir. A dilemma. But to set anyone's freedom against a matter of money, sir, is to my mind, well, scarcely moral.'

Mr Mayhew made no comment on that aspect. Facts had to be accepted as facts. And Mayhew was well versed in the ways of State. The Admiralty he knew to be a curious institution and all too often a devious one. He would have agreed with Admiral Watkiss that it was not a very efficient place; and reading between the sketchy lines of the decyphered cable he smelled a rat: although it was not an expression he would ever have used himself, he believed someone in the Admiralty had made a cock-up. The name of Captain Watkiss might never have been removed from the retired list at all. And, taking advantage of a cock-up, his retired pay might have found its way into an unentitled pocket and now a cover-up was on the way.

However any of this might be, it was now Mayhew's duty and Todhunter's to proceed with all speed to Santiago in order to represent, in the one case, the Secretary of State for Foreign Affairs and in the other the Secretary of State for Home Affairs – or perhaps just the Metropolitan Police Force – by way of Mr Todhunter's chief super.

vi

When Count von Gelsenkirchen had entered the chamber, wearing his uniform as Ambassador of the German Emperor, a quite unnecessary show of bombast Admiral Watkiss thought, Watkiss had sat on with his arms folded. He was not going to rise to his feet for any Hun, and Count von Gelsenkirchen was a square-headed Prussian of the worst sort, vain and arrogant to the point of looking as though he might well be a lineal descendant of Attila himself.

Watkiss made his own position quite clear from the start. He announced, 'Whatever that person has to say, it is a lie and I shall take no account of it.'

'But – '

'I shall not demean myself nor Her Majesty Queen Victoria by listening to the enemies of the British Empire.'

'There is no enmity between – '

'What nonsense.'

The Minister of Marine tried again. 'There is a blood relationship between Her Britannic Majesty and the Emperor of – '

'Balls.' Admiral Watkiss ground his teeth in anger against himself for having denied the undeniable, a foolish mistake. 'Oh, there may be. But Her Majesty has no time for damned upstarts who design to interfere with her shipping and her trading interests in Chile and that's fact, I said it. I – '

'Shipping, trading interests. Do I take it, then, that you admit – '

'I admit nothing. I have done nothing.'

The Minister of Marine lifted an eyebrow. 'Only listened?'

'Only listened, yes.'

'And passed on?'

'Oh, balls and bang me arse,' Admiral Watkiss burst out in a fury, 'things emerge, do they not, in civilized conversation, which is something blasted dagoes seem quite incapable of damn well understanding!'

'But His Excellency Count von Gelsenkirchen will say, if you will listen, Admiral, that – '

'I have already said I shall not listen to blasted Huns,

Minister. They never speak the truth and they are all jealous of the British Empire, their damn jealousy leading them to invent all manner of nonsenses against Her Majesty's interests. If I had had the buggers aboard any ship I've ever commanded, why, I'd have had them flogged round the fleet, ten lashes at each gangway! Dammit, it's well known that His Royal Highness the Prince of Wales detests his blasted Hun cousin and if he was here he would damn well support me!'

Count von Gelsenkirchen caught the eye of the Minister and stood up for his Emperor. 'The feeling is mutual, Admiral. His Imperial Majesty considers his cousin the Prince of Wales an ineffectual dolt of no intellect, and his grandmother, your Queen, to be an arrogant and bad-tempered old woman who attempts foolishly to meddle in international affairs which she does not fully comprehend.' The heavy square face and walrus moustache were thrust towards Admiral Watkiss, looking triumphant. 'What have you to say to *that?*'

Admiral Watkiss' answer was distant. 'I've not listened to a word. But had I done so I would have said it is a habit of blasted Huns to insult their betters and also to condemn themselves out of their own mouths, showing themselves up as – as *filthy barbarians!*'

Again there was an exchange of glances between the German Ambassador and the Minister of Marine. The latter shrugged and said *sotto voce* to von Gelsenkirchen that there appeared to be little point in his continuing his evidence until Admiral Watkiss was in a calmer frame of mind; he would, he said, hear the testimony of the British Minister in the meantime. The British Minister, waiting in an ante-room, was summoned and made his entry wearing a plain jacket and trousers of white sharkskin, which showed his moral superiority to the Hun, Watkiss thought – true British modesty and detestation of flamboyance were much to be admired, and in fact, Watkiss knew, most of the world did indeed admire them.

He rose to his feet in honour of Her Majesty's representative.

'Good morning, Your Excellency. I trust – '

'There is to be no conversation with the witness, Admiral Watkiss,' the Minister of Marine said sharply. Admiral

Watkiss glared and gave an audible sniff. Dagoes were always partial, taking sides in their own interest, loading the evidence. But of course His Excellency would be well aware of that. As the questioning of the British Minister proceeded, however, Watkiss became uneasily aware that evasion was taking place. His Excellency was not going to commit himself too far, and Admiral Watkiss knew why: his instructions from the Foreign Office would have been equally evasive because they were pandering to the blasted dagoes and if the British Minister misjudged the shoaling waters of Whitehall he would himself plunge into a sandbank or a rock. Watkiss listened in mounting anger and concern for his future. Yes, the British Minister said, Admiral Watkiss had had certain conversations with his staff. Yes, they might have spoken of trade and shipping but the position was not entirely clear: it would be perfectly proper for the Commander-in-Chief of the Chilean Navy to discuss shipping matters with the British, for the C-in-C had control of movements in Valparaiso, Puerto Montt and the other Chilean ports and anchorages used by British vessels.

'Exactly!' Admiral Watkiss interposed.

'Silence, if you please, Admiral.'

'I suppose you call this justice. I'm damned if *I* do.'

The Minister of Marine looked exasperated. His Excellency continued, after a warning glance at Admiral Watkiss. He did not consider the accused officer to have spied, a word much disliked by the Foreign Office who did not spy but merely gleaned information. Had Admiral Watkiss gleaned information, then? His Excellency didn't believe so; his mission would never have encouraged anything of that sort. He was quite certain that Admiral Watkiss, once of the British Navy, would never have reported anything said to him off the record by Count von Gelsenkirchen, for that would have meant breaking a confidence which was not a British habit and never had been. No, he himself had had no verbal contact with Admiral Watkiss. No, he was unable to offer comment upon Admiral Watkiss' service with the British Navy or under the Brazilian flag. Yes, he did understand that Admiral Watkiss (and this Watkiss thought most unfair and improper) was an officer of difficult temper and inclined to stress his British origins, at times with an unfortunate vigour.

'Oh, what balls,' Watkiss said with a long-suffering look. He then apologized. 'A slip of the tongue, Your Excellency. The term was addressed . . . elsewhere. Now perhaps I may be permitted a few questions of my own. In order to establish my own position, you see. I take it I am entitled to do that, even under Chilean law, such as it is?'

The Minister of Marine shrugged. 'Always we wish for justice to be seen to be done. If His Excellency has no objection?'

'No, no, Minister, I shall be only too happy.' His Excellency didn't look it; questions were never popular with diplomats, but on this occasion, with luck, he might later be able to sidestep the implications of his answers, for with typical Chilean inefficiency there was no note-taker present and denials would be that much the easier.

Admiral Watkiss came at once to the point. 'Since I am a British subject, Your Excellency – '

'I'm afraid I cannot accept that in full, Admiral – '

'But for God's sake, man – '

'The position is somewhat unclear. Legal advice is awaited from Whitehall. You were born British, yes certainly. But having taken service under first the Brazilian state and now the Chilean . . . I have to repeat that the position is unclear at this moment. There is perhaps a duality, and if so then half of this duality would render you subject to the laws of Chile – '

'And the other blasted half would surely render me subject to Her Majesty and an entitlement to the sending of a British warship to – '

'There must be no talk of that,' His Excellency interrupted quickly, his face paling. 'None at all. There are absolutely no suggestions, Minister,' he said, turning aside, 'that HMG would even remotely consider such an act, I do assure you.'

The Minister of Marine nodded: Watkiss was scarcely worth half a warship in his opinion. 'That is understood, Your Excellency.'

'Thank you, Minister.' His Excellency turned again to

Watkiss. 'I must warn you against improper suggestions, Admiral. I must also warn you to take nothing for granted in this odd situation. Nothing British, that is. You must not consider the Crown to be in any way involved – '.

'Blasted yellow-bellies the lot of you, damn Foreign Office pimps.' The words themselves were full of fire; but Watkiss himself was in danger of deflation. His face had sagged; the monocle he had placed in his eye when resuming his uniform dropped to the end of its black silk cord, tinkling against a brass button. The buggers were going to let him down as he had suspected they might. They had no backbone; Vice-Admiral Lord Nelson would have come to his aid with a battle squadron of sail of the line, his thunder being heard across the length and breadth of the Pacific Ocean. But there were no Nelsons left now; only pimps and loblolly boys in the seats of power. But it wouldn't do, perhaps, to say too much. There was one line of defence left, and Watkiss employed it. He pulled himself together and said, 'I am still upon the retired list of the Royal Navy. I am on the list as a post captain in Her Majesty's Fleet, and you may – '

'Ah.' Matters were approaching a nub. 'You have been in receipt of pay as such, Admiral? Retired pay?'

Reluctantly, Watkiss admitted what he knew His Excellency knew and said that he had not. A balls-up in the Admiralty, he said, which he had been intending to pursue.

'I'm afraid it may get you nowhere, Admiral.'

'What?'

'There is doubt as to your status. I understand the official view to be that you cannot be two persons at one and the same time. Either – '

Admiral Watkiss pounced on that. 'Yes – either! Either I am, or I am not. Which am I, pray?'

His interpolation had been a good one; His Excellency showed confusion. 'Either you are, or are not, whom?'

'Oh, God give me strength! Am I or am I not British, you fool –Your Excellency? Am I a post captain on the retired list of the British Navy, or am I the Commander-in-Chief of the Chilean Navy? If I am the Commander-in-Chief then this inquisition is entirely out of order and should stop instantly. Or I am British, in which case you must blasted well *act*!'

SEVENTEEN

Mr Mayhew and the detective inspector, accompanied by the latter's Gladstone bag stuffed with useful documents and aides-mémoire, took the train from Valparaiso to Santiago with Halfhyde into whose custody and aboard whose ship Admiral Watkiss was to be delivered after arrest by Mr Todhunter, always assuming such arrest could be carried out – preferably, as Mayhew insisted, with Chilean consent.

'And if there is no consent forthcoming, sir?' Todhunter had asked anxiously.

'We shall see, Todhunter. To some extent, events must dictate.'

It was an imprecise statement as usual but Todhunter had to be content. He sat in the hot, stuffy train with his bowler hat on his head, wearing his blue serge suit, and with the Gladstone bag held tightly to his chest. Also with the party, and next to Mr Todhunter, sat Mrs Weder-Ublick who had announced it her duty to be close to her brother at his time of stress. There was no talk now of his vileness or of the episode of the cut hammock lashing. Mr Mayhew had by this time dropped his suspicions that Mrs Weder-Ublick might be part of some German plot; and he had become fairly affable. Next to Mrs Weder-Ublick on her other side sat Canon Rampling, whose supposed malaria had been insufficient excuse for him not to accompany Mrs Weder-Ublick when she had such need of his support and his prayers. Opposite them, and next to Halfhyde, was Miss Penn, dressed for a day out in Santiago. Her hat was large and flowery, her skirt full, her bodice cut low, and she carried a parasol. All of this had been bought some months earlier in the port of Liverpool and had not been worn until now. As the train rolled without haste towards the Chilean capital she removed the hat and fanned herself with it and her decolletage grew a shade lower.

Mrs Weder-Ublick clicked her tongue and looked aside.

'What's up, eh?' Victoria giggled. 'Or is it that something's too far down – that it?'

Mrs Weder-Ublick refrained from comment but set her lips tight. Victoria murmured in Halfhyde's ear that she looked like a bloody tombstone, but she shushed when told. Looking forward to a strange city, she hummed 'Waltzing Matilda'.

Mrs Weder-Ublick spoke. 'We are not going to the music halls, Miss Penn. This is a serious occasion. You should show some restraint in my opinion.'

'I thought you didn't bloody like your brother. Tell me if I'm wrong, eh?'

Mrs Weder-Ublick's face reddened. She dabbed with a handkerchief at her eyes. 'You are an impudent hussy!'

Halfhyde, as Victoria seemed about to speak again, silenced her with a word. She said, 'All right, mate, I was just going to apologize, didn't want to bloody upset the old – lady.' She leaned forward and patted Mrs Weder-Ublick on the knee. 'I reckon it'll be all right. Me mate, he'll see to that, you c'n bet your knicker elastic.'

There was a silence, filled after the briefest pause by Canon Rampling whose years of reconciling the often warring ladies of his parish had given him the ability to calm stormy waters. He made reference to the Almighty and His works, one of which he seemed to suggest was the Chilean railway system, so much roomier than the stage coach, and a little faster. Why, he said, peering from the grimy window, they were very nearly into Santiago already.

ii

The party reported at the British Minister's residence, being taken there from the railway station in an open carriage drawn by a dispirited horse that ambled slowly through the busy streets. At the Residency Mr Mayhew produced his Foreign

Office authority and, of course, being expected, was accorded the speedy service of a junior diplomat. He was informed that Admiral Watkiss was still being questioned as to his activities and that so far nothing positive had emerged from the House of Congress. The charges, he was told, were grave and Admiral Watkiss was unlikely to impress his interrogators with his manner nor indeed with his protestations of innocence, since he was in fact guilty of passing on information.

'That is between ourselves, of course, Mr Mayhew.'

'Of course.' Mayhew knew the drill well enough. No-one in the diplomatic service was ever to be quoted and in any case he was there to remove Admiral Watkiss from his predicament and thus the question of actual guilt didn't arise. On the other hand, when guilt was proven, then he had to use all his wiles to see to it that the Crown's case was put for Admiral Watkiss, who might be British and might be Chilean, to be transferred to the custody of Todhunter of the Yard. 'A dilemma,' he said.

'Yes indeed. We are informed that the very fullest discretion is to be employed, Mr Mayhew.'

Mayhew eased his neck from his starched collar: his morning dress was hot. 'You've had further instructions from the FO?'

The answer was very careful. 'Yes. And no.'

'I see,' Mr Mayhew said. 'Er . . . the Admiralty?'

'The Admiralty is non-committal.'

Mr Mayhew nodded; he understood that as well. The Admiralty would wait to see which way the cat jumped and would then jump with it. This was certainly wise but would not necessarily be a help to Admiral Watkiss. Mayhew remarked as much.

'Yes, that's possibly true – possibly *will* be true I should say. But, of course, you're aware of how things go . . .'

'Yes, indeed. The greater good.'

'Exactly.'

They were in complete accord. Mr Mayhew reported on his conversation to Halfhyde and Mrs Weder-Ublick, adding that the diplomat had said permission had been obtained for Mrs Weder-Ublick, Mayhew himself, and Detective Inspector Todhunter to attend the House of Congress though not the hearing itself. They were to wait in the ante-room until an approach was made by the Minister of Marine.

Mrs Weder-Ublick asked, 'Has my brother been informed that I am here in Santiago?'

'I understand not.'

'I see. I wish Canon Rampling to accompany me to the House of Congress.'

'Oh, but I think – '

'I wish Canon Rampling to accompany me to the House of Congress.'

Mr Mayhew compressed his lips. An impossible woman . . . but he said, 'Oh, very well, I shall have further words with the member of staff.'

'Tell him that I insist.' Mrs Weder-Ublick, who had risen to her feet to make her statement, sat down again. Miss Penn remarked that the Residency was like a bloody morgue.

'All those pictures and statues, mate. Lot of old fossils.'

'Previous British Ministers,' Halfhyde said.

'That's what I meant. Stuck-up lot, eh?'

iii

The British Minister was allowed, by permission of the Minister of Marine, private words with the accused. He told Watkiss that he should be aware that he was not advancing his own interests by making rude and arrogant comments throughout. 'You must remember the Chilean national feelings, Admiral.'

'But they're blasted foreigners, Your Excellency!'

The Minister was patient. 'To you, yes. But do try to remember that to them *you* are the foreigner.'

'Oh, what balls, I'm not a foreigner, I'm *British* as I keep on saying, to no apparent effect . . .' Watkiss tailed off as something clicked in his mind. 'D'you mean to say they're trying to say I'm a blasted dago?'

'No, no, no, that was not quite what I meant – '

'Not quite?'

'Not at all.' The Minister was rapidly losing his coherence of thought. He changed the subject slightly. 'Of course, the present proceedings are not your trial. These proceedings are merely preliminary and you will have your chance to put your case again. At the same time, what is now going on is important and you should be careful not to antagonize anyone. Count von – '

'Oh, that oaf. Nothing but a blasted farmer.'

'Count von Gelsenkirchen's evidence is vital, oaf or not. It is his evidence alone, Admiral, that will be the deciding factor. I must warn you very seriously of this – '

'I shall never bow the knee to the blasted lies of a Hun, Your Excellency.'

The Minister gave a sigh of frustration. Pig-headedness he found impossible to deal with and he was now fearful of his own future and of his position as British Minister resident in Santiago. When the hearing resumed he would be very careful not to corroborate the evidence of Count von Gelsenkirchen for to do so would of course be to admit, by inference, his own duplicity or that of his staff; and Whitehall, his ultimate superiors, always made a very special point of stating very firmly indeed that Her Majesty's representatives abroad neither spied nor received illicit information that might be made use of against the host country. Her Majesty would be most grieved . . . and the British Minister had a poor ally in Admiral Watkiss.

Shortly before the Minister of Marine returned from the adjournment the party from Valparaiso was admitted to the ante-room. Mrs Weder-Ublick was accompanied by Canon Rampling, her request acceded to by the Chilean authorities on account of the high regard in which churchmen were held, the fact of the canon being in catholic eyes a heretic not being a bar on this occasion. Mrs Weder-Ublick sat with Canon Rampling on a settee close by the big doors through which her brother had earlier been taken. They conversed together in low tones, Mrs Weder-Ublick now and again using her handkerchief, and now and again they prayed briefly. Mr Mayhew sat with Halfhyde; Mr Todhunter remained standing stiffly, as if ready to spring to an arrest when the occasion demanded. Miss Penn was not present; leaving the British

Residency at the same time as the others, she had gone separately upon her shopping expedition.

Mr Mayhew, who had been promised an appearance before the Minister of Marine when he would back the British Minister by stating directly the views of Her Majesty's Government in regard to the disposal of Admiral Watkiss, drew from a pocket of his morning coat a turnip-shaped watch. He was examining this when the doors at the far end of the ante-room opened and a man came through with an air of importance and haste, a large man with a square head and a walrus moustache. Seeing the persons present he addressed Todhunter in what the latter took to be Spanish.

'Beg pardon, sir, I don't – '

'You are British?' The man spoke now in English.

'I am, sir – '

'The hearing, has it recommenced?'

'Indeed it has, sir.'

'Thank you. I am Count von Gelsenkirchen. I shall enter.' The large man moved forward. As he did so Mrs Weder-Ublick gave a startled gasp and stared after him as he went through from the ante-room.

'Mr Mayhew, what is that man here for?'

'He is the German Ambassador, Mrs Weder-Ublick. The one who is to give evidence against your brother.'

'Is he indeed!' Mrs Weder-Ublick rose to her feet. 'He is a man once known to my late husband. I shall not have him testifying against my brother, Mr Mayhew. Kindly fetch him out.'

'Really, Mrs Weder-Ublick, I have no jurisdiction – '

'If you haven't, Mr Mayhew, I have!' Mrs Weder-Ublick marched towards the doors into the great chamber beyond and upon reaching them threw them open with a flourish. Her voice was heard clearly in the ante-room. 'Willi!' she shouted. 'If you value your position and your reputation, you'll stop telling lies about my brother!'

iv

The doors had shut with a crash, hefted by Mrs Weder-Ublick.

183

Then they had come open again and Mrs Weder-Ublick had re-appeared in the grip of two Chilean officials who deposited her back on the settee alongside Canon Rampling. Her chest heaved with many emotions: anger, frustration, disgust, sisterly feeling for the brother whom she had disparaged for so many years and whom she had now glimpsed, old and florid but standing four-square, a Briton at bay before his tormentors.

'That appalling man,' she said in a low, tense voice, 'that German. So villainous . . . so *low!*'

Bewildered, Mr Mayhew tried to elucidate the facts. 'Perhaps you will explain, Mrs Weder-Ublick – '

'I cannot bring myself to speak of it, Mr Mayhew.' The handkerchief came out again and was made good use of. Three minutes later the great doors were opened again and Mr Mayhew was bidden to enter the chamber. The others waited in suspense while Mrs Weder-Ublick, seemingly a broken woman, sobbed on Canon Rampling's ample shoulder.

The minutes ticked past. Mrs Weder-Ublick, Halfhyde thought, would have cooked what was left of Admiral Watkiss' goose. One Watkiss was more than enough. After a little over an hour the doors opened again and Admiral Watkiss emerged, his face, like that of his sister earlier, a mixture of emotions. From the way he strutted, however, it seemed that a miracle had occurred and that he was a free man. Free at any rate of the Chileans. Mr Mayhew, following behind Admiral Watkiss, motioned to Mr Todhunter, who took the hint, stepped forward and, in the parlance of his chief super, felt Admiral Watkiss' collar.

v

Admiral Watkiss had angrily shaken off the feeling hand of Mr Todhunter and had stared in disbelief at his sister.

'You! I thought you were blasted well dead!'

'I thought the same of you, Edward.' She stiffened herself. 'What are they going to do to you?'

'Nothing the buggers can do,' Admiral Watkiss said, 'I'm British. That oaf didn't offer any evidence, in the end, or rather he withdrew it, said he'd been mistaken. Odd, really. It was

184

after you burst in with that blasted shout. All they've done is ask me to leave the country, and after all this, and the buggers' blasted ingratitude, I'm only too glad to accede to their request.' He turned round. 'Go away, Todhunter, blast you!'

'Beg pardon, sir, but – '

'I'm not a common criminal. Look at those two.' Admiral Watkiss moved aside as General Puga and Colonel Opago came from the great chamber engaged in bitter argument and mutual recrimination. 'They seem about to blasted well arrest each other since they can't touch me, the buggers! We British – we always win through in the end and that's fact, I said it.' He turned to Halfhyde. 'So you got here in the end – I was expecting not to be left in the lurch by Her Majesty, don't you know. She at least values my services. Have you a carriage, Halfhyde?'

'It will be arranged at once, sir.'

'I shall have to pack, of course. I've been given – I've agreed to leave the country within forty-eight hours. And I've no steward now, that bugger Washbrook had better stand well clear of me from now on. Get on with it, Halfhyde – a carriage.'

vi

They left Santiago that evening by the train for Valparaiso. In the interval Halfhyde had got the story from Canon Rampling, in whom Mrs Weder-Ublick had confided, using as many bowdlerisms as she could find in the telling. Put briefly, Canon Rampling said, Count von Gelsenkirchen had been a member some years ago of her late husband's Lutheran congregation in Germany. He had in fact sung in the choir and many of his singing companions had been boys.

'It occurred in the vestry,' Canon Rampling said in a hushed voice. 'He was caught *in flagrante delicto*, by the pastor himself, Mrs Weder-Ublick's husband. A very sad affair. Of course, it does happen from time to time. The pastor was a humane man and the sordid business was covered up – for the sake of the boy and the church, you know. But if it were to come out . . .'

'Quite. The end of an ambassadorship. So the Count back-tracked?'

Rampling nodded. 'As I gather from Mayhew, yes. Of course, the Chileans still consider Watkiss to be guilty, but they can do nothing with no sworn evidence. In its way, it's all very fortunate. Mr Mayhew is much relieved.'

'No war,' Halfhyde agreed. 'The Foreign Office comes through with colours flying.'

There were other repercussions and once aboard the train the emotions were mixed. Mr Mayhew had been informed by the British Minister in Santiago that on account of her violent outburst and her intrusion into virtual holy ground Mrs Weder-Ublick's presence was not desired in Chile. She would not be a good influence upon the South American Indians; and she was to be expelled from the country, taking passage back to England with Halfhyde and Admiral Watkiss. Canon Rampling, when this news had reached him, had shed twenty years in as many minutes. Brother and sister were not so happy; quarrelling broke out before the train had chugged into Valparaiso; a degree of vileness had returned and Halfhyde guessed that before long Mrs Weder-Ublick would regret her actions. As for Admiral Watkiss, no longer in fact an admiral at all, the future must be at best insecure, something that would dawn on him as the *Taronga Park* made the long voyage back around Cape Horn for the London River. It would not be an easy voyage with brother and sister thrown together, as was demonstrated during the train journey. After so many decades apart, the distant past was bound to come back into focus as the only shared ground; and the episode of the cut hammock lashing was disinterred.

'Such a *nasty* act. So typical of you, Edward.'

'Typical of you to blasted well sneak! And then marrying that damned Hun.'

'You will not refer to my late husband as a Hun.'

'Yes, I will and I have, so there.'

'If it hadn't been for him, Edward, you'd have been in a Chilean gaol at this very minute.'

'Why him? It wasn't he who buggered the choir-boy.'

'*Edward!*'

'For God's sake,' Admiral Watkiss said wearily, 'hold your

186

damn tongue, woman! Am I to be permitted no blasted peace, after doing my best for England?' He jabbed angrily at Mr Todhunter who, still fulfilling his role as arresting officer until his charge had been embarked beneath the British flag, was sitting alongside him. 'Keep your distance, Todhunter, I repeat I am not a common criminal.'

'Beg pardon, sir.' Todhunter shifted sideways, just a little. He impacted against Miss Penn, who was asleep. Her shopping expedition had included a little drink. She awoke in the instant that Mr Todhunter's elbow poked into her breast; she uttered a shrill cry.

'Leave me tit alone, do, I don't like gropers, mate. Not in a bloody train.'

Mr Todhunter's face became scarlet but he sat mute and transferred his thoughts to London and his chief super, to whom he would be able to render a most satisfactory report of duty well and truly done. Similar thoughts went through the mind of Mr Mayhew. The aberrations of an ambassador had obviated any need for diplomatic evasions, which Mr Mayhew did not think of as lies since lies were not told in diplomatic circles; and the Secretary of State would be very pleased.